ABOUT FACE

What Reviewers Say About VK Powell's Fiction

To Protect and Serve

"If you like cop novels, or even television cop shows with women as full partners with male officers…this is the book for you. It's got drama, excitement, conflict, and even some fairly hot lesbian sex. The writer is a retired cop, so she really writes from a place of authenticity. As a result, you have a realistic quality to the writing that puts me in mind of early Joseph Wambaugh."—Teresa DeCrescenzo, *Lesbian News*

"*To Protect and Serve* drew me in from the very first page with characters that captivated in their complexity. Powell writes with authority using the lingo and capturing the thoughts of the law enforcers who make the ultimate sacrifice in the fight against crime. What's more impressive is the command this debut author has of portraying a full gamut of emotion, from angst to elation, through dialogue and narrative. The images are vivid, the action is believable, and the police procedurals are authentic…VK Powell had me invested in the story of these women, heart, mind, body and soul. Along with danger and tension, Powell's well-developed erotic scenes sizzle and sate."—*Story Circle Book Reviews*

Suspect Passions

"From the first chapter of *Suspect Passions* Powell builds erotic scenes which sear the page. She definitely takes her readers for a walk on the wild side! Her characters, however, are also women we care about. They are bright, witty, and strong. The combination of great sex and great characters make *Suspect Passions* a must read."—*Just About Write*

Fever

"VK Powell has given her fans an exciting read. The plot of *Fever* is filled with twists, turns, and 'seat of your pants' danger…*Fever* gives readers both great characters and erotic scenes along with insight into life in the African bush."—*Just About Write*

Justifiable Risk

"This story takes some unusual twists and at one point, I was convinced that I knew 'who did it' only to find out that I was wrong. VK Powell knows crime drama, she kept me guessing until the end, and I was not disappointed at the outcome. And that's not to slight VK Powell's knack for romance.… Readers who appreciate mysteries with a touch of drama and intense erotic moments will enjoy *Justifiable Risk*." —*Queer Magazine*

Exit Wounds

"Powell's prose is no-nonsense and all business. It gets in and gets the job done, a few well-placed phrases sparkling in your memory and some trenchant observations about life in general and a cop's life in particular sticking to your psyche long after they've gone. After five books, Powell knows what her audience wants, and she delivers those goods with solid assurance. But be careful you don't get hooked. You only get six hits, then the supply's gone, and you'll be jonesin' for the next installment. It never pays to be at the mercy of a cop."—*Out in Print*

"Fascinating and complicated characters materialize, morph, and sometimes disappear testing the passionate yet nascent love of the book's focal pair. I was so totally glued to and amazed by the intricate layers that continued to materialize like an active volcano… dangerous and deadly until the last mystery is revealed. This book goes into my super special category. Please don't miss it."—*Rainbow Book Reviews*

Visit us at www.boldstrokesbooks.com

By the Author

To Protect and Serve

Suspect Passions

Fever

Justifiable Risk

Haunting Whispers

Exit Wounds

About Face

ABOUT FACE

by
VK Powell

2014

Credits
Editor: Shelley Thrasher
Production Design: Susan Ramundo
Cover Design By Sheri (graphicartist2020@hotmail.com)

Acknowledgments

To Len Barot and all the other wonderful folks at Bold Strokes Books—thank you for making this process so amazingly enjoyable and painless and for turning out a quality product every time.

My deepest gratitude to Dr. Shelley Thrasher for your guidance, suggestions, and kindness. You help me view my work through fresh eyes. Working with you is a learning experience and a pleasure.

For BSB sister author, D. Jackson Leigh, and friends Jenny Harmon and Joanie Bassler—thank you for taking time out of your busy lives to provide priceless feedback. This book is so much better for your efforts. I am truly grateful.

To all the readers who support and encourage my writing, thank you for buying my work, visiting my website (www.vkpowellauthor .com), sending e-mails, and showing up for signings. You make my "job" so much fun!

CHAPTER ONE

"Holy crap." Macy Sheridan ignored the insistent pounding on her front door, hoping the uninvited guest would take the hint. She considered hiding, but if she moved, the squeaky floors would give her away. More pounding. She clutched the hem of her baggy sweatshirt tighter, braced for the inevitable sales pitch mingled with cold air, and opened the door. "What?"

A cop stood on the porch, his right hand cocked toward the weapon on his hip as if she posed a serious threat, his left shoving a Greensboro Police badge toward her. "Ma'am, I'm Detective Shaver—"

"I don't care if you're Sherlock Holmes, the original or the latest movie incarnation. Get off my property."

"I'm looking for Macy Sheridan, forensic artist. Is that you?"

"Are my parents injured or dead?"

The detective's brow furrowed. "I don't know."

"Then I don't need to hear anything you have to say, and you're still trespassing." She tried to shut him out, but his expensive-looking shoe blocked the door.

"I called but didn't get an answer, and you don't have a machine." As if the statement justified his unwelcome presence.

"Is that a crime now?"

"Ms. Sheridan, please. I've been lost on back roads around Belews Lake all morning. This street isn't even on Google Maps." He shrugged like a fumbling football player waiting for the coach's disapproval. "I know you don't want to be bothered, but if you don't hear me out today, I'll keep coming back until you do. We need your help—again."

"I don't do that any more." She forced the words between teeth so tightly clenched her jaws hurt. The distance she'd tried to establish over the last six months vanished in winter's last gasp of frigid air and a wave of bad memories.

"Will you at least listen to me?" The detective stuffed his hands into the pockets of his heavy coat. "Won't take long. Promise." He looked like a young John Travolta—ebony hair, dimpled chin, and a smile that had probably broken hearts.

Her instincts screamed *run*, but Detective Shaver seemed as dedicated to his profession as she'd once been to hers. If she turned him away, he'd certainly come back until she heard his pitch. "Fine. Talk fast."

He peered around her into the small cottage. "Mind if I come in? It's brutal out here."

"Yes, I mind. Say your spiel and leave. You won't change my decision."

Flipping up his collar against another gust of wind, he said, "We've recovered a human skeleton and would like you to do a facial reconstruction for identification purposes. According to the forensic anthropologist, it's a female, probably in her teens at time of death. We found the remains in the Patterson Street area, near the railroad tracks…"

Patterson Street. Macy didn't hear anything else. Her heartbeat stuttered and she breathed in shallow gasps. The walls of the small room crowded in on her, and she stumbled backward. Detective Shaver reached for her just as she slammed the door. "Go away!" She clung to the doorknob and breathed deeply as if into a paper bag. *I'm okay. Just breathe.*

She slid into the past as easily as an addict succumbs to his poison of choice. She was running down the dark, deserted street searching and praying while music from the bar pounded ominously in the background. Years of waiting and wondering swallowed her again, and the outcome was the same—failure and guilt covered with a thick layer of loss.

The unwelcome feelings permeated her senses and then slowly ebbed with each breath. When she looked around the cottage, everything was as it had been. The worn sofa and two club chairs formed a horseshoe seating area and stood exactly two feet apart, the coffee table eighteen inches from each. Pillows on the sofa guarded their respective corners like sentries. Books in the built-in shelves lined up flush with the edges. Heavy window curtains were open only six inches. The butcher-block countertops in her compact kitchen were clear of unnecessary appliances and clutter. The meticulously organized space reassured her and centered her in the moment.

Looking toward the closed door that led into her studio, she cursed Detective Shaver. She'd finally decided to leave all that unpleasantness behind, but his intrusion had only caused a minor blip on her radar. Life was the same in her little corner of the world. She was in control. So, why was that door still closed?

She walked toward her studio as if on death row. Rubbing the heel of her palm against her chest, she tried to breathe normally. *It's just an art studio.* She repeated the mantra as she reached for the knob with a shaking hand. When she could no longer see the handle through her tears, she turned away. Maybe another day.

❖

"Jesus effing Christ." Nathan Shaver threw his briefcase into the chair across from Leigh and sat on the corner of his desk that butted up against hers. The small Youth Division office buzzed around them with the morning case shuffle and bitching about yesterday's investigative dead ends. "Women. I'll never understand them. Can you help me with that?" He looked at her as if she held the answers to all his ambiguous universal questions.

"No."

"Is that every woman's favorite word?"

"Pretty much a staple." She couldn't talk to Nate in his frustrated mood. Best to let him vent and offer an opinion when he really wanted to hear it. After six years as partners in the Youth Division, they agreed on many things, especially their confusion about women.

They were as close as male and female work partners could be who weren't sleeping together, and they respected each other's personal space—bonus.

"I guess the forensic artist turned you down?"

"Duh. I spent hours lost in East Jesus. I've never seen so many farm implements and tractor mailboxes. When I finally found the place, she made me stand on the porch and then slammed the door in my face. About froze my nuts off, not that I've needed them lately."

"Tell me again why you're doing the dirty work on a case that's not child-related?"

"I owed Sergeant Rickard in Crimes Against Persons a favor. He's dealt with Ms. Sheridan before but didn't bother to give me a heads-up about her charming personality." He leaned in and whispered, "But damn is she hot…or could be with the right clothes and some makeup. Looked like she'd seen a ghost when I told her what I wanted. Seemed like a bit of an overreaction."

"Hasn't she worked with the CAP guys for years?"

"Seven, to be exact, so I'm not sure what could've freaked her out. She's seen everything. I'm surprised we've never met her, and I'd remember a piece—"

"I get your point." Nate wasn't usually as bad as the other guys about objectifying women, but this one had obviously wound him up. "We don't have much use for forensic artists in our division. And that type of work requires specific equipment we don't have. Besides, she works on contract, probably from home or a studio somewhere."

"I guess. Rumor is she's become a hermit."

"Nobody really wants to be a hermit. It's not natural."

"Well, she did a great imitation. But you're probably right, because she's got a For Rent sign at the top of her driveway. But it *is* at Belews Lake. I couldn't even get a cell signal out there. You still looking for a place?"

The mention of house hunting reminded Leigh of her most recent disappointment—the failure of a three-year relationship with the woman she'd thought was *the one*. How could she have been so wrong? She'd sold her house, not her brightest decision, put most of her furniture in storage, and moved into Gayle's condo the first year and spent the next two flying back and forth to see her in Canada. "Yeah, I still need a place, but not sure I want to be at Belews Lake."

"If you ever go, definitely take your weapon and drop some bread crumbs. It's freaking *Deliverance* out there." Nathan slapped her on the back just as her phone rang. "You can always move in with me. We could trade castoffs." He winked as if the statement actually made sense.

"Detective Monroe."

"Leigh, it's Captain Howard. I need to see you in my office."

Anita Howard, commanding officer of the Youth Division, had trained Leigh as a rookie cop, was her sergeant in the field for three years, and had helped her secure a detective position in child crimes. Howard was the closest thing to a mother figure Leigh had ever known.

"Yes, ma'am, I'll be right there." It was the call she'd been expecting for a month. "It's time, Nate."

"Don't worry. Howard's fair. She'll treat you right. If you need backup, I'm here."

The guys had dubbed the hallway to Captain Howard's office the chute. Nobody liked to march that stretch of carpet lined with decorated detectives' photographs on both walls. The sergeant was usually behind you, and some form of discipline waited at the end. Today the walk seemed agonizingly slow. Captain Howard's secretary waved her toward the boss's open door. "She's waiting."

Under any other circumstances, Leigh would've loved to hear those words about Anita Howard. Though nothing personal had ever passed between them, she believed Howard cared about her and her career. Leigh squared her shoulders and stepped forward. "Captain."

Anita Howard greeted her at the threshold, her hand outstretched. She was the same height as Leigh, with a slight desk-riding bulge pushing at the waistband of her pants. The pinstripes of her suit followed her ramrod posture and seemed to point to her topknot of gray hair. When this woman was in the room, no one doubted who was in charge. She was the first African-American woman promoted to captain in the agency, and she'd earned the rank at every level. "Wanna sit?"

"I'd prefer to stand." Howard's office wasn't a typical commander's shrine. She didn't have any plaques, awards, or diplomas to flaunt her accomplishments, just a single framed photograph of her parents and one of her partner on top of a credenza.

Howard retrieved her reading glasses from the desk and put them on. "Sit. This could take awhile, and I prefer eye contact during a conversation."

Leigh positioned herself directly in front of the captain and met the stare that had always calmed and reassured her. "I guess Internal Affairs has finished its investigation?"

Captain Howard nodded. "And the State Bureau of Investigation finished the criminal part as well. I won't beat around the bush. It's not all good."

Leigh shifted as sweat stung her armpits and the backs of her legs.

"I'll summarize. Stop me if anything sounds off. Fair enough?"

Leigh slid back in her chair and scratched the side of her right index finger with her thumbnail, a nervous habit from childhood. She controlled it most of the time, but when her nerves were really on edge or emotions high, she regressed.

"Relax." Howard opened the file and pulled out two sheets of paper. "Lily Miller, eleven years old. Mother died of an overdose a month ago, father unknown. Mother's boyfriend, also a known drug abuser, lived in the home. Children and Family Services caseworker was Pam Wilkinson. Lily asked Wilkinson not to return her to the boyfriend after her mother's funeral because of alleged abuse. The child wanted to live with her grandmother in Detroit." Howard looked up at Leigh. "Right so far?"

"Yes, ma'am."

"The boyfriend wanted Lily back, presumably for the benefits, but CFS wanted to investigate the abuse charges and check on the grandmother's status. Here's where the stories vary. You and Wilkinson stated you took Lily to her mother's funeral and dropped her off at home later. The boyfriend insists you never brought her back and he hasn't seen her since."

Leigh's muscles tightened as she remembered the story Lily had told her and Pam about the boyfriend's abuse. "He's a doper, and he never had any standing with Lily. He wasn't a relative, and he couldn't collect benefits after the mother died. We told him that."

Howard gave Leigh one of the calm-down looks she'd gotten in her early days as a rookie. "Wilkinson contacted Lily's grandmother, but she couldn't get to Greensboro for three days. The question was, and still is, what happened to Lily? Where was she those days between her mother's funeral and her grandmother's arrival? She ended up in Detroit, safe and sound on the fourth day." Anita Howard could read Leigh's nonverbal cues better than most, so she blanked her face and met Howard's gaze.

"We dropped her off at her home." She didn't want Howard to think she was a screw-up who flaunted procedures for no reason, but she couldn't, no, she wouldn't, tell this woman a lie, nor would she betray a friend or a child—ever. It was best not to elaborate. The more she talked the greater chance she'd inadvertently reveal something.

"Did either of you walk her to the door, turn her over to a responsible adult?" When Leigh didn't answer, Howard continued. "Fortunately for you, the SBI couldn't find any evidence to contradict your statement. Neighbors remembered seeing the girl get out of a city vehicle in front of her home, so there will be no criminal charges."

Some of the tension drained from Leigh's shoulders, and she stopped worrying the side of her finger. "That's a relief."

"You're an excellent detective with good instincts and a big heart. That's why you're in this unit. But you can also be creative about skirting the law or procedure on behalf of a child. This time it turned out all right. Unfortunately, I can't run my division on outcomes alone and totally disregard policy. Adherence to the rules is essential in any organization. How does CFS or the department explain that we misplaced a child for three days? I have to suspend you."

"Suspend me? Really?" Leigh's eyes burned as she imagined not having the job she loved and the support group she depended on, especially now without Gayle.

"Unless you're willing to tell me where Lily was for three days, I have no choice. Contrition would go a long way."

"And what about Wilkinson? What's going to happen to her?" If necessary, she'd take the blame for everything. It had all been her hair-brained idea anyway.

"Her supervisors in CFS are handling that." Howard waited, her gaze fixed on Leigh. "Well, do you have anything to say?"

"How long is the suspension?" It really didn't matter. The discipline would be a permanent blot on her professional record. Every time she applied for a transfer or promotion, the unanswered questions would resurface. She'd feel the effects of this decision for the rest of her career. For a split second she considered telling the whole truth, explaining exactly what had happened that day. But she had no guarantee she could protect the others with the truth, and it might possibly harm them. She remained silent.

"One month." Captain Howard slid a piece of paper toward her. "Here's your official notification. Sign this copy for the file."

"Do I get time off for good behavior? I've already been riding a desk for a month waiting for the investigators to finish."

"You know it doesn't work like that, Leigh. Starts tomorrow. I expect you to check in at least once a week. Give Nathan your cases. He's familiar with them."

"Yes, ma'am." Leigh stood and offered her hand to Captain Howard. She was annoyed that she hadn't handled the initial situation better. "I'm really sorry if I've disappointed you."

Howard cupped her hand and held it until Leigh was forced to meet her gaze. "You've never disappointed me, and I doubt you ever will. You're holding something back, and I'm sure you have a good reason. Maybe one day you'll share it with me. Take care of yourself."

As Leigh walked back to the office, she wondered if Captain Howard knew more about what had really happened to Lily Miller than she let on. How could she? Aside from herself, only Lily, Pam, and one other person knew all the facts. It would have to stay that way. If a month off was the price for protecting two people who'd helped a child, she'd gladly pay it. Doing the right thing should be rewarded, not punished, but sometimes the two became indistinguishably intertwined.

"Well?" Nate stood with his hands perched on his hips like a mother waiting for a curfew-breaking child.

"Month off, weekly check-ins."

"A freaking month? Doesn't she understand the real world anymore? Sometimes we have to improvise." Nate didn't know for sure that she'd skirted the rules, but he knew her work style.

"I could use some time off to find a place to live and prioritize my life. Besides it's never a failure, always a lesson."

"Great, more self-help bullshit. You know that crap is annoying, right? I've got a better one for you. The beatings will continue until morale improves. Doesn't she understand you were just doing your job?"

It's all right, Nate. She's just doing hers." She packed her briefcase and slid her stack of open cases to his desk. "Happy new caseload."

"Half of those should've been mine to start with. By the way, you got a call while you were with the boss."

He handed her a Post-it and she read the name, Susan Bryce, and the number she'd memorized. She crumpled the note and threw it in the trash on her way to the door. When would Susan get the message and stop harassing her?

"You ever going to call that woman? She rings about twice a month. What did you do, sleep with her and then dump her?"

"Hardly." Leigh wasn't about to tell *that* story if she could help it.

"Want to go for a drink on the way home? Talk or something?"

"Not really in the mood, but thanks, Nate."

"What will I do without my wingman? Keep in touch…okay?"

She picked up her briefcase and choked out, "Will do, partner." The comfortable routine of daily life with Nate and Pam was a stark contrast to what lay ahead. She liked to process aloud, talk through things until they made sense. She'd need to do that now more than ever, but Nate was her idea bouncer and Pam her sounding board. She'd be like a muzzled dog in a barking contest.

On her walk home, ignoring the pitying glances from passersby, she released the feelings she'd battled since her meeting with Captain Howard. Tears slid down her face as she absorbed another disappointment. She'd made the right decision a month ago and stuck by it today, but the consequences still hurt.

When Leigh entered the condo she'd shared with Gayle, the emptiness enveloped her. She didn't hear even the annoying tick of a clock marking time. The air smelled stale and held a chill reminiscent of her last nine months alone. The contemporary furnishings—sleek, sophisticated, and eye-catching—reminded her of Gayle. Like their relationship, their decorating tastes were worlds apart. She preferred the warmth and timelessness of traditional styles. The only evidence of her presence in the condo was her solid-oak bedroom suite in the guest room. She should've paid closer attention when Gayle dodged her requests to integrate more of her belongings into their living space.

But Gayle always supported her position with numerous justifications: she was too busy working between the US and Canada to redecorate; it was too expensive; they needed to pool their money and buy together; they might decide to live in Canada. The list went on, and Leigh literally couldn't negotiate with her. Gayle talked circles around her while she was still thinking of a response to her first statement. But just because she could argue better didn't mean she was right. Like so many gifted attorneys, Gayle never gave a straightforward answer, especially about their relationship. Another clue she'd missed.

Why had she ever thought a long-distance relationship could work for her? The answer was simple—she'd loved Gayle enough to try anything. The old adage about long-distance love being hard to make and easy to kill was certainly true in their case. Sadness bubbled up again, but she refused to cry for someone who didn't care for her. Just because she'd imagined Gayle was *the one* didn't make it a two-way street. She dropped her briefcase beside the door and flipped on a torchiere.

Boxes half full of her belongings littered the floors like an obstacle course. She'd memorized the paths weeks ago and weaved her way into the kitchen. It was the only room that didn't torment her with soft things she and Gayle had lounged and loved on. Gayle had said she could stay in the condo rent free as long as she wanted, and initially it had been easier than moving. But recently she was suffocating in a place that didn't fit her style and memories that didn't offer any hope.

Digging into the freezer, she pulled out a tin of margarita mix, emptied it into the blender, and added ice and an overabundance of tequila. She wasn't a big drinker, but today called for something—not a celebration, but perhaps a new beginning. Maybe the suspension would force her to find a place of her own and reclaim her life. When the whirring stopped, she shoved a straw into the pitcher, grabbed a bag of cheddar jalapeño Cheetos, and retired to the guest bedroom she'd occupied since ending her relationship with Gayle.

CHAPTER TWO

Please stop. Leigh burrowed deeper under the pillows to block the annoying vibrations of her cell phone. When it didn't quit, she rolled onto her side, careful not to shake her gargantuan-sized head. She glimpsed the empty blender pitcher beside the bed just before she toppled onto the floor. "Hell." Her head throbbed, her mouth felt like she'd eaten insulation, and the taste of sour tequila and Cheetos rose in her throat. Pulling her knees up against her chest, she lowered her head between them and prayed she wouldn't puke. The phone buzzed and shimmied off the nightstand, and the doorbell chimed like Big Ben. "Double hell."

When the nausea passed, she grabbed the side of the bed and crawled upright. She made her way to the front door, kicking the boxes that had menacingly moved into her path overnight. Peering through the peephole, she saw her best friend, Pam Wilkinson, dressed in jogging clothes and waving two cups of coffee like toys from their childhood play dates. She opened the door and shielded her eyes from the sun. "Get in here and don't even mention the *j*-word." She didn't need a reminder of how loose and uncoordinated her body felt after months of bingeing and vegging following the breakup with Gayle. Her ass felt like a minibus following her around.

"Happy to see me?" Pam's gaze slid over Leigh and she shook her head. "Shouldn't drink tequila and eat Cheetos. It leads to hangovers and orange clothes…not to mention foul breath."

Leigh covered her mouth with her hand. "Sorry." She was still wearing her work clothes from yesterday and grimaced at the thought of adding them to the pile of dirty laundry already smothering the washing machine.

Pam offered her a cup of coffee and the newspaper. "Which do you want first?"

"Got a feeling the coffee might make me feel better, but not sure about the paper."

"Fukum." Pam's personal blend of *fuck* and *them* rolled off her tongue as easily as her own name. She scrubbed the top of her head with her knuckles, but her short hair remained pristine—she didn't have enough to be mussed by anything except a razor. "We did the right thing, and I don't care what they say."

Leigh waved her toward the kitchen as she went ahead kicking boxes out of the way again. "What did they do to you?"

"Same, month off."

"Who told you?" Leigh was too hungover to think clearly or she wouldn't have asked.

Pam gave her a *really* look and said, "Nate."

She brushed stacks of dishtowels off two chairs and motioned for Pam to sit. "How's he taking all this?"

"He's worried about you, like I am. Why else would I be here at seven in the morning with coffee? I've got a hot woman at home in my bed." Pam immediately looked out the window, probably berating herself for pointing out the obvious. "When's the last time you went jogging?"

Leigh held up her hand to stop the onslaught of helpful suggestions Pam was about to unleash in very colorful terms. "Don't start."

"I'm just jealous I don't have a stick figure and a tight little booty like you…without even trying, I might add." Coming from anyone else the comment might've sounded like a come-on, but Pam was offering a backhanded compliment to offset her awkward girlfriend faux pas.

"I know I've let a lot of things slide lately, but I'm getting my shit together."

"Oh, really? Let's recap. You helped Nate with his kitchen renovation this week, trimmed my hedges while I seeded the lawn, and worked overtime on cases that weren't even yours. When have you had time for your shit? These boxes haven't been moved in months, except the ones you stumbled over on the way to the door this morning. Am I right?"

She sipped the warm, perfectly doctored latte instead of answering Pam's question. Helping friends kept her from moping, but it was obvious she hadn't made any forward progress. Her belongings were still unpacked, stacks of real-estate magazines littered the countertops, and she hadn't been on a date since the breakup.

"Start today," Pam said. "You got nothing better to do. When you're ready, I'll help you pack, and then you have to leave. We can look through the classifieds and see if anything pops."

The idea was both appealing and depressing. She'd grieved and reasoned and convinced herself that moving on was for the best. But in the wee hours when loneliness cut deepest, she ached for a lover at her side.

"What're you thinking? Spill. You're like me. Introspection doesn't work."

"Maybe I should give her a call…try one more time." Pam set her coffee cup on the table with way too much control. Leigh could almost hear her counting to ten. "That's just the margarita effect, isn't it?"

"Exactly. Too much tequila kills brain cells, erases memories, and gives false hope. And God only knows what mind-altering crap is in that orange stuff on Cheetos. Besides, all you ever had was a vacationship. When you were there or she was here, you had a semi-relationship, otherwise nothing. When was the last time you heard from her?"

"She's busy with work." The excuse was so lame Leigh couldn't believe she'd parroted the very words Gayle had used the last time she'd called, three weeks ago.

"Yeah, like Canadian immigration attorneys work night and day. When are you going to get it? You were never the problem, Leigh. When one won't, two can't."

"Hey, that sounds like a neat bumper sticker." She offered a weak smile as the mental reality filtered down to her heart and soul, this time with a heavy thud. Pam was right. It was time. Love couldn't be bought, forced, or coerced. She'd waited nine months for Gayle to indicate she cared and wanted their relationship to continue. All she'd gotten were more platitudes and vague references to a future Gayle wouldn't commit to. "Let's get started."

Pam slid the paper across the table. "Brace yourself."

She opened to the front page and stared at the bold headline until the words registered and then distorted in a teary blur. DETECTIVE AND CFS WORKER SUSPENDED IN CHILD DISAPPEARANCE. "Disappearance? What the hell?"

"That reporter's getting his information from the boyfriend and not checking the facts. At least the boyfriend's not a known pedophile. You know how reporters are—anything to sell a few papers. Don't let it bug you. We know what happened."

"But our friends and family don't. The department won't clarify the story. They'll cite personnel policy and let everybody believe what they want." She lowered the paper and looked at Pam, tears welling in her eyes. "I'm sorry I got you suspended. Can you ever forgive me?"

"Nothing to forgive. I kept my mouth shut because I believed in what we did. And I'd do it again under the same circumstances. Wouldn't you?"

Leigh nodded.

"Enough said." She patted Leigh's arm and reached for the sports section. "And don't start crying on me. I get enough of that feeling stuff from my girlfriend du jour."

She gave Pam her best bullshit smile, remembering the kid who used to take home every stray animal she found. "Are you guys okay?" Pam had been dating a new woman for about six months, and it seemed to be going well.

"Sure, why wouldn't we be?"

"Just asking." Since the breakup, she worried about her coupled friends too much. She thought she'd found the one, and she'd been wrong. How could others be so certain?

"You worry about people too much. Nate is fine. I'm fine. Everybody's fine except you. But we're going to take care of that, aren't we?"

Leigh turned to the classified section and traced down to the real-estate column. "Nate said there was an apartment for rent at Belews Lake."

"You want to be out of town?"

"Might not be bad for a while, until this blows over. It's only forty-five minutes away. You've got the option of your parents' place in Asheville."

"Thought about it, but I'm staying put. Fukum. Why are you looking at apartments instead of another house?" She paused, and the space between her eyes looked like railroad tracks. "Is it money?"

"No. I've got enough from the sale of my house to buy a nice place."

"Then what's the problem?"

"I'm not sure what I want." The statement was more telling than she intended. It pretty much summed up every aspect of her life right now. She read the ad for the Belews Lake apartment and thought it was worth a look. "Want to ride out there with me?"

"Wish I could, but I'm babysitting my nephew so my brother and sister-in-law can have a free day. What the hell is that anyway? If they wanted free days, they shouldn't have had a kid."

"You love the little guy."

"True, I enjoy getting him juiced on sugar and caffeine and turning him loose on his parents. A return policy is a great thing."

"Spoken like a sensitive CFS employee. Does your new girlfriend know how you feel about kids?"

"I love kids as long as I can leave them. And yes, fortunately, we agree."

"Gayle and I never had a conversation about kids, and we were together three years. Aren't lovers supposed to talk about hopes and fears about the future? Isn't it a natural part of getting to know each other? Feels like we skipped a few steps."

"I got the impression Gayle dodged anything emotional. She was just a tough nut to crack, and I can talk to anybody."

"Yeah, intimacy wasn't her strong point." Leigh finished her coffee and stood. "Guess I better get to it then. Thanks for dragging me out of bed and for the coffee. I need to shower, take a bottle of aspirin for this headache, and hit the road if I'm going house hunting. Help yourself to whatever you can find."

"You mean like empty moving boxes, a sink full of dirty dishes, or a truckload of laundry?"

"Love you too."

After her shower, Leigh felt almost normal except for a slight pounding in her tequila-soaked brain and a nagging feeling that she should be working. She headed for the door but stopped when she heard a humming sound from the kitchen. "Pam, you still here?"

The room was empty and so was the sink. Pam had stacked the dishwasher and turned the machine on. She glanced toward the laundry area. The subtle wobbling of the washer confirmed her friend had also loaded her dirty clothes and started the cycle. She stood and let the feeling of love and gratitude bolster her sagging emotions. So her life was a little off-kilter, but with friends like Pam she'd make it.

Words for the day: If you don't step forward, you'll always be in the same place. This was her stepping forward. She dialed the number listed in the rental ad and waited as it rang and rang and rang. She was about to hang up when someone answered.

"Yes?" The woman's voice sounded distant and annoyed.

Not a very welcoming greeting for a potential renter, Leigh thought, as she considered what to say. She'd bought her home fresh out of the academy and never rented. How was it done? Did she introduce herself or ask about the place first? How much information should she provide before asking for further details? Before she could decide, the line went dead. She stared at her cell phone in disbelief and redialed.

"Yes." Same woman, same irritated tone.

"I'm sorry to bother you, again. That was me just now. Couldn't figure out what to say. My name is Leigh Monroe, and I'm calling about the apartment."

"Fine."

"The description in the paper was vague but intriguing. Could you tell me about it?"

"Need to see it."

Did this woman really want to rent her place? "How much are you asking?"

"Not sure."

"What can you tell me about the apartment?"

"You need to see it." Finally a complete sentence, though a little terse. "It's unique and won't suit everyone. If you like it, we'll negotiate price." As she spoke, Leigh caught the hint of articulation born of education and practice. Something in her tone sounded almost forlorn, as if talking at all was a struggle.

"Can I come out today?"

"I don't know, can you? You certainly may. My schedule is open."

She added retired English professor to her list of possible descriptors. "Thank you. What's the address?" After she obtained directions to Egret Lane at Belews Lake and negotiated an appointment time, Leigh pulled her sporty Mazda out of the garage and headed north.

❖

Macy hung up from Leigh Monroe and paced in her small living space, becoming more anxious with each pass. What had possessed her to think she could handle a renter on the property? She'd have to interact with her at some point: collect money, fix things, or make conversation. She reached for the phone to cancel the appointment but didn't have a number. The income would be helpful, especially if she hoped to pursue her passion. And the woman sounded friendly enough, maybe too much so. She grimaced at the sound of tires on gravel. Too late.

She crept to the window as if the woman could hear her footsteps and peered out. Leigh Monroe unfolded herself from a red compact vehicle and stretched languidly against the side. She looked like a rusty nail, tall and lean with a shock of curly copper hair falling across her forehead. She pulled the tail of a white polo shirt toward the waistband of low-rider blue jeans, shrugged into a leather jacket that reflected her hair color, and strode toward the house with the confidence of an athlete and a swagger Macy associated with cockiness. Flashes of vivid red and rich purple conveyed power and sexuality. The closer the woman got, the more nervous Macy became. If she could trust her first impression, this might get complicated.

Opening the door before the woman could knock, Macy waved her off. "I'm sorry. I've made a mistake." She folded her arms over her chest, determined to stand her ground.

"Something I said?"

Up close, Leigh Monroe would never be mistaken for a rusty nail. Barely perceptible lashes fluttered like a thin veil, revealing and concealing eyes an unusually brilliant shade of green. Her alabaster skin offered a perfect palette for a light dusting of freckles. A close-cut hairstyle did little to tame her natural waves. The angles of her jaw and chin were strong but softened by a quick, genuine smile. She looked as hopeful as a Girl Scout selling cookies when she extended her hand and her perfectly shaped lips moved. Macy realized she was speaking. "Sorry?"

"I'm Leigh Monroe." Macy was torn between the mental decision she'd already made and the benign woman standing in front of her. "And you are…?"

"Macy. Sheridan." She glanced at Leigh's outstretched hand and shook her head.

Leigh looked down and laughed, the kind of laugh that permeated a room and begged you to join in. "Don't blame you." She wiped her fingers up and down the sides of her jeans, leaving orange streaks. "Cheetos. Breakfast of champions."

This was definitely not going to work. Macy liked things neat and tidy. This woman couldn't even keep her hands clean. "I've decided not to rent the place." When the words hit their mark, something softer replaced the playfulness in Leigh's eyes.

"I'm sorry to hear that. Have I upset you already? Usually takes at least an hour."

"Not at all." Was she upset? Was that the right word for the tingling sensation pelting her skin like tiny raindrops? No, she just wasn't ready to be in close proximity to another person, any person. And she certainly didn't want to interact with a tenant daily.

"If I have, I'm sorry. I'd love to see the apartment. The setting's absolutely beautiful. It's on the water, lots of trees for privacy. You must have at least two lots."

"Four, actually. My parents are classic overachievers."

Leigh looked toward the lake, and when she spoke again she sounded distant, almost mesmerized. "I can imagine this as a family home. Kids charging off the end of the pier into the lake. Dad grilling hot dogs and hamburgers. Mom setting the picnic table with a red-

and-white-checkered tablecloth. Must've been great growing up here. As the old saying goes, 'As the twig is bent, so grows the tree.' This would be the perfect place for me right now."

Macy hadn't exercised her one-on-one skills much lately, but she was a student of life and art. She was accustomed to the nuances of body language and verbal tone, the degrees of shadow and light, and the powerful unspoken word. She recognized the telltale signs of pain.

When Leigh turned toward her again, she offered an apologetic smile. "Sorry I bothered you. Have a good day."

As she walked away, Macy heard herself say, "Maybe you should at least see the place. You drove all the way out here." The Girl Scout was back, her grin broad and infectious, body seeming to vibrate with excitement. This one would never be able to hide her feelings, which probably caused her a lot of pain. She was like a walking billboard of emotions: reassuring in a world saturated with subterfuge and misdirection, but threatening to Macy's comfortably stoic existence.

She pulled a key from her coat pocket and walked toward the lake. "The apartment is over the boathouse." Why hadn't she just kept quiet? Leigh would be gone. She didn't want a tenant, but she kept putting one foot in front of the other in that direction.

"On the water?"

"Is that a problem?"

"Sweet. I didn't even know that was possible."

"It's amazing what a little ingenuity, family political clout, and cash can do." She couldn't seem to keep from offering tidbits of useless information about her parents, none of which Leigh Monroe needed to know. Maybe she had been alone too long.

When they reached the dock, Macy pulled the stairs down and locked them into place on the floater. "This serves as steps when down and a door when closed, just like in an attic."

"Jeez, this is huge. It's a house on stilts."

"It's just an A-frame, really—one large room, like a loft. The only light comes through the front windows and sliding door."

Macy glanced at Leigh as she moved toward the steps, uncomfortable with her closeness. She started to ask her to back up, but Leigh's look of unfiltered awe as she gazed at the lake stopped her.

She'd never seen an adult so captivated by a simple view. Her emerald eyes were wide, her lips slightly parted, and her cheeks flushed. Macy stared, drinking in the wonder she didn't know still existed in the world. How long had it been since she'd looked at anything with that kind of enjoyment and expectation? Not even her art carried that thrill anymore.

She turned back toward the stairs, her legs unsteady as she climbed the first few steps. She was halfway up when a motorboat whipped through the cove pulling a skier in a wetsuit. Waves rocked the floater and it bobbed up and down. Losing her footing, she grabbed for the railing to regain her balance but failed. She seemed to tumble in slow motion until landing unceremoniously in Leigh Monroe's powerful embrace.

Macy thought for a moment she'd lost consciousness because she wasn't breathing and was entirely rigid. Then she realized she was lying on the dock on top of Leigh, whose arms were still tightly clasped around her. She struggled but couldn't break the hold. "Let go. Take your hands off."

"Okay, okay. Are you all right? Are you hurt?" Leigh released her and sprang to her feet, as if the whole incident hadn't fazed her.

"I'm fine." Not exactly true. She was still wobbly, and her skin was too warm for the cool spring temperature. Leigh's embrace had felt confining but also non-threatening. She didn't like being touched, especially by strangers. Her body seemed to be saying otherwise.

"That's what I call sweeping a girl off her feet. Well played." Her shock must've been evident because Leigh said, "I was kidding."

She backed as far away from Leigh as possible and pointed to the steps. "Look if you want, but hurry. I'm busy." She wasn't going to rent the apartment. Decision made, again. She couldn't even spend ten minutes in a social situation without freaking out. Leigh probably thought she was an emotional basket case.

When Leigh came back down the steps, she kept a careful distance between them, but her eyes flashed like beacons atop her flushed cheeks. "It's gorgeous. The pale-yellow paint is perfect with your antiques and the bright sofa and side chairs. Could use a few paintings on the walls, but otherwise, it's real homey. Traditional is my favorite style. The kitchen is small enough that I won't feel pressured to cook. And the view…well, you know what that's like. I'd love to rent it…if you're still willing."

"No, I'm sorry. It's not a good idea." Leigh's smile vanished, making Macy feel like she'd robbed the day of a bit of sunshine. "I can't."

"I feel like I've offended you in some way, and if so, I apologize, again."

"It's not you. It's me." She'd never spoken truer words. Leigh Monroe seemed like a genuinely nice, considerate person who would probably make a relatively unobtrusive tenant. *She* was the problem.

"Sounds like my last girlfriend, but she wasn't being totally honest," Leigh said.

"I just don't think I can be a landlord right now. I have…issues."

"I'm a sucker for sappy sayings, and one of my favorites is, if you think you can or you can't, you're right."

"Exactly."

Leigh started to offer a handshake but pulled back. "Okay, I won't push. If you change your mind, please call me. I don't need managing, wouldn't be intrusive, and I'm also pretty handy—do my own repairs and such. A quiet, private place would be great for a while. I have issues too." Leigh pulled a small notepad from her inside jacket pocket, scribbled her phone number, and extended it to Macy between two fingers. "Please?"

Leigh's eye color reminded Macy of the first vivid leaves of spring and the promise of new beginnings. She could create an entire ensemble of pieces from that single shade of green. She knew having a renter was unreasonable and destined to fail, but something inside her softened. Scribbling the rent amount on the note, she handed it back to Leigh. "I don't have wireless, just an unreliable cable connection, and the cell service is spotty, especially on the dock. I don't allow kids, pets, or loud parties. Can you live with that?"

Leigh's smile hijacked her entire face. Her eyes filled with excitement, the corners of her mouth stretched wide, and the freckle bridge across her nose deepened to a golden tan. "Absolutely. I'm not tethered to my electronic devices. And if you want, I can rent month-to-month, in case it doesn't work out. I want you to be comfortable."

"Good idea. I assume you're employed?" Leigh hesitated, and Macy's antenna vibrated. If she wasn't, she couldn't pay the rent and would be home all the time, with more chance they'd have to interact. Not a good combination. Before she could withdraw her wavering offer yet again, Leigh answered.

"I am, and I promise I can pay."

Leigh pinned her with those eyes and she acquiesced. "Security deposit and first month's rent." When had she become a sucker for Little Orphan Annie look-alikes, or any looks for that matter? She based decisions on facts and logic, not an attractive package or a charming line.

Leigh pulled out a roll of bills. "Thank you so much. You won't regret it. I promise. When can I move in?"

"Whenever you're ready, but one more thing."

"You sure do have a lot of rules…but I can adapt. Fire away."

"I don't really socialize. I prefer to be left alone." Leigh's look of surprise stopped her momentarily. Was it so unusual that she didn't want to be surrounded by people and their problems? Or had her unsolicited comments about her family indicated she'd be open to more interaction? "You have the number here. It's an unlisted landline. Share it with your emergency contact, but I won't be your personal secretary. Sometimes you can get a cell signal at the top of the driveway."

Leigh gave her a quick salute, a smile tugging at the corners of her mouth. "Yes, ma'am. No problem. I know I can be chatty, but I'll keep my distance. Thank you again. Really."

A few minutes later Leigh Monroe's car pulled out of the driveway and Macy stared at a handful of cash, wondering what she'd gotten herself into.

CHAPTER THREE

L eigh threw the last pair of jeans from her closet into a packing box and looked around the bedroom for the final time. Gayle hadn't been surprised when she told her about the move, and she hadn't offered to help her pack. They weren't likely to remain friends, if they ever were, and that stung. She'd spent three years trying to be what Gayle wanted. Note to self, *You can't be happy with anyone else unless you're happy with yourself.* She hated to sound like a self-help slogan, but her dad used to say the truth was welcome in heaven.

She carried the box into the living room and stacked it with the others near the door. As long as she kept busy, the roiling emotions that came and went without reason or announcement weren't so bad. "I will not let this woman control my life one second longer."

"That's the spirit." Her younger sister, Hedy, grabbed another box from the doorway and handed it off to Pam, who shuffled it to Bo, who was packing the truck. "Too many fish."

"You know, I could've gotten these boxes into my trunk and backseat, and you guys wouldn't have wasted half a day."

"But we love you and want to help. Besides, we're gagging to see the new place."

She loved her baby sister and sometimes even sought her advice on matters of the heart. Hedy had married Bo, a bald, bearded, long-distance truck driver, the polar opposite of her trendy, petite self, fresh out of high school. Fourteen years later they were still together and seemed happy. Where had she gotten that gene? Leigh certainly hadn't inherited it.

"Speaking of fishes in the sea," Pam plopped down on the steps and took a gulp from her water bottle, "what about the one you're renting from? Deets."

"You get no details because I don't have any. She's my landlord. End of story. Now get back to work. I want to get there before dark."

She'd been thinking about the apartment at Belews Lake and about Macy Sheridan for the past two days. The small cottage seemed more suited to the beach, but its green siding blended nicely with the woodsy lakefront lot, making it almost disappear into the surroundings. It was exactly what she needed, a private setting away from the city, prying eyes, and questioning reporters. No one could say they were just in the neighborhood, if they could find her at all.

Her new landlord was more of an unknown. Nate had been right and wrong about her. She was a looker but didn't need makeup or a makeover to prove it. Her chestnut hair was thick like a stallion's mane, straight with just a hint of curl at the ends. She'd never seen eyes quite that blend of brown and black, reflecting and absorbing light. The blackish tint fluctuated based on Leigh's proximity, and she'd enjoyed watching the subtle changes more than a little. Macy had worn a beige sheepskin coat two sizes too large and black baggy jeans that tapered to a pair of scuffed Durango boots. She'd constantly hugged herself as if protecting herself from the world.

Macy Sheridan seemed perfectly contained, until she'd fallen into Leigh's arms. Then she unraveled. But in those brief seconds before the panic set in, Macy had felt comfortable against her, as if the universe had purposely flung them together. She'd held on longer than necessary to absorb the heat that rose between them. Leigh missed the luxury of a lover's arms, but clinging to a stranger had been a little unexpected. She'd jumped to her feet and made a joke to cut the tension. But that feeling stuck to her like a tiny piece of lint to a statically charged blanket.

"I think that's the last of it," Hedy said. "Who knew moving a few boxes was so exhausting?" She glanced toward the door before stepping closer, and Leigh got the awkward feeling that always preceded their taboo topic. "Did you call her yet?"

"No, and I'm not going to." Her stomach clenched into a knot of nervous energy.

"Why?"

"Come on, Hedy, you know why. I've got nothing to say."

"It's been a long time, and things happened that you don't know about. Did it ever occur to you that she might have something to say?"

"I don't care what happened. Besides, it's too late to change anything. You may think of her as your mother, but she was never mine."

Hedy placed her hand on Leigh's shoulder and forced her to look at her. "*You* were my mother, cook, housekeeper, tutor, protector, therapist, and best friend. You were my sanity, and I'll never be able to repay you. But I've learned to forgive."

"Then you're a better person than I am." Leigh didn't like feeling at odds with her sister. They consistently disagreed on the subject of their mother and seldom discussed her, mainly because she refused.

"Hey, are we leaving or—" Pam spun around and headed back outside. "Never mind."

Leigh grabbed her backpack off the floor and waved Hedy out the door. "Coming?"

"Yeah." Hedy's frustrated sigh signaled her disagreement and her promise that the conversation wasn't over. "Bo and I'll follow you."

"Can you drop Pam back here when we're finished?" Hedy nodded. "And don't let your trucker get lost. Everything I own is in that vehicle."

"Including a very nice bed and dresser for my guest room, thank you very much."

The atmosphere in Leigh's car was strained for the first part of the drive to Belews Lake. Pam was obviously trying not to mention the tense scene she'd witnessed between her and Hedy, but she didn't do quiet or restrained very well. "Go ahead. Say whatever's on your mind."

"Oh, thank God. I was about to bust. Hedy brought up the *M*-word again, didn't she?"

"What was your first clue?"

"The daggers in your eyes or maybe the fiery cheeks? You know she just wants to help."

"Yeah, but there's no help for the situation…and I really don't want to talk about it." She gave Pam what she hoped was her I'm-serious look to end the discussion.

"Fine, so tell me about your new landlord. I noticed a little flush when I mentioned her earlier. Give me ten words that describe her." Pam loved this game.

She sighed and gave in. The more she avoided, the more determined Pam would become and the more pointed her questions would get. "Educated, refined, unusual, reclusive, aloof, controlled, afraid, and attractive."

"That's only eight."

"Very hot." Leigh couldn't believe she'd said exactly what was on her mind. But even bundled up in heavy clothes with her arms wrapped around herself, Macy Sheridan was hot.

"Woot!" Pam fist-pumped the air and sang, "Leigh's got a crush on her landlord. That rocks. And you know I'm totally kidding, right?"

Leigh shook her head and tried to reason with the unreasonable. "Even if I do have a crush on her, and I'm not saying I do, nothing would come of it. She's made it very clear she wants privacy."

When Pam got an idea, it was like the proverbial thorn in her side. And if Leigh's love life happened to be involved, she showed no mercy. "Just be open. That's all I'm asking. You totally rock that innocent redhead thing. Before you know it, she'll be eating out of your hand."

That was an image Leigh could not associate with reserved Macy Sheridan. Nate believed that underneath every uptight woman was a tiger clawing her way to freedom. Maybe this one was a scared kitten needing to be comforted. Whatever her desires, Macy had made it clear she didn't want to be bothered. They both had reasons for hiding out in the boonies. She wasn't going to pry into Macy's and hoped Macy wouldn't pry into hers.

❖

Macy dropped a bag of ginger tea into the pot, set the timer for three minutes, and placed her favorite "Starry Night" mug on the counter. Looking toward the lake, she wondered why time disappeared so quickly during happy times and crawled during the hard ones. She'd planned to at least approach the art studio today, maybe even open the door, but she'd said that for the past three months. However, something substantial had distracted her—that woman. Her *tenant* was moving in, and it hung over her like a lopsided halo ready to crash. She couldn't possibly tackle the studio with such a disruption to her normal schedule.

A tickle of discomfort raced up her spine, and she retreated to the safety of her afternoon routine. She adjusted the curtains to diffuse the late-day sun, placed the items she'd chosen for dinner on the same rack in the refrigerator, and checked the woodpile in case she wanted a fire later. Everything was set. In a couple of hours, she'd fix her meal and relax, maybe read or listen to music.

When the timer sounded, she poured a cup of tea and moved to the wall of windows facing the lake. Would it be possible to relax knowing another person was on the property? What did she know about Leigh Monroe? She hadn't asked enough questions, but after her clumsy back flip from the steps, she'd been emotionally frazzled. Now every time she glanced toward the boathouse, she'd wonder if Leigh was looking back or if she would appear at any moment. What had she been thinking? It was too late for self-recrimination as she heard the distinctive sound of two vehicles coming down the gravel drive.

Suddenly her backyard was a cacophony of people and voices. A bald man with a full beard backed a red pickup toward the dock, and she held her breath as he edged closer to the water. Twangy country music and a woman's off-key singing caterwauled from the vehicle's windows. Leigh and another woman bailed out of her car, and the other woman ran to the floater, yelling and jumping like a kid at summer camp. The boathouse rocked as if a tidal wave had passed. It took all of Macy's considerable restraint not to rush out and demand order. Taking a calming sip of tea, she reasoned it would take only a short while for Leigh to unpack.

An hour later, it seemed like forever. What was taking so long? Music blared from the truck as four people darted back and forth carrying boxes that were haphazardly wrapped with tape and spewing clothes and papers. Who were these people? Would they be regular fixtures at the apartment? She'd made it clear she preferred privacy, but she couldn't prohibit Leigh from having guests. She sipped her tea, unable to look away from the almost comedic scene. It would've been funny if it weren't happening in *her* backyard. Feeling her world shrinking, she opened the window and breathed in a cool breeze from the lake. But her respite was short-lived as the wind also carried the voices from below.

"You're so lucky," the petite woman with hair almost the color of Leigh's said.

"I know, right?" This from the butchy woman with spiked locks.

"You must be living right," the man replied, with a slap to Leigh's ass.

"Watch where you put that hand or you'll draw back a nub," Leigh said. She grabbed him in a headlock and pulled him toward the lake. "Can you swim, Bo?"

"Hedy, help! Your crazy sister is trying to kill me."

"If I let go, will you get back to work? I want to be moved in before midnight."

"Promise." He backed away and pumped a few fake fist jabs in her direction. "I was just about to bust loose on you." Leigh waved him off and bounded up the apartment steps as if she'd done it for years.

Macy tried to remember the last time she'd been with friends, much less enjoyed them in such a casual way. Had she ever been as playful, even as a youngster? Maybe as a child when she and Jesse… The picture froze in her mind, and when she blinked, it shattered into millions of pieces, each a shard of pain slashing through her. It had been so many years. Why hadn't time dissolved the aching? She loosened her white-knuckled grip on her tea mug and took another sip as the man's voice wafted up from the dock.

"Last box coming through. Time to celebrate."

Leigh swung from the apartment opening, hanging upside down like a monkey. Dear God, did her insurance cover such shenanigans? She started to call out to be careful, but Leigh did a flip and landed cleanly on the floater. "Let's go for a celebratory swim."

"Hello, it's probably freezing in there?" The butch woman huddled closer to Bo.

"What's the matter, Pam, chicken?" He was teasing her.

"No."

"You guys go ahead. I'm going to dabble my toes," Leigh's sister said as she sat down on the dock and dangled her feet in the lake.

Macy definitely needed to call this off before it went any further. She didn't need four hypothermic people on her dock waiting for an ambulance. As she started to set her mug on the counter, Leigh grabbed the tail of her polo, shucked it over her head, and stripped off her jeans, leaving only a sports bra and hipster boy shorts. Warmth snaked through Macy like a shot of moonshine, and she licked her dry lips. Leigh stood tall and proud, as if being almost naked on a stranger's dock with these three people was the most natural thing in the world.

She envisioned Leigh standing in that very spot, posing in the nude as her brush replicated her exquisite form. She'd enjoy touching the subtle curves and dips of her body in order to express them on canvas. Capturing her skin tone would require expertise Macy wasn't sure she still possessed, but she longed to try. The scene before her played out in real time, and the one in her mind crept in slow motion. Just as slowly her mug slipped from her hands and smashed on the kitchen floor.

"Shit, shit, shit." She stalled, momentarily torn between the spectacle of Leigh Monroe and the tea soaking through her pants. It had been too long since she'd seen anyone except a student model nearly nude, but more than Leigh's nubile body and gentle curves gave her pause. She was drawn to the freedom and enjoyment of life Leigh expressed so easily. Her joking when they met had seemed off-putting, but after seeing her with friends, she realized that was Leigh—jovial, engaging, and so alive.

As she picked up the pieces of broken glass around her feet and mopped the floor, she wondered what Leigh must think of her. She'd been distant and unwelcoming, to say the least. She hadn't even recognized when Leigh was kidding—and God knows she could use a good chuckle. When was the last time she'd laughed until she cried and her sides ached? If it was possible to lose a sense of humor, hers was surely missing or so dormant that it needed resuscitation.

Strange how it took only a couple of brief encounters to reveal how disconnected she'd become.

The last sixteen years of her life had been alternately intense and achingly bland. She hadn't given up entirely, but she'd certainly become more circumspect. Translation, she was boring and predictable. Could she resurrect her artistic muse, or had it also vanished after years of suppression? She'd spent so long trying to solve one mystery that everything else had become secondary.

❖

"Oh. My. God." Leigh collapsed on the squishy sofa and propped her feet on the oak coffee table. The sky over the lake was packed with stars, and she couldn't get enough of the view. She pulled a bundle from one of the boxes, unwrapped the layers of tissue paper, and pointed her old sock monkey toward the sky. "Don't get skies like this in the city. Right, Toby? Sorry for leaving you in solitary confinement so long. The Grinch didn't like you."

She'd been in her longest relationship with Toby, since her seventh birthday. He'd been a gift from her father, just before he died. Toby's ears were frayed and the seams around his hat were unraveling, so she held him gently under the arms, careful not to stress the fragile lines of stitching. Gayle had thought he was ridiculous and insisted she put him in storage. "What does she know?"

When her friends weren't around to bounce ideas off, she talked to Toby. Often just hearing the situation out loud helped, and he was a great listener who didn't give cheesy advice. Talking to a stuffed toy wasn't the most mature thing in the world, but everybody had quirks. She loved motivational adages and Toby, number-one sock monkey.

"We never had a place like this. The furniture is older than you, but it's solid and comfortable, the way a home should be."

After her father's death, home was a series of government-subsidized apartments that coincided with her mother's flavor-of-the-month boyfriends. Susan wasn't one to bake cookies or play dress-up, and her daughters were seldom a priority. How had she and Hedy grown up so optimistic about love and life? Their role model sucked.

She'd spent many nights covering Hedy's ears to block the arguments so she could sleep. Learning to cook had been a necessity, housekeeping falling a distant fourth behind taking care of Hedy and schoolwork. She'd kept up with her studies just enough to ensure Hedy didn't fall behind in hers. And they'd grown closer. But Leigh still had an inner void that longed to be filled. Why had she never been important enough? How could a mother be so unavailable and unconcerned about her children?

"Her loss, that's what I say. We got along without her then…and we sure don't need her now. Right, my friend?" Holding Toby to her chest, she enjoyed the stars' reflections off the glassy surface of the lake. She loved quiet, simple moments like these when nature rocked her in its lap and she belonged. As she looked around the cozy little apartment filled with antiques and starlight, she felt at home for the first time in three years.

"Guess I better unpack. We'll be staying, if our landlord doesn't change her mind again."

As Leigh divided her clothes between a small dresser and a portable hanging rack, she thought about Macy Sheridan's behavior the day they met. Her responses to Leigh had been erratic—but predominately aloof, bordering on rude. The perfectly packaged woman seemed on the verge of becoming undone every time Leigh was near. What was Macy afraid of and how did Leigh's presence threaten her?

Macy had treated Nate the same way when he approached her about the facial reconstruction, but for some reason his request had upset her. Maybe her last case with the CAP detectives had ended badly. If so, she might be wise to keep her occupation secret. Toby seemed to stare at her from the sofa as if to say, *Why didn't you tell her you were a cop?*

"I didn't want to…I thought I should…wanted to give her… Hell, I don't know. It's not like I have anything to hide. Why should she care anyway, as long as I pay the rent?" Toby's embroidered eyes drilled into her, demanding the truth. "Okay, maybe I was worried she hates cops now. What if she'd seen the newspapers? Would she have rented the apartment to me? Maybe I just wasn't ready to face one more person who'd judge me without knowing all the facts and dismiss me out of hand."

That felt right, but she'd have to come clean sooner or later. She'd give Macy a chance to warm up to her first. They'd shared a moment of connection, in a heap on the dock; at least *she'd* felt it. When they settled into a comfortable living routine, she'd have plenty of time to gently reveal the details of her not-so-stellar history. Leigh just needed to figure out how to get close to someone who preferred to be left alone—and why it mattered to her.

Based on Macy's off-handed comments about her parents, she had a few skeletons of her own. Maybe that was why she acted so unapproachable and disinterested. Such behavior reminded Leigh of her mother, and that hadn't turned out well. She placed Toby over her shoulder and stepped onto the small balcony overlooking the lake. "But I can warm a sock monkey's heart. Macy Sheridan doesn't stand a chance."

CHAPTER FOUR

Pictures of Leigh Monroe shucking off her clothes, half naked, and diving into the lake had chased away Macy's much-needed sleep. The evocative images clung to her as tightly as her damp, tangled sheets. She awoke groggy and hypersensitive, almost agitated. Why did her body respond so viscerally to a woman she'd just met? She was used to nude bodies, artistically, but this one wasn't like the graduate students she sketched periodically to keep her skills sharp. Leigh Monroe had the curves and telltale signs of maturity that appealed to her creative eye and her prurient interest. She'd love to combine her passions for art and the female form by painting a nude of Leigh. *Stop it.* Their arrangement was business, best to keep it that way.

Yesterday she'd marveled at Leigh's uninhibited physicality and ease with her friends. But Leigh's indifference to social decorum in her new landlord's backyard worried her. What if Leigh was a reckless thrill seeker with no regard for anyone but herself and her desires? She'd need to clarify a few more ground rules if this regrettable rental arrangement was going to work. And in order to do that, she'd have to talk to her again. Shit.

It wasn't that she couldn't carry on a decent conversation. She didn't want to. Conversation gave others the mistaken idea that she wanted to share. Nothing could be further from the truth. She had no energy for or interest in having a getting-to-know-you chat with another woman. Sharing led to relationships and eventually to pain.

As little contact with Leigh Monroe as possible was the order of the day, every day.

Macy finished her coffee, glanced at the studio door, and stepped outside just as the morning started to bleed color. She loved the dance between the tendrils of darkness still clinging to the sky and the shocks of light breaking through. She'd painted this scene many times but never quite perfected the magic feeling of promise that was daybreak.

Grabbing her gardening gloves and trowel from the potting table outside the door, she headed for the first of several flowerbeds that ringed the house. The last frost of the season had passed, and it was time to plant annuals. She'd helped her parents sow the original perennial seeds when she was a child and knew exactly where each black-eyed Susan, iris, and daylily would sprout. She visualized the location for the marigolds, zinnias, and petunias she planned to disperse among the existing plants. Just the thought of color surrounding the house lifted her spirits and erased the troubling thoughts of Leigh Monroe.

When she settled on the ground, the cool dampness of the morning earth seeped through the knees of her sweatpants. She turned the weathered mulch and inhaled the musty aroma of fertile soil. Sliding her gloves off, she buried her hands in the black richness and sifted the textured dirt through her fingers. She felt a part of the earth, joined with the energy of new life that sprang from it. She carefully lifted a squirming worm from the hole she'd started and relocated him to the back of the flowerbed. "You'll be safe here."

"Guess it's true then."

"Shit." She scrambled backward on her hands, her butt dragging the ground like a backstroking crab. "Don't sneak up on me like that. What's true?"

"About the early bird getting the worm—that was a worm I saw you fondling, wasn't it?"

Blood and heat rushed to her face. "I wasn't fondling—" Leigh grinned. "You're teasing me again. It's a shame I can't tell the difference anymore. I need to—"

"I was wondering—" They spoke at the same time and Leigh waved her hand graciously. "Go ahead, please."

With Leigh in front of her now, fully clothed, the objection to her behavior yesterday seemed less important. "I hope you aren't planning any more semi-nude bathing parties. The neighbors may not be next door, but this is still rural, conservative North Carolina. A little more restraint would be appreciated." *And a little more warning.* Leigh was like a ninja skulking around the property.

Leigh's amused grin didn't fade. "Did I embarrass you?"

"No, of course not. Don't be ridiculous. I've seen plenty of nude women, just not in the backyard in broad-open daylight. I mean, I've..." She pulled on her earlobe like a kid unable to explain bad behavior, babbling about something she probably shouldn't have broached in the first place.

"No one was actually nude, you know. We were just as clothed as if we'd been in bathing suits, except it was tighty-whities. But I promise to be more discreet."

The image of a stuffy principal disciplining an errant student flashed through Macy's mind. "Just be careful and have respect for the neighbors." She was anxious to move on before she trussed herself any tighter into an ill-fitting moral straitjacket. "What were you going to say?"

"Could you give me a lay of the land? I'm all keyed up this morning. Thought a run would help me unwind. I need to get back into my routine, and I'd like to avoid any flesh-eating varmints. I also need a grocery store. Is there one close by?"

"You should be relatively safe running along Egret Lane. As for grocery stores, Smith's is about half a mile down Pine Hall Road, but the selections are limited, mostly emergency stuff. You'll find two or three smaller places in Stokesdale with the basics. If you're looking for anything healthy, you'll have to go to Food Lion in Walnut Cove, and even that's suspect."

"Wow, I'm really not in Kansas anymore, am I? But that's good. I love it out here. Thanks again for renting to me. See you later."

She watched Leigh's retreating ass, cupped by jogging tights, with too much interest: the slight bounce of flesh, the self-assured swing of arms and planting of feet. She'd tried to capture that curve and confidence of the human body in her art but usually fell short. Leigh would pose a greater challenge. She was fluid and graceful, tall and lean, secure, open and engaging. Leigh was everything she wasn't.

As Leigh trotted off up the incline, an official-looking vehicle pulled into the driveway. The driver stopped at the side of the narrow path and allowed Leigh to pass. Not this again. As she started toward the house, Detective Shaver waved her down.

"Ma'am, please. If I could just have a minute?"

"I heard you last time and the answer is still no. Why are you back?"

"Because I'm a persistent, bordering-on-annoying cop who hates to disappoint a victim's family or my supervisor."

She sensed Shaver's priority was more about the victims than his supervisor, and in some small way that pleased her. A lot of cops she'd worked with were more interested in the exciting aspects of the job and career advancement. As she searched Nathan Shaver's eyes for any indication of deceit, her resolve slipped a little. "Do you expect to wear me down by just showing up every day, or do you have a more detailed plan?"

"Honestly, I'd camp out on your doorstep if I thought it would change your mind." Shaver scuffed the toe of his polished shoe into a lump of soil she'd dug from the flowerbed. "I wanted to apologize too. I got the feeling I upset you last time, and I'm not sure how. If I did something wrong, I'm real sorry."

This was a first, a cop apologizing for anything. Most would rather gnaw off a finger than admit they'd done anything wrong, much less make a public statement about it. "Wasn't you, Detective."

"Good. If you refused to help us because of something stupid I said, I'd never forgive myself. Finding a missing person and bringing a family some peace is much more important than pride or ego."

She was starting to like the attractive, modest young man, and her empathy gene was vibrating. "Again, it wasn't you."

"Then would you reconsider?"

"I didn't say that."

"Could I possibly leave a copy of the file with you? Just look at it? Please, Ms. Sheridan."

Macy remembered the families she'd encountered in her years as a forensic artist and how her efforts had comforted and eventually brought them closure. Just because she'd gotten out of the business didn't mean people had stopped doing horrible things to each other or that she would be insulated from them forever. "If I let you leave the file, will you go away?"

"Forever. You'll never see me again."

"Leave it. I don't promise anything, but I'll look at it—sometime. Tell your cohorts in CAP not to push me or these copies will end up in a bonfire roasting marshmallows."

Shaver lacked the arrogance most of the Crimes Against Persons detectives wore like a badge of honor, and she liked him more for it. He handed the file to her and almost bowed as he backed away. "Thank you, really."

"Tell Rickard *if* I decide to take the case, I'll contact him." She wanted to add "prick" to the end of the sentence. Sergeant Kevin Rickard had obviously sent Shaver to do his dirty work. He wouldn't have the balls to approach her after their last conversation. She'd asked for a favor and he'd refused without a real discussion. She'd quit the next day, and it had taken only six months for him to send someone knocking on her door begging for help. Now it was her turn to blow him off, but could she? Rickard wasn't the one who would suffer if she did.

"Thanks again, ma'am." Shaver nodded and rushed to his car as if afraid she'd change her mind if he lingered.

She held the heavy manila envelope in her hands, staring at it until her muscles ached, and then dropped it on an old stump that served as a seat. Already regretting her decision, she felt the weight of responsibility settle uncomfortably on her shoulders. She grabbed the trowel and returned to the mindless safety of the earth and new plantings.

❖

Leigh almost did a one-eighty when Nathan pulled into Macy Sheridan's driveway. She hadn't told him yet she'd moved to Belews Lake and wanted to keep her cop status quiet for the moment. To his credit, he didn't yell in disbelief when he saw her. He slowed, rolled down the window, and started to say something, but she shook her head and kept walking. They'd both worked undercover and understood the subtle signal for *don't acknowledge me*.

She'd spent most of her run thinking about what to tell him and how she'd gotten so out of shape. The latter question was much easier. She'd ignored her own desires in order to accommodate Gayle's every whim. Her exercise routine, friends, family, and even her work had suffered in the years she'd tried to single-handedly maintain their relationship. Today was the first step back to her life, if she lived through it. She checked her watch. Her time was way off her usual pace, she was breathing hard, and her stride was awkward, but it felt good to be running again.

When Nathan's vehicle approached on Egret Lane, she took a deep breath and waited for him. He pulled over and motioned for her to get in. "What's the big freaking deal, Leigh?"

"Did she take the case?"

"What?" Not the response he apparently expected, but she needed to explain in her own way. "She took the file, no guarantee she'll help."

"I haven't told her I'm a cop, and you don't want her to know right now. Trust me. She'll think we're trying to gang up on her. Besides, I don't want her to hear all the bad press and dislike me before she gets to know me."

"Plenty of time for that once she does know you."

"Smart-ass. I need a little time and I'll tell her." She felt guilty about evading the truth, but Macy was as skittish as a new colt already. Leigh didn't know the reason or why she was so protective of Macy, but she seemed vulnerable. Maybe she was just the type who needed to warm up to strangers. Leigh could be patient. "So, will you keep it quiet for the time being?"

"No problem, partner. I promised she'd never see me again if she took the file. Now get out. I've got work to do back in civilization." He flashed a white toothy grin and put the car in gear. "Stop by next time you check in with the warden. Later." He spun off, leaving a puff of dust on the shoulder and a streak of rubber on the pavement.

"Juvenile." She mumbled under her breath as she jogged back to the cottage. When she reached the top of the driveway, she stopped. Macy was crouched over the flowerbed, her shoulders drawn forward as if trying to exclude the world. She kneaded the soil like a chef mixing ingredients for a gourmet meal. The rhythmic back and forth of her body was hypnotic, and the tension of the last few days drained out of Leigh's shoulders as she enjoyed the sight and sound of woman and water.

"What *are* you staring at?" Macy's voice shattered her reverie.

"Sorry, just admiring the scenery."

"Are you always so…bold?"

"Some people call it honesty, and I hear it's a fine quality. You're the first person I've met who objects."

"Maybe if it wasn't so, I don't know…"

Macy was obviously struggling with the innuendo, and a stab of guilt prompted another apology. "I seem to offend you a lot, when I'm trying to express my feel—"

"I'd just appreciate a wider berth, the privacy thing. Thought I made that clear."

She was having trouble keeping up with Macy's shifts. One minute she was spouting unsolicited information about her parents, and the next she was throwing up barriers. But an occasional spark in her dark-brown eyes hinted at an opening. "You were clear about your preference, but I'm such an extrovert I talk aloud to myself when no one's around. It's hard to resist the opportunity for a real conversation. I can be annoying like that. I'll try harder." As she started to walk away, she saw the thick envelope on the tree stump. "Homework?"

Macy looked up from her digging. "Is this you trying harder?"

"Just wondering. That looks serious."

"You just don't quit, do you?" In spite of her annoyed tone, Macy took a seat on the stump closer to Leigh. "I used to work with the police as a forensic artist…but I quit. They don't want to take no for an answer. This," she tapped the envelope with a dirty finger, "is their idea of a subtle request."

The revelation, another divergence between words and actions, surprised Leigh. But she wasn't complaining. Nor would she admit she knew the police were asking for Macy's help. "So, you're an artist? I admire anyone with creative ability."

"I was. Not sure what I am anymore."

"You're whatever you want to be."

"If only life were so simple."

"The police must really need you. Would it do any harm to take a look? Beats boredom out here with no cell or Internet service." She was half joking, but now her own situation seemed more dismal. "You know what they say. Never test the depth of the ocean with both feet."

"What makes you think I'm bored? Did it ever occur to you that I actually enjoy the peace and quiet? And I'm working my way up to painting again."

"How do you work your way up to painting?" Macy gave her a skeptical look and she hurried to explain. "I'm not being funny or dense. I just don't understand the whole creative process."

"I do nude sketches. The complexity of the human form is great for honing your skills."

"Nudes?"

"Don't look so surprised. I'm an artist, not a prude."

"I didn't mean that. Who poses for nude sketches? I thought that was a ploy that lecherous old men used to seduce young women. Shows how in touch I am."

"Lots of graduate students paying off college loans are happy for the work, and it is just work."

Leigh imagined Macy staring at a naked woman all day and re-creating her body on canvas. The idea was appealing in a way she'd never considered. "I can see how that might spark some creative juices."

Macy's eyebrow arched like Leigh's first-grade teacher's when she'd misbehaved in class. "Anyway, back to the point. I'm not bored."

"Are you going to help the police?"

"I haven't decided. It's not really a simple decision, but you wouldn't understand."

"I'd like to." She wasn't sure what prompted Macy's sudden candor and didn't care. She just wanted it to continue until she knew everything about her.

"The work was satisfying for a while, but it slowly leeched the joy out of my life like ultraviolet light fades a painting. My art became more about resurrecting the dead and completing a horrible story and less about creating something beautiful."

Macy wrapped her arms around herself, and tension tightened the corners of her mouth. Her palpable pain made Leigh almost sorry for prying. She understood losing something you love and the emptiness that lingered. That she and Macy shared this most human of experiences seemed fitting. "I'm sure you helped a lot of families."

"But eventually the cost became too great." Her eyes closed, and when she opened them again, the moment had passed. "I'm sorry. That was inappropriate." She left her gardening tools on the ground, picked up the file, and started toward the cottage.

Macy's openness fascinated Leigh, and she wanted to prolong the connection. "I was wondering…would you maybe consider having dinner with me…tonight? I don't know anyone out here, and I'm not much of a cook. A good meal would be nice…to share with someone. With you." She was rambling, but her feelings were all over the place.

Macy didn't even look back. "No, thank you."

"Maybe another time?" When Macy didn't answer, she tried another tack. "Do you have anything I can do? To keep busy, maybe help out?"

"No." She wasn't sure which question Macy was answering.

"What about that woodpile out back? Could I split some logs if I get bored?"

"If you're that desperate," Macy said as she closed the cottage door.

Macy's abrupt departure reminded her of her mother's segregation behind bedroom doors. The situations were very different but the message was the same. She'd enjoyed the few moments of intimacy with Macy. Knowing another person's secrets and guarding their trust was one of the most precious gifts of a relationship, and she'd missed that with Gayle. But in her desire to get to know Macy, she'd overstepped and fittingly been rebuffed.

Was it the memory of past rejections that stung so much, residual pain from losing Gayle, or the fact that Macy had said no without giving her dinner offer serious consideration? Either way, she got the point loud and clear—Macy Sheridan was not interested.

❖

Macy closed the door between her and Leigh, leaned against it, and shook her head. What the hell had come over her? Some very personal thoughts had oozed out of her like liquid mercury seeking a level plane. She didn't know Leigh Monroe or if she could be trusted, but she'd spilled her guts like they were best friends.

She'd even told her about sketching nudes. What she hadn't said was how connected she felt when her two passions were combined—the beauty of women and her love of the artistic process. It was the only time she felt truly still alive and vibrant. She indulged her deepest feelings in art without having to expose them to anyone else. Leigh would've thought her pathetic. Moving to the kitchen table, she dropped the file and slumped into a chair. What about Leigh compelled her to talk about her life and desires—compelled her to talk at all?

She hadn't been as forthcoming with her lover of two years. She'd tried to rationalize the distance between her and Julia, blaming work pressures, family responsibilities, and general ennui, none of which went over well with Julia. A year later, it made perfect sense. She hadn't been in love with Julia. She cared for her but never experienced the link that tugs on the heart when the other is joyful or in pain. She'd drifted on the wave of Julia's infatuation until stagnation set in. Now, she was ashamed to admit, she thought about their relationship only when she felt guilty about the breakup or found herself emotionally lacking again.

She wasn't in a relationship because she couldn't handle one. The give-and-take, constant togetherness, and analyzing every comment simply made her feel inept. Maybe she didn't process like coupled people seemed to. How did one *explain* feelings anyway? You either felt them or you didn't, and once you said so, what else was needed? Perhaps she had the emotional genes of a man—shit happens, don't dwell on it, carry on. Her failure had to be in the genes or hormones, something she couldn't control, because she'd tried everything within her power to overcome the deficit. Would she ever know that all-encompassing love that romance novels and best-selling movies depicted?

Jesse. The name floated to the surface as easily as color dyed the faces of flowers. They'd shared the joys and pains of each other's lives from the time she was old enough to recognize feelings. They were best friends, confidantes, and never seemed to tire of talking. Could they have been more if circumstances hadn't intervened? Their friendship had been the most genuine relationship of her life. When it ended, she'd never let another woman close and never explained why. How could she describe something she'd spent sixteen years trying to understand? Work had become her savior and her oppressor until the memories and pain became unbearable and she left the job as well. She hadn't consciously chosen to isolate herself from future involvements, but it had probably worked out for the best.

She pushed the thick envelope back and forth on the table. Maybe Leigh was right. What was the harm in looking at the case? Before she could second-guess herself, she ripped open the tab and emptied the contents. A copy of the witness's statement detailing the discovery of the skeletal remains lay on top of a stack of old missing-person reports. She was amazed and saddened by the sheer number of people still unaccounted for in the area.

As she shuffled through the reports, an envelope fell on the table. She recognized the handwriting of Trudy James, forensic anthropologist. Macy always read Trudy's notes first because they provided the preliminary information she'd need if she decided to take the case.

She scanned the pages looking for specific details she desperately wanted but dreaded finding. The remains contained no soft tissue at the time of discovery, making it more likely identification would come from forensic anthropological results and her reconstruction rather than from the pathologist or medical examiner. Trudy determined the age of the victim to be between fourteen and nineteen, based on bone length and fusion. The victim was female, based on differences in the pelvis, skull, and femur. She was small-boned and of Caucasian ancestry, concluded by teeth and skull measurements.

All the elements were there. This could be the one she'd waited for. Macy looked away from the reports and registered the tightening in her gut that always accompanied the conclusions segment of the document. She took a deep breath and read the last few lines of Trudy's report.

Possible cause of death, massive antemortem blunt-force trauma to the posterior right parietal segment of the skull. No indication of perimortem or postmortem trauma. No identifiable surgical procedures or healed bone fractures. Small portion of denim fabric and dark leather boots recovered with remains and sent for material analysis. Possible time of death 15–20 years ago.

The timeline fit. Denim fabric. Boots. No surgical procedures. No bone fractures. Oh, God. She picked up the phone and dialed Trudy's home number. When she answered, Macy didn't wait for pleasantries. "Trudy?"

"I know what you want to hear, Macy, but I'm not sure. All I can say is it's possible. But listen to me—"

Trudy had never offered the slightest hope that Macy's nightmare could be reaching an end. She dropped the phone in the cradle with a shaky hand and sat down on the sofa. She didn't pick up when Trudy called back.

CHAPTER FIVE

*A*sheer turquoise blouse, top two buttons open. Dark-blue straight-legged jeans tucked into scuffed brown cowboy boots. Jesse was gangly, sixteen-year-old thin, long blond hair, and silvery blue eyes that danced with mischief.

They walked the ragged path along the railroad tracks, Jesse's coconut shampoo scenting the air. A full moon gilded the night sky. Music from the club vibrated her insides as they neared the entrance. Gray concrete building. Flashing neon lights. Lines of people. Perfume and cologne mingled with cigarette and marijuana smoke. A T-shirt-and-jeans-clad bouncer waved them in.

Black lights swirled awkward shapes across a crowded dance floor. White shirts shimmered like beacons in a sea of color. Jesse swallowed by a mob. Teenagers indulged in alcohol and sex urged on by blaring music. Hours passed.

"Going out for a smoke," Jesse said.

"You don't smoke."

"Duh, I'm just outside the door. You'll be okay, right? Be back in five."

"Jesse, don't..."

Five minutes, ten, and then thirty. No Jesse. Not inside the club, not in the toilets, not outside. The full moon was like a lamp guiding her path to nowhere. The night air reeked of stale cigarettes, and the alleys stank of urine and vomit. She gagged as she searched again. Jesse had disappeared.

As morning dawned, she ran home, along the tracks they'd followed. "Jesse." She yelled, but no Jesse. "Jesse, please!"

Macy woke to the sound of her own screams. Her cheeks stung from tears and her clothes were matted to her body with sweat. *Why?* Sixteen years later the sights, sounds, and smells of that night were still painfully vivid, as were the last words she and Jesse had spoken to each other. No matter how precise her recall, she still didn't understand what had happened. The only true thing was that she was responsible. She was older and should've taken care of Jesse. It was a familiar mantra, and like a flagellant, she let the penance sink in. Through the years, the pain had dulled, but the guilt had grown inside like a malignancy devouring any hope of real happiness.

She rose from the uncomfortable sofa and stretched the kinks out of her back on the way to the shower. Hot water and hot coffee— then the studio. If this new case could help her find Jesse, she'd take it, but she had to start in the studio. Searching the file last night, she prayed she'd find parallels between this case and the circumstances of Jesse's disappearance while praying she wouldn't. She didn't want to believe her friend was dead. After so long, it seemed the most logical conclusion, but the thought brought only a renewed wave of guilt with no comfort.

As she downed her last sip of coffee, the phone rang. "Hello."

"Macy, are you all right? You didn't answer when I called back last night."

"I'm fine, Trudy. I just needed some time."

"You read the file, didn't you?"

"Yeah."

"I'm sorry I couldn't tell you more, but every detail I could make out is in the report. Are you taking the case?"

"Not sure yet."

"Let me know if I can help."

"I will." The sadness in Trudy's voice made her wince. She hadn't been fair to her colleagues, friends, or family since her self-imposed exile, but she needed time to make decisions about her future. Everyone had been patient, but they were also anxious for her to resume their idea of a normal life. "Thank you."

Macy hung up, collected the file from the table, and turned toward the studio. If she opened the door without over-thinking, she might have a chance of facing what was on the other side. She pulled on the dingy-white lab coat hanging beside the door and wiped at stains that never brushed or washed away. The extra layer of clothing made her feel more protected as she turned the knob and pushed the door wide.

The age-progression sketches she'd attempted were everywhere: hanging on easels, tacked to a giant corkboard, and taped to the walls. She hadn't completed a drawing yet. The only element she was certain about was the look around the eyes, which changed little through a lifetime. Everything else was a guess. If she'd only had more pictures of Jesse and her family, the results would've been different. The single faded photograph of the two of them on the hood of her mother's car didn't provide enough detail for a computer application, and her memories had faded. Jesse deserved more.

Macy recalled the day she'd asked Sergeant Kevin Rickard to reopen Jesse's case. They'd stood in this very room as he collected the results of her last reconstruction.

"Please, Kevin, just have a detective review the case file and let me look at the photos of her. It won't take long."

"We don't have time to dredge up old cases. We've got enough fresh ones to work."

"Can you let me look at it then? I've seen plenty of police files before. You know I'm trustworthy."

He squirmed as if she'd caught him in a lie. "There is no file, Macy."

"What do you mean?"

"It's been purged. We don't keep sixteen-year-old missing-persons files anymore. There's no point. If they haven't turned up, they're probably not going to."

"Your sensitivity is touching. Surely, there's something on the computer about the case. Everything can't be gone. I'd like to try anyway. She was my best friend."

"No."

"Why?"

"We've got other cases we need your help on. Cases that have a better chance of being solved."

She stared at his back as he headed toward the door. "If you don't do this, I'll quit. I've never asked you for anything before."

"Then I guess you're quitting."

She'd worked for three months trying to reconstruct Jesse's face from memory and then avoided the studio completely for three more because she couldn't cope with Jesse's faceless eyes asking for help. Now Jesse stared at her in every conceivable gradation of morning light. Her heart pounded in her throat. She failed Jesse every day that passed without answers. Was she alive or dead? Either way, Macy needed details so she could move on with her life. Jesse would want her to be happy, not shuffling through her days like a barely functioning zombie.

She collected all the incomplete sketches one at a time, careful not to rip the delicate paper or smudge the drawing. She stacked them neatly in a box, placed them on the corner of her drafting table, and put the new file beside them. Thirty sets of silvery blue eyes begged for answers. This new case *would* be her last, no matter what the outcome. She'd either find Jesse or find a way to forgive herself.

Pushing up the bangle bracelet on her left wrist, she stroked the noticeable scar and flinched. Was she really just taking a break as she'd told everyone, or was she skirting another bout of depression? Her renewed obsession with solving Jesse's case could be a precursor to a relapse.

She thought about what Leigh had said about being bored. Boredom wasn't the problem. Failure and lack of confidence were her issues. Maybe it was time to get her hands dirty again. In life, as in art, little was accomplished painting inside the lines.

❖

Leigh had tossed and turned all night, replaying Macy's curt refusal of her dinner invitation and listening to the droning hum and click of cicadas. The rhythmic sound should've lulled her to sleep, but it seemed to echo a single word, no-o, no-o. What had she done to deserve the personification of her mother in other women? She and Hedy had fended for themselves as children, her past relationships had failed for various reasons, and Gayle had been mostly absent. The experiences left her searching for someone who shared her priorities and actually wanted a commitment. But she kept stumbling into women who wanted only a one-night stand or a continuous fling.

Macy's rejection stung longer than she imagined it could, obviously striking that old unhealed wound. They'd just met, but she already cared what Macy thought of her and how they got along. Unable to rest, Leigh got out of bed, stretched, and started up the driveway for a predawn run. She was still a bit stiff from yesterday, but if she wanted her endurance back, she had to keep at it. The small cottage was dark as she passed, and she turned onto the street at a quick jog, trying to ignore the pang of disappointment.

House lights flickered on along Egret Lane as residents began to stir, and her stomach growled at the smell of cooking bacon. A rooster crowed, but otherwise the pounding of her feet on the deserted road was the only sound. She checked her watch and settled into a comfortable pace, enjoying surroundings much simpler than she'd been accustomed to. She'd almost forgotten how uncomplicated life could be. The city was never this quiet, even in the twilight hours. It was one of the things she loved and hated about urban life and her work.

Her job and the month-long suspension were never far from her mind, even in this tranquil setting. She was basically lying in her professional and personal lives: not being totally candid with the investigators about Lily Miller's case and not telling Macy she was a slightly tarnished, temporarily unemployed cop. She hated lying. Dishonesty, no matter what the magnanimous reason, took too much effort and brought everything she did into question. She wasn't one of those cops who believed the end always justified the means. Fortunately, she'd never lied before, but it felt right this time…or the lesser of two evils. When had her life become so convoluted? *About the time Gayle Braxton showed up.*

She'd isolated herself by throwing money at round-trip tickets to Canada, being at her lover's beck and call, and serving as the caboose on Gayle's long train of priorities. She'd dreamed of devoting her time and energy to the woman she loved, but in her dream her lover reciprocated. Hedy and Pam had tried to keep her grounded, but she'd become a cliché, blinded by love. Hopefully, that trend would end when her suspension was over and she found a place to live. She might even start dating again.

The image of Macy kneeling in the flowerbed digging with her hands surfaced. She'd been so engrossed in her plantings, reverently kneading the soil barehanded, that she hadn't noticed Leigh's blatant staring for several minutes. Leigh had seen her share of attractive women, but never one who tried so hard to appear otherwise.

Macy didn't seem to take special interest in her physical appearance, preferring to blend into the background in baggy clothes and humble surroundings. But underneath Macy's roadblocks and modesty she detected a woman of complexity and challenge whose feelings wouldn't be easy to mine, a woman of passion. Was she willing to risk more rejection to uncover the real Macy Sheridan?

The question brought her up short and she doubled over to catch her breath. She'd been daydreaming and was almost back home at a full run, her pace shot to hell. She gasped for air and steadied her heart rate. The idea of opening herself to another woman who seemed uninterested had the appeal of stepping in front of an oncoming train. She'd been run over too many times to take another careless leap. But something told her she'd make the leap regardless of the outcome.

The sun was just breaking through the trees as she walked up to the cottage, and a dim light shone from the windows. She started to knock but didn't know what to say. Just seeing Macy or talking to her wasn't a good-enough reason to intrude on her first thing in the morning. Still feeling antsy, she walked around the side of the cottage to the woodpile. Maybe a little manual labor would calm her or exhaust her enough to let her nap.

As she passed the small window at the back of the house, she heard what sounded like crying from inside. She started toward the back door to make sure Macy was okay but stopped just shy of the threshold. Would Macy misinterpret her concern as meddling and give her another sermon about privacy? If Macy was hurt or upset, would she even accept comfort from her?

She crept to the side of the window and peeked in. Macy was slouched over a stack of papers on a drafting table, rubbing her left wrist as if it ached. She clutched a stained grayish-white lab coat around her like a shroud. Her face was splotchy and her tearful wails echoed through the room. She appeared fixated on the papers, upset by their contents but unable to look away.

Leigh traced a path down the windowpane with her fingers. She could almost feel Macy's grief seeping through the glass, but what could she do? She had no idea what had caused so much pain and had no right to ask. Maybe Macy had lost someone close to her, possibly a lover. That would account for her need for privacy and distance. She turned reluctantly from the window, feeling like a cross between a Peeping Tom and a stalker.

She should leave Macy to grieve in her own way. Whatever was going on in her life wasn't Leigh's concern. Macy hadn't gone overboard to make her feel welcome since she arrived, and she'd been adamant that she wanted space. Still, Leigh thought it cruel to turn her back on someone who was hurting. She wanted to be nearby, just in case.

The woodpile provided a legitimate reason to continue lurking. Placing a piece of wood on the stump that served as a chopping block, she reached for the ax. Splitting wood would exercise her arms, and since she hated weight training, this seemed a good substitute. She eyeballed the log, repositioned it on the stump, and hefted the ax over her head. She took a deep breath and swung. Her strike skimmed the side of the log, which went flying through the air. The ax stuck in the ground between her legs.

"Jeez, are you trying to kill yourself or me?" Macy was standing behind her with the airborne log at her feet, her face a mask of tenuous composure. "Have you ever split wood?"

Leigh's face and neck burned with embarrassment. She'd lost serious butch points with that display. "Not exactly, but it seemed pretty simple." She'd never been so happy to see anyone, in spite of her failed attempt at macho chores. Macy's eyes were puffy and her face still splotchy, but at least she wasn't crying. Leigh would take anger, censure, disappointment, or anything over crying. "Sorry, guess I should've asked, huh?"

"You should know what you're doing before you play with sharp instruments." Though Macy's voice was stern, a hint of a smile tugged at her lips. "This stack," she nodded to her left, "is green wood. It's harder to split than the seasoned wood over there." She pointed right.

"I didn't know."

"And, you're using an ax. It's okay if you're experienced, but a maul is probably better, and you have less chance of slicing your leg open. You can still do serious damage with a maul, but it's more likely to produce a deep bruise, break, or dull cut."

"Charming. Who knew log splitting could be so complicated? I thought you just swung the ax and presto."

Macy picked up the log next to her foot and pointed to the top where Leigh's strike had careened off the side. "You were going against the grain. Always chop with the grain and use the natural cracks as a starting point. Let me show you."

Leigh stepped back, watching Macy more than her log-splitting demonstration. The soiled lab coat was gone, and her short pajama bottoms, worn T-shirt, and bedroom shoes revealed more of her body than her usual camouflage of layered clothing. Her legs were thin though well-muscled, small breasts high and tight, but her shoulder blades poked at the T-shirt at sharp angles. Leigh wondered if she'd be able to hoist the maul, much less split a log.

"Pay attention. You're staring again." Macy positioned the piece of wood on the stump and sighted the maul along the cracks as Leigh might sight her weapon. Stepping back so her arms were straight and her dominant hand forward on the handle, she swung with surprising strength and precision. The log separated with a whack and lay in two pieces on top of the stump.

"Impressive. Where did you learn that?"

"Right here. Splitting logs was my punishment as a teenager. My parents didn't believe in corporal punishment, but manual labor was fine. You try." She handed the maul to Leigh and moved well out of range. "Remember what I told you and you'll be fine."

She followed Macy's instructions and split the log on her second try. "I think I've got this now. Not quite as easy as I'd hoped, but nothing worthwhile ever is, right?"

"More motivational wisdom?"

"Am I that transparent?"

"It can be annoying. How are you so upbeat all the time? Does anything bother you?"

"Hearing you crying this morning bothered me, a lot."

"Leigh...I..."

It was the first time Macy had spoken her name, and it was almost a whisper. Hearing Macy call her by name meant she recognized her as an individual and not just part of the mass of humanity or a faceless tenant. It was a form of validation. To her it was the equivalent of Macy saying, *I really see you*, and that was huge. "I didn't mean to make you uncomfortable. Heard you as I passed. Is there anything I can do?"

"No, but thank you. If anything could be done, I'd have done it years ago." The tone of Macy's voice left no doubt that the subject was closed.

"You're a complicated woman, Macy Sheridan. I thought most artists were creative, spiritual, nonconformists, but you seem more—"

"Careful, I might take offense."

"Yeah, guess I better stop while I'm ahead." If she was ahead, which was always hard to tell with Macy. "Would you like to go for a walk? It might help to exercise and breathe some fresh air."

"Looks like you've already been." She nodded to Leigh's wet jogging clothes. "I'll be fine." Macy looked on the verge of tears again as she turned and walked back into the cottage.

"Damn, damn, damn. Why can't I say anything right to this woman?" She just wanted to help but kept getting shot down. Her second refusal of an invitation in twelve hours had to be some kind of loser's record.

Chapter Six

For the next three days Leigh gave Macy a wide berth, going only as close as the woodpile out back after her morning jog. In her experience, crowding an emotionally distraught person seldom helped, especially one who'd asked for space. The only sign she'd seen of Macy was light coming from different parts of the house. Macy probably thought she was a pathetic woman with no life beyond jogging and chopping wood. Sometimes it seemed that way to her as well. After all, she'd given up everything she cared about for a dead-end relationship. Pathetic pretty much covered it.

"Okay, I've had it," she said to Toby, who gave her his usual impassive stare. "That's right, you ignore me too. I have to get out of here or I'm going crazy. Not that you're bad company, but I'd like to hear a voice besides my own occasionally. Maybe I'll call Hedy or Pam and have lunch while I'm out. I'll give them your regards."

She pulled on a fresh pair of jeans and a clean T-shirt and jumped down the stairs onto the dock. Maybe she'd check in at work. It had been barely a week since her suspension and a phone call would suffice, but she needed human contact. Even unpleasant contact beat nothing. Forty-five minutes later she walked into the Youth Division office to a round of boos.

"I can see nothing has changed around here. You guys are still a rowdy bunch."

"We miss our workhorse. Our clearance rate is down, and the sergeant is on our ass every day." Nate grabbed her in a bear hug. "Nice of you to drop by."

"I had to see people. Living in the sticks is harder than I imagined."

"I told you, freaking *Deliverance*." He nudged her toward the canteen, dropped coins into the machine, and plunked two coffees down on the table. "So, any headway with the recluse?"

"What am I, your only source of entertainment? Or do you expect me to soften her up so she'll work the case?"

"I'm just having a conversation with my partner. We've got an understanding." He waggled his forefinger between them. "Besides, you don't have to worry about the case. She called Rickard this morning and said she'd do it. He's on his way to drop off the full case report and hand over the skull for reconstruction. He thinks I walk on water now. I figured it must've been you."

"Nope. She made that decision on her own."

"Even better. I do walk on water." He poked his index finger into the dimple on his chin and twisted. "Have you told her you're a cop yet?" She shook her head. "Don't wait too long. If she's as schitzy as you say, that won't end well." Nate lowered his voice, sounding almost reverent when he spoke again. "I thought you two might hit it off. At least somebody you can talk to, be friends with. Know what I mean?" She'd seldom seen this sensitive side of him.

"Yeah." She understood the concept. She longed for a lover who would also be a best friend, easy to talk to and a companion. Why did she expect more from a lover than she did from a friend? Is that why her relationships failed? Or did sharing her deepest vulnerabilities justify expecting a higher level of trust, respect, and commitment? Whatever her needs or desires, Macy Sheridan was not the answer. "That might not be so easy, Nate, but I promise to tell her the truth soon."

"All right then." He finished his coffee in a gulp and started back toward the office, obviously finished with their tête-à-tête. She followed, not anxious to see Captain Howard. "Got something to help you pass the time out there in the boonies."

"What?"

"You'll see. Go check in. I'll have it ready when you come back."

The captain's administrative assistant wasn't at her desk when Leigh reached the complex, so she tapped on the boss's closed door. "Yeah?"

"Captain, it's Leigh."

"Come in." By the time she opened the door, Captain Howard was at the threshold, greeting her with an outstretched hand and the smile Leigh associated with genuine warmth. "You doing all right?"

"Yes, ma'am."

"Not too bored?"

"Didn't say that."

"I'm sorry you have to check in with me, but since I issued the discipline, I feel better doing the follow-up. The guys will give you a ration of crap, but you can handle it." She didn't wait for a response. "I'm sure you've reflected on your situation over the past week. Anything you want to tell me about Lily Miller's case?"

"No, ma'am."

"You sure there isn't something else I need to know? I could probably make this all go away if I knew what really happened."

"It's best if you don't know, Boss."

"Okay. You've always been stubborn—or maybe determined is a better word—but I'm sure you have your reasons. You don't deserve this blemish on your record. It's my job to take care of my people, not vice versa."

"I know. Thank you." As she left the captain's office, she reviewed her actions in the Lily Miller case again and came up with the same answer. She'd done what was best. Consequences be damned. Her record be damned. Period. She stopped by Nate's desk on her way out and collected a sealed accordion file he'd left for her with a note attached.

To keep your mind sharp. Don't open this in the office.

She was in the parking lot about to get in her vehicle when one of the youth detectives called from across the lot. "Hey, Monroe, someone here to see you."

"In case you didn't get the memo, I'm suspended. Handle it."

"Said it was personal, but I can tell him to get lost. Fine by me."

Sometimes her cohorts' lack of sensitivity astounded her. "Never mind. I'll talk to him. Where is he?"

"Hallway outside interrogation."

When she entered the small corridor beside the interview rooms, she saw a boy about fourteen or fifteen sitting on a straight-backed chair scuffing his worn sneakers on the floor. His jeans appeared relatively new, T-shirt fashionably wrinkled, and his leather bomber jacket could've been fifty years old or a replica fresh off the rack. He wasn't poor or homeless, and he definitely wasn't a regular she'd worked before. She would've remembered his almost-white-blond hair and the intense gray eyes he focused on her as she approached.

"Detective Monroe, nice to meet you." He held out his hand and gave her a firm handshake. "I need your help."

"And you are…"

"Call me Jack. I understand you're the best detective in the police department."

"Excuse me, but you told the other detective this was a personal matter. I don't recall meeting you before."

"I might've fudged a little." His smile started at the corners of his mouth, sprouted across his cherubic face, and radiated from eyes the color of liquid silver.

"How did you get my name and what do you know about my work?"

"Research."

She'd never seen this kid before, had no idea how he knew her, and wasn't about to commit to a pig in a poke. "If you need police assistance, I'll refer you to one of my colleagues. I'm not taking cases right now."

"Because of the suspension?"

She silently counted to ten. She didn't like anyone having the upper hand, especially in her job. "How do you know about that?"

"Read it online. Sounds like you did something good, maybe not by the book, but good for a kid. That's what I need. Or did I read too much into the situation?"

"Are you in some kind of trouble?"

"Need you to find my dad's family. He died recently. They should know." The boy looked down at his sneakers, and a connection vibrated between them like a current.

"I'm sorry, Jack. It's tough to lose a parent." She placed her hand on his shoulder, remembering the night her father was rushed to the hospital and never returned. The loss was a hole in her heart that could never be filled. "What about your mother? Doesn't she know how to get in touch with his family?"

"I don't know who she is."

Jack's situation was similar to many cases she'd worked—absentee, addicted, or deceased parents whose kids suffered from lack of love or adequate direction. She recalled her childhood after her father died and her mother withdrew, and her chest tightened. There should be a universal law to protect children, the elderly, and animals. But she'd seen too much to the contrary in her career. Her first instinct was to help Jack. But the suspension prohibited her from taking police action or assisting in any active investigation.

"Talk to one of the detectives in here." She walked to the office door and held it open for him. "They'll get the ball rolling."

Jack didn't move from his chair. "I'll wait."

"For what?"

"For you to change your mind."

"It's not going to happen." She called into the room, "Guys, would one of you take care of this young man? I've got to go." She walked past the boy and out the door. As it closed behind her she heard him say, "I'll be waiting."

❖

Macy stood in her studio holding the box and case file Sergeant Kevin Rickard had handed over to her without even a thank you. He'd barely managed a greeting, as if he'd been the wounded one in their last encounter. It was petty to hold a grudge, but he'd dismissed her request to review Jesse's case without much consideration. After seven years of working together, she'd expected more deference or at least a bit of professional courtesy.

But she wasn't doing this for him. She placed the box in the center of her refectory table and picked up the file. The official case notes might contain new information, but Jesse's eyes stared at her from the corner of the table, making concentration impossible. Who was she kidding? Could she really do this again? At least she'd made it back into the studio after months of avoidance, though not doing what she really wanted—painting. She tucked the file under her arm, poured the last cup of coffee from the pot, and took a seat on the back deck in the morning sun.

The yard seemed empty without Leigh's sweaty body hunched over the chopping block swinging the ax like a lumberjack goddess. She'd spent the early morning hours of the last three days here, careful not to intrude on Macy's space but close enough for contact. Macy hadn't made the effort because her only option had been to tell Leigh about Jesse, and she couldn't do that. Sharing hers and Jesse's story with anyone would be like tearing off a chunk of her heart and handing it over. Detachment seemed more merciful than asking another woman to share an emotional burden she could never relinquish.

Why did she run from the simplest act of kindness? Guilt flourished while her other emotions were in a vegetative state, unresponsive and unreachable. What was wrong with her? She didn't want this floating, disconnected existence, but she could barely remember any other. Leigh's compassion made her wonder if she was still capable of anything else, made her almost want to try.

She hugged her waist and closed her eyes, remembering the feel of Leigh's arms around her, the slow-motion fall and soft landing. Her heartbeat trebled and a jolt of excitement drizzled through her. The sensation oozed to places that longed to be touched, and she absorbed it like a medicinal balm. Deprivation had sucked away her energy and creativity like a black hole. She wanted—no, she needed—to touch again. *No!* Her mind intervened like a splash of water on fire. The pleasurable feelings disappeared behind her bulletproof shield that protected but also distorted everything.

The crunch of paper brought her back to the deck and her hands gripping the sides of the file folder. Best to leave Leigh Monroe to her life and get on with hers. But she couldn't help wondering where Leigh was, what she did with her time. Did she work from home? Was she retired? She'd avoided the question when they met and now Macy couldn't help speculating. Maybe she just missed having her around, her unending optimism and annoying motivational sayings. How was that possible when she'd been here only a few days? How ludicrous.

She scanned the reports and officers' notes and didn't find anything new, so she returned to the studio.

The red-and-black evidence tape wrapped around the box cautioned her not to open it, and for a second she considered heeding the warning. She'd already accepted the case, and if she didn't follow through, she'd always wonder about it. She wiped her sweaty palms down the front of her coat along streaks as clearly delineated as ruts in a muddy road. *This is the last one.* She lifted the box cutter with a trembling hand and slit the tape.

A border of Styrofoam peanuts encircled the bubble-wrapped skull. She tipped the box, and the weightless pieces scattered like snow flurries. Wriggling her fingers underneath, she cupped the skull and lifted it gingerly from the container. Trudy's report indicated the skull had been shattered on the posterior right parietal, but she'd reassembled the fragments. Macy knew the more she handled the fragile bones, the greater chance of damage. She placed the bundle on the desk, tweezed up the edge of each piece of tape, and pulled slowly until the wrapping separated.

This was where the process started for her, actually touching the skull. She lightly traced the uneven surfaces of bone, skimmed the orbital openings, and avoided the ragged edges of glued fragments on the back right side. She focused on the mandibular profile, symmetry of the nasal bones, dentition, and any unusual markings, all of which affected an individual's appearance.

A potential powerhouse of knowledge, cognition, and memory had once thrived in this casing. Was it possible to divine a person's history from the shape of her head as phrenologists once believed? Macy imagined she could recreate a victim's story through touch alone. The energy was profound and humbling, but her need to be so connected to her subjects had taken a toll. This time she vowed to maintain a professional distance and remain objective.

When she completed her scan of the braincase and viscerocranial bones, her hands were shaking. She couldn't possibly glue the mandible to the cranium with her hands trembling like a detoxing alcoholic. A facial reconstruction required attention to minute details and steady hands. She could alter the facial outcome or completely destroy the skull with the slightest tremor.

She shivered as fear swept over her like a cold breeze. What if her refusal to connect emotionally had stifled her professional abilities along with her artistic muse? Her past failures danced around in her mind like skeletons. Maybe accepting this case had been a very bad idea. She secured the skull on a cork ring and slid out of her lab coat. At least she was back in the studio. Baby steps.

❖

"Hey, Leigh, I'm so glad you called. A late lunch slash early dinner was perfect. Bo's been home for three days and he's driving me nuts. Time to fend for himself." Hedy started talking when she walked into the small deli beside the police station, nodding at familiar faces from the cop shop, and didn't stop until she sat down in the booth across from her. "Don't ever get married unless she lives far away so you can have alone time. I'm sorry. That was as tactless as my husband."

"It's okay." Her sister would rather bite her tongue than say anything to hurt another person. Kindness was her double-edged sword. That she'd said something insensitive meant she was truly stressed. "What's going on besides too much Bo?"

"Your mind-reading thing is really sweet and I love that we're so close, but it's also a little freaky. You know that, right?"

She nodded, returning Hedy's grin.

When the waitress walked away with their drink orders, Hedy's eyes finally met hers and her smile faded. "We *have* to talk about Susan."

"Hedy, please. You know how I feel about her."

"Like it or not, she's still our mother, and you need to know some things."

Tension crept up the back of Leigh's neck and her temples pounded. She couldn't think clearly or objectively about Susan Bryce. She'd given birth to them, but she'd missed the important things that would've earned her the title of caring mother. "No, I don't."

"I love you more than anyone in my life, bearded Bo included, but you're totally unreasonable when it comes to her. If you'd just listen, you might be able to get past it. Let your little sister help you, just once."

"How is it so easy for you to forgive her?" Tears stung her eyes as another round of pain surfaced. "After everything she did, correction, *didn't* do for us."

"Because of you." Hedy reached across the table and entwined their fingers. "You didn't let me give up on anything—brushing my teeth, reading, learning math, making friends in school, and certainly not on love. You made me believe anything was possible."

"I was naïve."

"You were right…and you still are. You've just lost sight of that because you've been hurt again. And hurt compounded with no relief festers and infects everything."

"Did you just call me an infected, festering sore?"

"Don't deflect. I see through you, sister. Why do you hate Susan so much?"

"I don't hate her. I just seriously dislike the way she treated us, and it's hard to look at her without remembering that."

"Maybe if you gave her a chance to explain."

She couldn't be upset with Hedy, ever. If she managed to work up a decent pout, Hedy defused it with her blazing smile or one of her stories about life with a long-distance truck driver named Bo. "I'm not sure I believe in the happy ending any more, Hedy." She'd never said those words aloud and didn't like how they sounded hovering in the air around her. She wanted to believe, had spent years encouraging Hedy to keep the faith, but now she needed something tangible she could hold on to. Words were no longer enough.

"You wouldn't spout those annoying bumper-sticker slogans all the time if you didn't believe some of them were true. People change, even Susan. And as for the happy ending, Gayle wasn't the right woman for you. But when you find the right one, you can't embrace love if you're holding on to negativity."

The tightness in her chest eased as the truth of Hedy's words registered. She'd never thought of herself as a parent, but at this moment she couldn't have been prouder. Her little sister had grown into quite a woman, and now she was getting a dose of her own medicine. "Okay…why is this suddenly so important, and what does it have to do with Susan?"

"I'm pregnant." Hedy's face glowed like when she'd passed her first algebra test in high school or won the head-cheerleader position, but deeper. She wasn't that kid anymore. She'd turned into an adult, headed for motherhood, right before Leigh's eyes.

"Preg...pregnant?"

"You *do* know Bo and I have sex, right?"

"Ewww...I mean when, how?"

"The how part is easier than the when, but we've been trying for years. Waited until after my first trimester to tell you. I threatened to castrate Bo if he leaked the news. He hasn't said a word."

She moved to the other side of the booth and hugged Hedy until she begged for air. "I'm so happy for you and so very proud."

"Thanks. We're both over the moon, really. Bo is like a kid himself. I can't wait to see what kind of parent he'll be."

After placing their meal orders, Leigh forced herself to ask the question hanging over them like the sword of Damocles. "So, what does Susan have to do with your pregnancy?"

Hedy sat taller and squared her shoulders, assuming what Leigh called her fighting stance. "I want my child to know his or her grandmother."

There it was: the turd in the punch bowl, the only bone of contention between her and Hedy ever—Susan Bryce, mother from hell. "You've *got* to be kidding. She sucked as a mother. Why do you think she'd be any better as a grandmother?"

"I want both of you to be part of my baby's life. Family is important, especially to children."

Leigh was suddenly light-headed, and her stomach churned like she might throw up. "I can't believe you said that. Are you serious?"

"I've forgiven her...and we've been spending time together."

"Why don't I know anything about that?"

"Look at your reaction. Do you think I enjoy getting a smack-down every time I bring up the subject? I don't need additional stress in my life right now. This pregnancy could get tricky because I'm not a young woman anymore."

"You're not that old. Is everything okay?" She placed her hand on Hedy's belly, already protective of the life that grew inside her.

"Fine so far, but you can't be too careful. I don't want to fight about this anymore. Susan isn't the person you remember. Just listen to what she has to say."

"Why can't you just tell me about these miraculous changes?"

"Because you wouldn't believe me."

She moved back to her side of the booth and took a gulp of water. "Come closer to believing you than I would her."

"Some things you need to see and hear for yourself. Everything isn't what it seems…and never has been."

"What the hell does that mean? Stop being so cryptic."

"Susan deserves a chance to speak for herself, and you deserve the truth."

"Hedy, you know I'd do anything in the world for you, but I'm not sure about this."

"Will you at least think about it? For me and the baby?"

She couldn't imagine not being able to see this child because of Susan—not being able to spoil her, read her nursery rhymes, or teach her sports any time she wanted. She'd dreamed of this day ever since Hedy and Bo got married. To have Susan Bryce jeopardize her dream was just another nail in the coffin of their relationship. The words almost wouldn't come. "I'll think about it."

"Come home with me. Spend the night. Bo wants to tell you all about his plans for a play area out back. You know he'll need your help."

"Sure, as long as he doesn't brag about how he knocked up my baby sister. Some lines should never be crossed."

CHAPTER SEVEN

L eigh had spent most of the day with Hedy and Bo talking about the baby and all the plans they'd made for her, like a real family. She drove along Egret Lane enjoying the view of lakeside homes in full sunlight that she'd seen only in the hazy glow of dawn as she jogged. She'd hoped the winding drive through the country would help her understand Hedy's request that she reconcile with Susan. So far she'd succeeded in avoiding the subject by counting farm implements, stubbornly refusing to give Susan Bryce one more second of her time. *Real mature, Monroe.* As she approached the cottage driveway, her cell phone rang. She debated letting the call go to voice mail until she saw Nate's number.

"Miss me already?"

"Got a minute?" When Nate started talking without a smart-ass comeback, she knew it was business.

"Sure, what's up?"

"Remember the kid you spoke to before you left yesterday?"

"Yeah?"

"He's disappeared or run away."

"And…? I'm suspended, remember?"

"I tried to talk with him after you left. He refused to give me his name, age, address, next of kin, anything. You know what that means."

It meant that without proof of age and/or someone to take care of him the state considered him a dependent child, basically a runaway, and headed for protective custody. "What am I missing? What's that to do with me exactly?"

"He kept asking to see you. Said you'd spoken and he would only talk to you."

"Nate, you know how I hate to turn any kid over to CFS, but if I do anything work-related during this suspension, I could be fired."

"All I'm asking is if we find him, maybe we could have a milkshake and chat, completely off the books. If you're the only one he'll talk to, you're our best hope of finding out who he is and getting him back to his family."

Nate knew she'd do almost anything to keep a child out of the legal system, sometimes to her own detriment. "How did he manage to disappear?"

"Collins and a uniform took him out for a burger, and the kid bolted. Hefty Collins didn't have a chance. The uniform guy was in the restaurant. If I'd been there, I'd have caught him."

She tried not to laugh. She'd always been the chasing component of their partnership and Nate the brawn. But this was no laughing matter. She'd been at this crossroads before—to walk the narrow path of proper procedure or to help a child. If she chose the latter, she could get into more trouble than even Captain Howard could help her out of. "Fine, what's the plan?"

"Thanks, partner. When I find him, we'll rendezvous."

"Send out some feelers about missing boys fitting his description. Update it when you get new information. Check the airlines for a young kid traveling alone, and put the word out at the bus and train stations. He had to have gotten here somehow. And don't let anybody know I'm involved in this. Do you understand?"

"Yeah, yeah, I know how to do my job…and keep you out of it. Don't worry. I'm following your lead—help the kids, no matter what." Before she could insist that she wasn't the best professional example, Nate hung up.

As she drove up to the cottage, Macy's wild locks and bundled frame came into view on the front porch. She sat forward in one of the Adirondack chairs, her back straight, arms wrapped around her as if for protection. Leigh imagined she could feel the heat radiating from her dark eyes as she neared. The reason became clear as she parked—Jack sat beside Macy chattering away and smiling like they were the best of friends. As if she didn't have enough trouble getting close to this woman. Jack's appearance would require more than a little explanation, which she didn't have.

She approached slowly, hoping some witticism would present itself before she spoke. No such luck. Macy's stare cut through her like a samurai sword on silk. One of the rules of her rental agreement was *no kids*. But it wasn't like this was her kid. "What's going on?" Lame.

"Good question." Macy's voice was an octave lower than usual and held the barely contained tremble of anger. "This young man has been waiting over an hour. Take care of it."

She expected an exclamation point at the end of Macy's order. She rose and closed the door behind her so quietly that Leigh flinched.

"She's wound a little tight," Jack said.

Leigh wanted to be angry. His appearance out of nowhere placed her in another professionally untenable position and put her at greater odds with Macy. But when she looked into his big gray eyes, she felt only compassion for a lost child. Though his methods were unconventional, his cry for help was no less genuine.

"Why don't we walk down to the lake? You hungry? Thirsty? It's been awhile since your prison break." She smiled so Jack would know she was at least partially kidding.

"Yeah, a little…about the break…sorry. I needed to talk to you."

"How did you manage to find me and get here all on your own?" Leigh offered him a seat on the dock while she went up and retrieved a couple of sodas, Cheetos, and three slices of cold pizza from the day before yesterday. When she came back down, he'd removed his shoes and was dipping his toes in the water.

"I told you I got skills. Finding you wasn't hard. Your buddies were talking about you moving to Belews Lake, renting from an artist who used to build faces for the police, or something like that. Took a bit of research online to find Ms. Sheridan's name and then a long cab ride and a few chats with the neighbors. And before you ask, I've got money. Didn't rob a bank or anything. As a matter of fact, I haven't done anything illegal, yet."

Jack could've been a much older person. Kids these days were smarter and savvier in the ways of the world than in her day, but this one seemed head and shoulders above others she'd worked with. She waited for him to scarf down a piece of pizza before questioning him.

"This pizza is a bit rubbery. How long you had it?"

"Beggars can't be choosers." She elbowed him and took a bite of her slice. "Jeez, you're right. So, why do you need to see me specifically? Any of the other detectives could help you find your father's family. They're all very good."

"But you put yourself at risk to help a kid who needed you. That's the kind of detective I want on my case."

The same dilemma swirled through her head again—help this boy or follow the rules. The professional stakes were clear, but she wasn't sure how, or if, helping Jack would affect her tenuous relationship with Macy. And it shouldn't matter. If Macy would turn a needy child away, Leigh wouldn't be interested in her anyway. She'd help Jack, no matter the consequences, but they'd have to reach an understanding first.

"I knew the story of the young girl you're talking about, and she definitely needed help. I don't know anything about you or why you've suddenly shown up here. If, and it's a very big if, I agree to help, you have to be honest with me. Will you?"

"I'll tell you everything you want to know, but only after I'm sure I can trust you."

He made a good point. If she'd been in his shoes, she wouldn't trust the police either. Actually, she *had* been in his shoes and had reacted the same way. One night when she and Hedy were home alone the police had come to their apartment. She'd lied to keep them out of foster care and her mother out of jail. Jack was smart to play it close to the vest.

"What do you propose?" She wanted Jack to feel he had some power in the situation. Often children ran away from home because they were kicked out, had intolerable living conditions, or someone died. The death of Jack's father had obviously been his catalyst, but was there more?

"I'll go to a foster home, for a while, so you can look for my dad's family. I won't cause any trouble, but I'll expect regular updates. Otherwise, I'll run away again."

"And what do I get out of this?" It wouldn't be much, but Jack needed to know he could trust her and that he also had some responsibility. As long as he was safe and off the streets, she'd go along with his quasi-plan.

"I tell you my dad's name and stay put." He stuffed the last piece of pizza in his mouth and chew-grinned, obviously pleased with his negotiating skills.

"I'd prefer to keep you out of the foster-care system, but if you won't give me any more details, I don't have a choice. You drive a hard bargain." She tousled his blond hair and faked pushing him in the lake. "Deal." For several minutes, they played back and forth like she and Hedy had done as children. When their laughter settled, she asked, "What's your dad's name?"

"Steven Temple."

"Can I assume that's your last name?"

"You could, but what do you guys say about assuming? Jack isn't my real name either, so don't get any ideas."

"What makes you think your dad's family is in Greensboro?"

"I heard him and my mom talking years ago about where they lived as children. Not sure what the big deal is, but nobody wants to say anything about his relatives or my mother's. Makes me wonder if I'm adopted or something, you know?"

"Yeah, but don't worry. I'll find out what I can. Any idea when he might've lived here?"

"Maybe fifteen, twenty years, long before I was born."

"Is there anything else that might be helpful? That's not a lot to go on."

"Not really." His voice cracked. "We didn't look anything alike. He was tall, brown hair and eyes, worked as a building contractor, just a normal guy." The gray of Jack's eyes turned dark as he spoke about his father. They'd obviously been close and the pain was still fresh.

"I'm so sorry, Jack." Where was this boy's mother, and why hadn't she been around to help him through the grief? Maybe she was like Susan—an absentee mother who could care less about her children. Her desire to help Jack doubled as she remembered her own childhood. "If your dad's family is still in the area, I'll find them, but you can't tell anyone what I'm doing. Understand?"

He nodded.

"I'm serious, Jack. I could get in even more trouble if anyone knew I was working while I'm suspended. I'll have my partner Nate Shaver help us. Be nice to him."

"You got my word and it's good."

"One more thing…did you tell Ms. Sheridan why you wanted to see me?"

"No, just that I needed to and I'd wait until you returned. She wasn't exactly cordial."

"I can imagine. Promise you won't tell her anything about our arrangement, if your paths cross again."

"Keeping secrets, Detective?"

Leigh gave him her sternest cop look.

"Okay."

They shook hands to seal their deal, and forty-five minutes later she turned him over to Collins for transport to a foster home. Collins didn't know about her conversation with Nate or Jack, and it would have to stay that way. As far as he knew, she'd just spotted him on the street and was returning him to custody like any other cop would do. Right now she had a more pressing problem—what to tell Macy about Jack.

She circled the edges of the property on her way back to the apartment, not wanting Macy to know she'd returned from her errand. As she crept up the steps from the dock, a quote from Abraham Lincoln rattled around in her mind: *You cannot escape the responsibility of tomorrow by evading it today.* But she was damn sure going to try.

❖

Macy paced around the cottage, sneaking an occasional peek out the kitchen window to the dock where Leigh and Jack sat chatting. She'd been seriously annoyed when he showed up unannounced at her door looking for Leigh. He hadn't offered any explanation except that he needed to talk to her.

While they waited, Jack told stories about kids he went to school with and his desire to join the FBI when he was old enough. It took a degree of confidence and character to talk intelligently to adults at his age. His strange-colored eyes and facial expressions captivated her as he told his stories. She'd even started to warm up to him when Leigh returned. But the list of rental agreements flashed through her mind, and she grew irritated again. Damn it, she should've put everything in writing. Why did Leigh insist on pushing every one of her buttons?

When she glanced out the window again, Jack was dangling his feet in the water, munching on a slice of pizza, while Leigh continuously plunged her hand into a bag of Cheetos. Their laughter floated through the open window, bringing with it the memory of her last carefree time at this place. She was sixteen and Jesse was fifteen, the year before she disappeared. Jesse's mother agreed to let her spend most of the summer with her family at the lake. They were in heaven, claiming the dock apartment as *their* home, going for late-night and early morning swims, and surfacing sporadically for meals to satisfy her parents.

She and Jesse talked about everything, especially sex. While Jesse was interested in the boys on the football and basketball teams, Macy was interested in her, the initial indication their desires weren't mirror images. Jesse kissed her the first time in the apartment, anxious to perfect her technique. Macy lost her heart in that instant to a technique she assured Jesse was already perfect. They'd become closer that summer and she flirted with telling Jesse about her feelings, but every time she tried, Jesse laughed her words off. She vowed to be patient until Jesse was ready to hear her and accept her love. That day never came.

Laughter from the dock returned Macy's attention to the scene of a young boy and a grown woman splashing water on each other with their feet. She envied Leigh's ability to hold on to her playfulness in spite of the demands and challenges of adulthood. She'd ignored that part of herself after Jesse disappeared, seeing laughter and frivolity as blasphemous. Now she'd give anything to reconnect with the humor in life, if only occasionally.

Macy paced again, trying to persuade herself to work on the case, but she couldn't concentrate, wondering instead about Leigh's connection to Jack. She reasoned that her irritation was about Leigh's violation of the rental rules, but actually she didn't like adding one more thing to the list of unknowns about Leigh Monroe. Maybe she'd learn to enjoy having someone on the premises, just for occasional conversation, and if that someone happened to be a lively, attractive woman, all the better. She was so lost in the pleasantness of that particular thought she jumped when someone knocked at the door.

"Macy, it's Leigh. May I come in?" She denied the acceleration of her pulse had anything to do with Leigh or her voice that oozed kindness through every crack in the door.

"Macy?"

The place was clean and orderly as usual, but she looked a fright. Her hair was falling from the French braid she'd carefully arranged this morning, and her clothes were vintage house wear. What's all the fuss about, she asked herself as she reluctantly opened the door. She and Leigh needed to talk about what was and was not allowed on her property—stick to business. "Yes."

Leigh stepped inside. "Before you get—" She stopped in the middle of the floor and turned in a complete circle as she took in the room. The green of her eyes changed shade as she saw things she liked and others that didn't appeal. Macy could almost feel the emotions pouring off her as she studied her paintings on the walls.

"Oh, my God. Are these yours?" She waved her hands as if they stood in the Metropolitan Museum of Art surrounded by great works.

"Yes." Her face flushed and heat spread downward, filling her with gratitude for the genuine appreciation. How long had it been since anyone looked at her paintings with such obvious enjoyment? This was what she craved, the pursuit of her passion and the pleasure of sharing it with others, but it also made her feel vulnerable, exposed. She joined her hands in front of her and inched farther away from Leigh.

"These are fantastic. You should really do this full-time, not that I'm an art critic. But I know what I like, and these are amazing. I love that they're abstract and let the viewer see whatever they want in the piece. They seem a little dark for you, maybe more light."

Leigh walked to the window and pulled the heavy curtains back, allowing the afternoon sun to stream in, then dropped her leather jacket on the floor at the end of the sofa.

"Make yourself comfortable." Macy noted the sarcasm in her own voice as she picked Leigh's jacket up and hung it by the door.

"Sorry. This is such a wonderful surprise. I've never been inside your cottage."

Was that true? Leigh's presence in the room was like the return of a treasured artifact, the centerpiece of a rare collection. Her over-familiarity was annoying, but she added such vitality that the walls seemed to breathe with her. Macy squeezed her clasped hands tighter, desperately wanting to touch Leigh, to connect with the excitement that radiated from her in waves. She'd never met anyone as openly expressive as Leigh, and diving into her energy would be like sinking her fingers in paint and creating a masterpiece. The image evoked a sharp breath, and she caught only the end of it as the rest escaped in a strangled cough.

"Are you okay?"

She dipped her head, afraid that a full nod would break the spell Leigh had cast over her. "It's just been a very long time since anyone appreciated my work. Thank you."

Leigh stuffed her hands into her jeans pockets and rocked back and forth, her curls of red hair falling across her forehead. "Does it violate some rule to touch an artist's work? That one just seems to invite it." She nodded toward the last canvas Macy had done almost two years ago, an acrylic abstract of sunset from the apartment balcony.

"Go ahead." Macy watched her approach the painting almost reverently, removing her hands from her pockets only after she'd stared at the piece for several seconds.

"I won't knock anything off, will I?" Leigh asked over her shoulder.

"No." She stepped closer but stopped just out of reach. Her clenched hands trembled. She wanted to help Leigh experience the literal feeling of her work, but the warning signal in her head blasted like a foghorn. The pull was too strong. She couldn't resist—a gorgeous woman and art—the combination was too compelling.

Moving within inches of Leigh's body, she felt heat radiating between them and almost leaned in before catching herself. The last time she'd been this near a woman was Julia, and she'd felt only the certainty of good-bye. She reached for Leigh's hand, then withdrew. What if she touched her and Leigh pulled away? What if she touched

Leigh and didn't like it? What if she did? Why did she feel the need for physical contact, now, with this woman?

Leigh placed a hand gently in the small of Macy's back and pulled her closer. "Show me." When Leigh captured her hand and extended it toward the painting, her touch was like sticking her arm in an open flame. Brilliant white light, pure and crisp, flashed behind her eyelids. Her body felt liquid and languid and raw. Dust particles floating on late-evening sunrays felt like pinpricks against her skin, delicately stimulating but tortuous. *I want. I want.*

"Macy?" Leigh's breath against the side of her face was a slow caress down her body. "What's wrong? You looked flushed."

"F…fine." She willed herself to remain lucid and slowly guided Leigh's hand to the art piece in front of them. Her long, slender finger fit like a paintbrush in Macy's, and as she traced the lines of the painting, she lost herself in the binary beauties before her. Curved lines of acrylic, sweeping curvature of Leigh's back, the dip of a brushstroke, the sway of Leigh's backside against her, vibrant color on canvas, sex on legs. Their fingers fused in a singular motion across the face of the image, their arms moving in unison. She watched her hand, wrapped around Leigh's with almost a sensation of disembodiment.

"I love the texture, it's so sensuous." Leigh's elbow brushed lightly against her breast as she turned to face her. "Don't you think?"

She searched Leigh's face for intent, but her gaze stopped at her mouth. Her lips, the color of ripe pomegranates, called to her like a bold splash of paint on naked canvas. Something foreign and fierce ignited inside her. *Oh no.*

"Are you going to get that?"

"What?" The telephone rang behind her, and Leigh nodded toward it. "Sorry." Was she apologizing to Leigh for not hearing the phone or to herself for breaking contact? God, she'd been so totally absorbed in the touch and feel of Leigh. She shook her head to gather a coherent thought and picked up the handset. "Hello? What? Yes, of course. Hold, please." She motioned to Leigh. "It's for you."

Leigh looked as surprised as Macy felt, but for completely different reasons. She was trying to figure out how she'd let herself get so out of control. She'd actually allowed Leigh, a woman she barely knew, to touch her, and she'd liked it. Needing distance and wanting to give Leigh privacy, she escaped to the back deck. Leigh's voice still carried through the open windows, and she felt like an eavesdropper.

"Why are you calling me? I'm not ready to talk to you. I said I'd think about it, not that I'd do it. I need more time. Don't call me again, especially not here. This is not my number." The phone clanked back into the cradle, and a few seconds later, Leigh joined her on the deck. "I'm sorry about that. Hedy, my sister, gave her your number. I asked her not to call back."

"Ex-girlfriend?" She couldn't believe she'd asked exactly what she'd been wondering.

"Mother, in name only." Leigh's usually expressive eyes were a dull shade of green and devoid of animation as if a deep, black pain had settled there. "Sorry, that was unkind."

"I take it you don't get along."

"Understatement. I should be going. I'm sure you don't want to hear this."

She reached for Leigh's hand but stopped before making contact. "Actually, I do. Please, sit." She was surprised that she felt the same sincerity she heard in her voice.

Leigh pulled a chair closer, kicked off her shoes, and tucked her feet under her, her gaze focused on the lake. "It's a common story really. My father died when I was seven, but my mother never missed a beat. She found a long line of men to fill his shoes, four husbands at last count. Hedy, my younger sister, and I were pretty much on our own. Now she's having a baby and wants Susan to play grandmother. I don't mean to sound bitter, but what does a woman who nearly abandoned her own children have to offer a grandchild?" Leigh worried the side of her finger with her thumbnail, her attention no longer on the lake but on some distant memory shadowing her face with pain.

"I'm sorry, Leigh. It must've been hard for both of you. Surely you had relatives, a grandmother?" Her parents weren't perfect, but she always knew they loved her and wanted only the best for her.

Leigh shook her head. "Hedy was only three. I did the best I could, but I still worry it wasn't enough."

The air was so thick with the weight of Leigh's commitment she could almost breathe it in. She couldn't imagine fending for herself as a child, and with a dependent sibling. Her pulse quickened as admiration swelled for this woman she'd initially likened to a rusty nail and dismissed as too frivolous. An important piece of Leigh Monroe's puzzle snapped into place.

"I doubt if Hedy sees it that way. You both made it to adulthood, which is more than a lot of kids in your situation do. You appear to be fairly functional, except for an annoying habit of spouting self-help slogans. I'd say you did an amazing job."

"Thank you, that's nice to hear, but it doesn't solve the mother problem. I can't ask Hedy to choose between us."

"I'm the last person to ask for parent advice. My folks and I aren't estranged, but we're not in regular contact. They're busy being self-indulgent in exotic places and I'm..."

"You're what?" Leigh asked.

"Here, doing God knows what."

"What do you want to do?"

Without a moment's hesitation, Macy said, "Paint a collection of pieces for my own show." She hadn't said those words aloud since she was sixteen and shared her dreams with her parents. They'd encouraged her to get a degree in something more substantial and continue painting as a hobby.

"Your parents can't see how talented you are?"

"I think they're just worried I can't make a living on talent alone, without the supplement of my forensics work."

"Well, as I've said before, I'm no art critic, but I wouldn't bet against you on that score. I believe if you have a passion for something, you can earn a living at it. Sorry, that sounded like one of those annoying sayings you hate."

"In this case, I appreciate it." Macy dangled her hand off the chair arm, dangerously close to Leigh's. She was reaching for a lifeline, afraid of being swept away but just as afraid of the mooring. When had she become so hungry for human touch, or was it just this human's touch?

They sat in silence, listening to the rising rapture of cicadas and the occasional hum of a powerboat in the distance. Leigh slouched in the chair beside her, feet tucked. She raked her hand through wavy copper locks that promptly fell back across her forehead. Macy had never been around anyone who seemed so comfortable in her own skin. When Leigh finally stirred beside her, the moon and stars competed for brilliance in the blue-black sky.

"Guess I better go. It's getting late."

Leigh retrieved her jacket from inside and started toward the steps leading to the dock, but Macy wasn't ready for her to leave. She fished for a delay tactic that didn't involve touching Leigh again and said the first thing that came up. "What about that kid today?" Her tone wasn't as casual as she'd intended, and the relaxed expression on Leigh's face vanished.

"Oh, yeah, sorry. That's really why I came over. He won't be back."

"Who is he? He's a nice boy, very intelligent too. Wants to join the FBI someday."

"Really? There's nothing to worry about. He just needed to talk. He won't be a problem. See you later, and thanks for sharing your art."

Leigh hadn't really answered her question, which seemed counter to her usual candor. Was she trying to hide something? Maybe she'd made a mistake opening up to Leigh about her parents. In the span of an evening, she'd gone from being fireball angry with Leigh to vertical spooning and handholding, ending with confusion and suspicion.

❖

Leigh vaulted off the deck and sprinted to the dock, shucking clothes as she ran. The temperature had been a respectable seventy degrees today, but the lake would still be cool, exactly what she needed. Her blood felt like it was boiling, and her loins couldn't have been hotter if they were splayed across a grill. Underneath her shapeless clothes and tightly spun control, Macy Sheridan oozed sexuality like a sieve leaked water. She'd felt it the second she stepped into the small cottage. Macy's sensual energy saturated the space, and with no outlet it hung in the air. She'd braided her hair into a French twist, and Leigh had wanted to run her tongue along the square angle of her jaw to her unadorned earlobe. After their intimate hand fondling over the art pieces, sitting on the deck hadn't relieved the tension between them. She could barely breathe for wanting to press their bodies together and relieve the ache between her legs that throbbed like a fresh wound.

Diving off the end of the floater, she gasped a mouthful of lake as the frigid blanket covered her. She surfaced sputtering water from her mouth and nose. The hurt was so hellishly good her teeth chattered and she didn't think about Macy for at least five seconds. Then she made the mistake of looking toward the house. Macy stood silhouetted by the kitchen light, staring toward the lake as if she could see her. She imagined an arc of electricity between them plunging into the water and deep into her center. She forgot to tread and her head went under. When she did, the water coursing between her legs was an unpleasant reminder of what was missing.

Damn it to hell. Ever since they'd met, Macy had deliberately kept her at arm's length, until tonight. She'd inched so close that the anticipation of touching was almost as painful as its withdrawal. When their fingers finally touched, it was as if they'd been forged as one. What had changed? She'd treated Macy with the same deference as always.

The paintings had surprised her, but she'd enjoyed seeing Macy's creative side. Had Leigh's appreciation meant that much to her, enough to soften her resistance? She continued to tread water as the night air chilled her shoulders…and Macy still watched from the window.

She couldn't guess what made Macy Sheridan tick. They'd talked about their families, a rare moment of vulnerability from Macy. Had she felt something between them tonight as well, or was Leigh looking for connections that didn't exist, willing Macy to show an interest? She'd wanted to spend time with Macy, and tonight she had, quality one-on-one time. She should be pleased. *The secret to getting there is to know where you're going.* The saying stuttered through her mind as her toes grew numb. She had no idea if she and Macy were going anywhere, but if she didn't get out of the lake soon, she'd be going to the hospital for hypothermia.

Leigh hauled herself up the side of the dock and flattened like a beached seal. Her arms and legs felt like popsicles. She reached for her pile of discarded clothes and drew them closer. As she took long, deep breaths of the warmer air, her extremities tingled and regained feeling, and with that reawakening came a wicked idea. If Macy was still watching, she was about to get a show.

She stood, bringing only her T-shirt with her, and distanced her legs shoulder-width apart. Holding the shirt like a towel, she started at her breasts, rubbing in slow, rhythmic circles until they were dry and her nipples puckered. She slid the fabric down the center of her chest, stopping just above her pubic mound. The desire Macy had kindled earlier flared and chased the chill from her body. A moan of arousal clawed up her throat, reverberating across the lake. She hoped Macy *was* watching and feeling just as uncontrollably horny. She couldn't bring herself to check or she wouldn't be able to complete her coup de grâce. Lowering the T-shirt she grasped it with one hand in front and the other behind and seesawed it back and forth between her legs.

Her knees buckled. She'd intended her evocative show to be just that, but when the fabric touched her slick folds, it turned serious. She bit her bottom lip to keep from crying out again and increased her pace. The release she hadn't allowed herself in months was surprisingly close. Then another wail echoed off the water—a sound like that of a wounded animal. Leigh stopped mid-stroke and looked toward the house just as the lights went out.

Glancing down at herself, she suddenly became self-conscious and a little ashamed of her naked demonstration. She was expressive, yes, but not *this*. Maybe she could blame it on her frigid dip in the lake. Macy had sparked yearnings in her that she'd neglected for too long. She gathered her clothing and shimmied up the ladder, part of her eager to see what tomorrow would bring, part afraid to face it.

CHAPTER EIGHT

Macy was in her studio before dawn, a cup of coffee at her side and a human skull in her hands. She'd already glued the mandible to the cranium and was positioning the skull on an adjustable stand in the Frankfort horizontal position that closely approximated the natural position of the head. She gathered her tools and materials for the first phase of work from the tidy cubbies and cartons in which they'd been stored since her last reconstruction. Clicking off a mental list, she arranged each item on her work table: Duco cement, X-acto knife, vinyl eraser tips, drawing boards, T-square, triangle, masking tape, drawing and vellum paper, pencils and erasers, and camera.

She'd slept poorly, restless after allowing Leigh to touch her as if they'd already been intimate. Her behavior seemed like a dream, edging gradually closer to Leigh, almost begging her to reach out. And when they connected, the dream ended and her senses focused razor sharp on the physical. The energy between them hummed and she found it difficult to restrain herself. Control had always been like breathing, natural and effortless, but for several delicious moments she'd slipped into a belly crawl through the wading pool of arousal. She'd wanted to ask Leigh to stay but the words wouldn't come, trapped in a place where guilt trumped longing.

She admired Leigh's spontaneity, but what was she trying to prove by that show on the dock? What must it be like to be so uninhibited? Maybe Leigh was an exhibitionist who got off on public displays, or maybe she was symbolically offering herself? She'd chosen the latter and gone to bed with a sexual ache so severe that multiple rounds of self-pleasuring hadn't satisfied her. She was acting like a hormone-crazed teenager and had woken a bit confused by the whole evening. Maybe work would redirect her urges into something more productive.

Grabbing her X-acto knife, ruler, and tissue-depth table, she began the two-dimensional portion of the reconstruction process. She measured the first piece of eraser to coincide with the measurement on the depth table and cut it to size. After writing the number one on the end of the marker, she glued it to the skull's forehead just below the hairline. She positioned number two between the orbital openings. Falling into a familiar working rhythm, she cut, identified, and glued the subsequent pieces in place. When she attached the last marker, twenty-one pieces of vinyl eraser stuck out from the skull like a pincushion. These tissue-depth markers would guide her photographs, sketches, and later clay molding of the skull by indicating the thickness of muscle, tissue, and skin on specific points of the skull.

When she finally stepped back to evaluate her progress, she'd been working for five hours without a break, but she hadn't felt so energized in months. Suddenly her objections to this project disappeared and she was optimistic about the outcome. She glanced at the unfinished sketches of Jesse staring up from the corner of the table and knew she'd made the right decision. She placed a lid on the box and slid it under her work counter. Perhaps she was one step closer to the creative, carefree artist she'd once been.

She made a cup of tea and looked out the kitchen window toward the apartment. She hadn't seen Leigh all morning. Maybe she was avoiding her after that rowdy show on the dock, unable to explain her behavior any more than Macy could understand it. Her mind flashed to last night and her clit stiffened. Leigh's moans had echoed across the lake, answered shortly by her own as she'd fisted her genitals in an attempt to stop the pain. As she remembered the heat of that scene, the cup in her hands suddenly felt too hot and she placed it on the counter.

When was the last time she'd thought about getting involved with another woman? Did the occasional tryst with a grad-student model count as involvement? Would Leigh consider a purely sexual relationship, or was she the type who'd want more? Macy couldn't do more, but sex was a basic human need and could be as casual as eating, sleeping, and drinking. Before she became too invested in her ill-conceived thought, she returned to the studio. When she focused on a task, little penetrated her concentration.

Now that the tissue-depth markers had dried, she photographed the skull from every angle. She'd use these shots as the basis for life-size enlargements and attach them to boards for her facial drawings. These drawings were one of the creative parts of the process that Macy enjoyed. Several new computer software programs could produce the two-dimensional images for her, but she preferred doing the work by hand. The programs were quicker but missed subtle variations, and in her opinion, the end results were more generic than her hand drawings and much less artistically satisfying.

By the end of the day, she'd finished the photo enlargements, attached them to the drawing boards, and taped the delicate vellum paper over the skull photographs. She was ready to begin the artistic phase of the reconstruction, but she wanted to start fresh. Would this be the face she'd waited years to sketch?

As she closed the door to the studio, the phone rang and she considered not answering. She didn't have a message machine, so annoying telemarketers couldn't leave messages. It could be the police with more information about the skull. Since she'd agreed to take the case, she picked up. "Yes?"

"Mace, it's Trudy. How's it going?"

"Pretty well, actually. I'm ready to start the drawing."

"Wow, when you make up your mind, you don't waste time. Anything else going on?"

She recognized Trudy's subtle way of asking about her personal life. "Not really. I took on a renter in the apartment."

"Really?" The tone was pure Trudy, genuine surprise laced with a hint of disbelief. "Who is it?"

"Woman named Leigh Monroe. She answered my ad in the paper. It's probably a short-term thing. Not sure I like having someone else on the property."

"Leigh Monroe? Seriously?"

Now the tone was starting to annoy her. "Yes, why? Do you know her?"

"Not really know, know, but I know of her…"

"Know what, Trudy? Spill."

❖

Leigh purposely started her jog before Macy woke and hoped to be finished before lights came on in the cottage. After her shindig on the dock, she still hadn't figured out how to explain her behavior. Her options were to make up an excuse about the effects of cold water on brain cells or to tell the truth. Which was what, exactly? That she'd been so overcome with head-spinning, crotch-burning lust that she'd resorted to fondling herself in public? Or that she wanted an intimate connection so much she'd reached out to a woman who obviously had no interest…and then resorted to fondling herself in public. However she spun it, the fondling-in-public part was the kicker. Maybe she should just let Macy believe whatever she wanted, but for some unfathomable reason, her opinion mattered. At least she could put off the inevitable a bit longer.

As she approached the house, she slowed her pace to cool down and left a message for Nate at the office. She asked him to search for information on Steven Temple: criminal history, driver's license and record, tax documents, title search, military status, and credit reports. He probably wouldn't find anything because they didn't have enough information to eliminate potentials. She wanted to help Jack, but he was hiding more than his name and date of birth.

After a quick shower, toast, and coffee, she settled on the small balcony overlooking the lake. If she sat with her back to the cottage, maybe she wouldn't be tempted to watch for Macy or go talk to her. She opened the accordion folder Nate had given her and pulled out the contents—computer-generated copies of an old missing-person report, not the original case file. A pink handwritten Post-it note was stuck to the top sheet.

In your spare time, give this a look. Let me know if you find anything of interest. And don't discuss it with ANYONE. AAH

Captain Anita Howard's horrific handwriting rivaled any surgeon's illegible scrawl. She'd gotten used to it during training, but it wasn't something you picked up quickly. Flipping the cover, she looked at the front sheet of the case report and the victim's name highlighted in yellow, Jesse Quinn. The toast and coffee she'd had for breakfast threatened to claw its way up her throat. This case had initially left a bad taste in her mouth, and it was still there.

The Jesse Quinn case was the first major crime she'd worked on, while still a trainee with Anita. They hadn't handled the call but assisted with the neighborhood canvass and grid search. Anita had quietly shadowed the lead detective's progress on the case until it was closed only two weeks later. They'd both wanted to do more to find the missing sixteen-year-old girl, but neither of them was in a position to buck the system. Now it seemed Anita Howard, as a command-level officer, was in a perfect position to do so and had chosen Leigh as her instrument. Why now? Was it because of the new skeletal remains CAP had Macy working on or simply because Leigh had time and Anita knew she hated being bored?

Nate's instruction on the outside of the folder not to open it in the office had to have come directly from Howard. Though the lead detective had retired years ago for health reasons, several patrol officers who'd worked the original case were now detectives, and others were supervisors. The captain wouldn't want anyone to know about this unofficial review. She doubted that Nate even realized what he'd passed along.

She closed her eyes and recalled the feelings surrounding this case at the time. The parents were understandably distraught—their teenage daughter had gone out with a friend and disappeared without a trace. The best friend was hysterical, near shock, and inconsolable with grief and guilt. But the officers working the case were skeptical, certain she'd run away with a boyfriend and would show up in the morning. Leigh and Anita hadn't shared their theory, believing instead that foul play was involved. They'd been partially vindicated when the girl failed to reappear the following day, the day after, or two weeks later.

But once the scene was cleared and potential evidence lost, a shoddy investigation was permanent. The investigators were screwed and so was the victim. The only person who won was the suspect, if a crime was committed. Leigh had been disappointed in her fellow officers for not going the extra mile. Though she had no direct contact with the family and friends of the missing girl, her heart ached for them. Maybe this was her second chance to speak for the victim.

Leigh moved a side table from the living area onto the balcony and separated the file by preliminary reports, forensic evidence, photographs, witnesses' statements, follow-ups, and detectives' notes. With a yellow legal pad on her lap, she started at the beginning, as if seeing the case for the first time. The hard part was ignoring her initial feelings and the nagging sense they'd missed something important.

Three hours later she'd made it through everything except witnesses' statements with little to show for her effort. The officers had done an adequate job but hadn't recanvassed the area in case neighbors had been away or remembered something later. The photographs were useless, pictures of a vacant club parking lot and the girl's bedroom. Forensic evidence was nonexistent, because no one wasted time or resources on a teenager when they'd decided she'd simply walked off.

She had written only three entries on her notepad, reinterview and recanvass, which would be nightmares after sixteen years. Her other note—why no picture of the missing person? Had it been removed, destroyed, left out of the original file, or simply not included in her copy? Her stomach tightened as she picked up the witnesses' statements. Was she frustrated because she lacked useful leads or because she was grasping at straws? Was she just trying to keep busy so her mind wouldn't wander to the two subjects she desperately wanted to avoid—her mother and Macy Sheridan? No. This case had been important to her then and was even more important now. The Quinn family deserved answers. They needed to know the truth, even though the chances of Jesse being alive were miniscule. As she picked up the stack of witness statements, she heard someone walking on the dock.

"Hello?" Macy called from below.

Her reprieve was over. She sickened at the possibility of having to explain her behavior last night. "Yes, I'm here."

"Would you come down, please?"

Leigh backed down the stairs slowly, not anxious to face Macy's censure. They'd shared a comfortable evening and confided in each other, but now her tone sounded like an order instead of a good-morning welcome. When she looked into Macy's eyes, she knew something had gone terribly wrong.

"I don't think this arrangement is going to work."

"What? If this is about last night—" Leigh's stomach tightened and she started to reach out, but Macy's expression stopped her.

"It's not, but that was certainly…interesting. It's about you lying to me. Should've gone with my gut the moment I saw you."

She wasn't sure if Macy was still speaking to her or berating herself aloud. "What are you talking about? When have I—"

"A cop? A cop, for God sake! Were you in on this whole let's-get-Macy-to-take-the-case exercise? Is that why you encouraged me?"

"I had nothing to do with trying to convince you to take the case. Honestly." Her mind raced like a gerbil on a wheel but produced nothing helpful—no witty comeback, no words of wisdom, no truthful explanation that wouldn't make her look like a complete dick.

"Poor choice of words in your situation. And it gets better—a cop suspended for hiding a child. Is that why Jack was here? If you've involved me in something illegal…I can't believe you'd bring this to my door, but then I don't really know you, do I? For all your emotional candor, you sure have a lot of secrets."

"Who told you?"

"Is that really the question you want to ask right now?"

"I…I can explain."

"Don't bother. The time for explanations has passed. Just make other living arrangements as soon as possible."

"Macy, please listen. It's not what you think."

"Did you purposely withhold this from me?"

Leigh struggled for the right words, but they wouldn't come.

"Then it is *exactly* what I think."

"What difference does my profession make anyway? I'm just renting an apartment, not sharing your bed or your life."

Macy's mouth twisted into a sneer, as if sharing her bed or life with Leigh was the most distasteful thought imaginable. Her reaction seemed a bit over the top, but Leigh didn't know if she had trust issues from past relationships or was just happy for any excuse to get rid of her after the closeness they'd shared last night.

"I don't appreciate being misled, and I don't want anyone on my property who isn't trustworthy."

Leigh tried again. "If you'd just let me explain."

"Not necessary. I won't feel comfortable having you around anymore. Sorry."

"Can I have a few days to find another place? I don't have anywhere else to go." Not at all what she needed to say, but her usual calm demeanor evaporated under Macy's dark eyes that sparked like flints.

"You have two days."

As Macy walked away, something sad and familiar settled in Leigh's chest. She'd been summarily dismissed, deemed insignificant, like she had in the past when she hadn't spoken up for herself. She'd been a child when her mother's absences and indifference seemed so personal. With Gayle she'd tried too hard to be something she wasn't, denying herself for the relationship. What about Macy made her feel so off balance? Why didn't she just assume her cop persona and tell her everything? Maybe because she already cared too much?

Looking out over the lake, she realized that wasn't it. She was scared, afraid if she told the truth Macy would still find her lacking, which disturbed her more than being insignificant. But she'd take the risk. If Macy rejected her, it would be because she knew everything. She'd let Macy cool off until tomorrow while she decided exactly what to say.

Chapter Nine

M acy crumpled another sheet of vellum paper and flung it in the direction of the overflowing trash bin. She couldn't concentrate enough to actually make progress on the drawing, though she'd been trying since daybreak. Her surprise at the news about Leigh had quickly morphed into anger and left her too agitated for the delicate work.

She'd harbored animosity about the shoddy investigation of Jesse's disappearance for years. When she began working for the police as a forensic artist, she'd expected to purge those feelings and have other chances to find Jesse. Her plan worked for a while, but Sergeant Rickard's denial of her final plea had renewed her distrust and dislike for anyone wearing a badge. Finding out Leigh was a cop had broadsided her. She'd reacted impulsively and abandoned her usual control for the satisfaction of being pissed off and venting.

Now she was choking on regret—for renting to Leigh in the first place, for not checking her out, for trusting her, for caring enough to be bothered by her, and for letting anger dictate her actions. Leigh wasn't responsible for the entire police department, but she was responsible for intentionally lying. She wasn't really sure why it mattered so much. Honesty wasn't part of their landlord-tenant relationship, and she had no right to Leigh's entire life story. Sharing a few moments of candid conversation didn't give her special privileges. She'd simply dropped her guard last night and enjoyed it, and Trudy's revelation had surprised her.

But Leigh had stood there and taken her angry rant without offering one word in her own defense. Why, when she'd been so forthcoming about other things, would she not try to explain? Then she remembered, Leigh had tried, but she'd cut her off, refused to let her speak, too high on outrage to listen. *This* was the reason she didn't do relationships. She lacked the get-along gene, the compatibility component, or something. Her foul moods, led strongly by guilt and anger, always blocked her path to anything lasting. The thin vellum she was drawing on ripped beneath her heavy-handed strokes, destroying another attempt, and she dropped the pencil on the desk. She couldn't get anything right.

She'd tried with Julia, but they'd drowned in lesbian-bed-death-but-everything-else-is-fine-itis—the malady that couples suffered when they were too oblivious to face their issues or too afraid to end it. The real fault had been hers, and she'd quickly agreed to the separation when Julia asked. What made her think, even briefly, that she could or should impose her dysfunction on anyone else?

She thumbed the jagged scar on her left wrist, a reminder of how precious life was and how quickly it could disappear. *What do you want, Macy?* The answer was immediate—she wanted to talk to Leigh, to apologize and actually listen to what she had to say. If she was going to dismiss the first woman who'd sparked an interest in years, she wanted the reason to be a damn good one, not something she'd concocted.

She hung up her lab coat and opened the front door, but Leigh's car wasn't in the driveway. Macy hadn't heard her leave, but it was possible she'd gone after her tirade. Who could blame her? Would Leigh move in with one of the people she'd seen on the dock? She wanted to be the person Leigh turned to. Illogical as that sounded, it felt right, though she hadn't really listened to her gut for months. When she closed the door and turned back to the safety and comfort of her retreat, only an empty chill greeted her.

❖

"Turnabout is fair play," Leigh said when Pam opened the door in her sleeping shorts and tank top, though it was after eleven a.m.

"Yeah, but I brought coffee."

"Sorry." She'd been driving around since early morning waiting for a decent hour to show up at Pam's door. She hugged Pam and dropped onto the sofa as if the burden she carried were a visible weight.

"Don't move while I put on another pot of coffee."

Pam's house was like a well-decorated mini sports stadium. Her leather furniture was comfortable but not gaudy and her accessories tasteful contemporary, but the flat-screen TV against the wall dominated the space. Her favorite motto to any prospective partner was love me, love my flat-screen.

In a few minutes, Pam returned with the coffeepot and two cups of hot caffeinated heaven on a serving tray. "I'm not sure how cops, nurses, social workers, and probation officers would survive without coffee twenty-four-seven. Breakfast, lunch, and dinner of champions. So, what's going on?"

Leigh took a sip before launching into a story that had no good points. "I've messed up, big-time."

"Again?"

"Not funny. I mean more, in a different way this time…with Macy."

"Uh-oh. I thought she was *just* your landlord."

"Not helping, Pam."

"You're right. My feeling antennae aren't activated yet. Please, go on."

She wasn't sure where to start—with the lie, the sharing, the touching, or the feelings. They'd all lead back to the same screwed-up place anyway. "I lied to her. A lie of omission, but she found out."

This time Pam didn't have a smart-ass comeback. She sipped her coffee, choosing her words carefully. "You didn't tell her about the job?"

Leigh shook her head. "I know, you told me it was a bad idea. But if she got to know me first, she might not think I was a complete loser."

"Now she thinks you're a lying loser. Not sure you've gained any ground." She held up her hand before Leigh could respond. "I know, also not helpful. Did she give you a chance to explain?"

"Nope. She told me to pack my stuff and be out in two days."

"Ouch. That seems harsh, maybe a little overreaction. What does she care as long as you pay the rent? Did something else happen?"

Hiding anything from Pam was like trying to hide it from her own reflection. "Not really. I guess, technically, we had a couple of moments."

Pam placed her coffee on the side table and turned toward her. "My best and dearest friend, *having a moment* is not technical. Either you did or you didn't, and you'd feel it."

She relayed their interaction at the woodpile, Macy's metamorphosis from ice queen to touch-receptive hottie, and their conversation about family. As she retold the story, her stomach tightened into a mass of nerves. They were developing trust, but they'd built it on a lie, her lie. No wonder Macy was irate. She didn't seem the type to take emotional risks lightly, and Leigh had proved she wasn't worthy of this one. Maybe if they hadn't had those moments, Macy wouldn't be so upset.

"I've got to talk to her, make her understand it wasn't personal."

"Whoa, whatever you do, don't say *that*. I'd bet money she thinks it's personal. And from the look on your face, so do you. Have you fallen for this woman?"

She couldn't answer immediately, too many conflicting feelings warring inside. "I've only known her a few days." Why had she thought she mattered to Macy Sheridan anyway? They'd talked a few times, which didn't mean they were bonded for life, but the loss settled in that sensitive spot deep in her gut that always knew the truth.

"That's not really a denial. If you care about her, give her time to calm down. She's not thinking clearly while she's angry. In the meantime, decide what you want."

"Guess you're right."

"I'm always right." Pam topped up their coffee cups and her look softened. "You've never been afraid of taking an emotional risk…except where your mother's concerned."

The mention of her mother brought up the other two-ton weight around her neck. "And that's another thing. Hedy is pressuring me to talk to Susan."

"When your mother's gone, you'll see things differently. Trust me."

"But you and your mother were best friends. Susan and I will never be."

"How exactly is Hedy pressuring you? This ought to be good. That little sister of yours is almost as cute, feisty, and smart as you."

"She's pregnant."

"About damn time. I was beginning to think Bo was shooting blanks." She gave Leigh a sideways glance. "That's a great reason to reconsider. Family is family, no matter how dysfunctional. And Hedy will need all the support she can get with a new baby. It's not like having a puppy. Well, it sort of is, but more time-consuming."

Leigh shook her head. "Why did I come to you? So far you haven't told me anything I wanted to hear."

"That's why I'm your best friend. I give you tough love." Pam rimmed the top of her coffee cup with her finger. "You need to know something else, and you're not going to like it."

"Great. As if this day could get any worse."

"Brace yourself, it's about to." Pam took a gasp of air as if it might be her last. "Susan Bryce is a new foster parent with Children and Family Services."

Leigh stood so quickly her coffee cup tumbled off her knees and skidded across the hardwood floor, leaving a dark, wet trail. "What? How the hell did that happen?" She cringed at her shrill voice, several octaves above her usual contralto.

She retreated to the kitchen for a paper towel, as if leaving the room could distance her from the unwanted news echoing in her head. When she returned, Pam stared at her like a scolded dog, contrite and eager to please. As she cleaned up the spill, Pam struggled to explain.

"I didn't have anything to do with it, and I'm not sure how it happened."

"Who told you?"

"Nate called this morning to get some background on a new foster parent. I about lost it when he told me it was Susan. He thought it was odd because you've been getting phone messages from this woman but don't return her calls. You never told him she was your mother?"

"We're partners, not best friends. We don't really get into personal stuff. So what did you tell him?"

"The truth, and I'm sorry if that pisses you off, but he needed to know. He's in a bit of a situation…and so are you."

"What do you mean?"

"He told me about this kid you're helping, off the books. You could get fired."

"Not if he keeps his mouth shut. But what has one got to do with the other?" Pam's face twisted in that odd way that preceded more bad news. How could it beat what she'd just heard?

"Susan is Jack's foster mom."

The room felt like it was spinning. Was the entire universe conspiring against her, forcing her to interact with this woman who had done nothing but make her life miserable? "Oh, hell, no! You've got to stop this. Get it changed. Have her removed. She's unfit, and this kid needs somebody he can talk to…and somebody *I* can communicate with."

"Have you forgotten we're in the same boat—suspended? If our bosses find out we're anywhere near an active case, we'll be in deep shit."

"Do you have any idea what she's like? She didn't take care of her own children. Why would she care about someone else's? They don't mean anything to her. Come to think of it, neither did we. She's got to be in it for the money."

"Oh, yeah, because it's such a high-paying career?" Pam had been looking at her lap for several seconds, avoiding Leigh's gaze, but her tone was thick with sarcasm. "Did it ever occur to you that she's changed?"

"Sure, just like a zebra. You sound like Hedy, but she's naïve." Leigh couldn't believe what she was hearing. She wouldn't be shocked if Susan popped out of the bedroom and yelled, *surprise*. Now she'd gotten herself entwined in Leigh's professional life, and that was not okay. When she'd knocked on Pam's door, Macy Sheridan was her most immediate problem. How had the Earth tilted so sharply, and what could she do to right it?

Pam put her arm around her and guided her back to the sofa. "I know she hurt you, Leigh. But you're a caring person not afraid to show your feelings or put yourself at risk for someone else. Don't let your pain change that. If you resolved these issues with Susan, maybe you'd find a woman who sees how great you are, and maybe you'd finally believe it yourself."

"When have I ever said those things to you?"

"Never, but I'm your best friend and I see things."

Pam was right about one thing. Susan Bryce was the only black hole in her life. When it came to forgiving her for the pain and neglect of childhood, Leigh had a blind spot as big and cold as Alaska. Maybe it was time to at least consider talking to her. It didn't mean they'd ever be friends, but maybe it was time to make an effort—for Hedy and the baby.

"As I told Hedy, I'll think about it. Subject closed. Now, did Nate say anything else about Jack?"

"He said to tell you he's going to see him at noon. He tried to reach you on your cell, but it went straight to voice mail. One of the joys of living in the boonies, I guess."

Fifteen minutes until noon. She calculated how long it would take to drive to Susan's and whether she wanted to go. She really had no choice. She'd made a promise to Jack and didn't intend to break it, certainly not because of Susan. That would make them alike, and Leigh railed at that with everything inside her. "Want to go with me?"

"Not unless you need me. Nate can back you up. Besides, I'm enjoying sleeping late, drinking coffee all day, and being a suspended bum. Maybe next time." Pam gave her a final hug and followed her to the door. "Let me know how it goes. Love you."

"Love you too. Thanks for the chat…I think."

On the short drive to Susan's, Leigh vowed to keep her visit professional, update Jack, and leave as quickly as possible. She didn't have any reason to engage Susan in a personal conversation today. By the time she pulled in front of the tidy contemporary townhome, she questioned her sanity for coming at all.

Nate parked behind her and got out of the car without speaking. His usually handsome face was tight around the lips, and parenthesis wrinkles blemished the space between his eyes. She decided to let him make the first move because she had no idea what to say to the man she'd worked with for six years.

"Your *mother*, really? Why didn't you tell me? As I recall, I made a smart-ass comment every time she called, about her being one of your pieces of—never mind. That's just sick now."

"Sorry, Nate. We don't get into each other's personal business, probably why we're good partners. Susan and I haven't been in contact for years. She thinks it's time. I don't. End of story. Do you forgive me?"

"It stings a little, but sure. Your business is your business, but if you ever need to talk, I'm here. So, why did you come if you don't want to see her?"

"I promised Jack I'd update him and keep in touch. Any news on his family?"

"Not really. Only ten Temples live in North Carolina, but we're not even sure his dad grew up here. Even if we were, it's impossible to narrow the field. Ten isn't really overwhelming, but more information would make it a lot easier. I tried the obits, but nothing popped. If we have to expand beyond NC, you can imagine what kind of nightmare that'll be. Let's see if he'll give us anything else."

"Thanks for doing this and for keeping me in the loop."

"Bullshit. You're my partner." Nate knocked, and when the woman opened the door, he said, "Holy freaking...sorry, ma'am. I'm Detective Nate Shaver and," he motioned behind him, "I'm sure you know who this is. Jeez, you two could be twins."

"No, we couldn't," Leigh mumbled under her breath as she nudged him into the house, but he was right. If she'd been a few years older, had a spattering of wrinkles around her eyes, and added ten pounds, at a distance they could pass for twins. It wasn't a comforting revelation. Now every time she looked in the mirror, she'd see her mother staring back.

"Detective Shaver. Leigh. Please come in." Susan Bryce stared at her as she entered, and her green eyes misted. Was she tearing up? Not likely. She refused to give Susan the satisfaction of acknowledging her by returning her gaze.

"We're here to see Jack." Leigh got to the point before Susan had a chance to engage them in idle chitchat. This wasn't a social call.

"He's just having lunch. Could I offer you something, either of you?" Susan walked toward the back of the house, and they followed.

The home was open and spacious, with dated but clean furniture throughout and live plants near every window.

"No." Nate gave Leigh an evil glare. He was always hungry and took a free meal whenever and wherever offered. She shrugged and took the opportunity to assess this woman she hadn't seen in several years. Susan had taken care of her body—still relatively trim, her face showing little sign of her sixty years. The jeans and fitted blouse she wore were tasteful, not too trendy but not frumpy. If she'd passed Susan on the street, she would've thought her an attractive middle-aged woman…if she didn't know her. But actions spoke louder than words or appearance, and Susan's actions still screamed in Leigh's head like a bullhorn.

"Detective Monroe," Jack rose from the kitchen table and offered his hand, "so good to see you again. Do you have news about my father? I'm sorry. I forgot my manners. Would either of you like something to eat? Mrs. Bryce made spaghetti with real meatballs, garlic bread, and salad, my very favorite meal."

Leigh looked from the arrangement of food on the table to Jack's plate. "Is it edible?" The thought popped out and Jack looked confused.

"Yeah, real good. Want some?"

"No."

"Yeah, I'll give it a try." Nate smiled at Susan, who took two more plates out of the cupboard and set them on the table. Leigh felt like she'd fallen down the rabbit hole into some alternate universe where the evil step-monster was the good guy and she was the demon.

"Sure I can't tempt you, Leigh?" The food smelled delicious, but she remembered all the meals she and Hedy had missed because Susan was never home to make them and all the ones she'd ruined trying to be a surrogate mother. If she'd been hungry, her appetite vanished.

"I said no."

"What about some tea then? Surely that won't hurt?"

As if she'd already accepted, Susan prepared two more glasses and handed them to her and Nate, then stood beside Jack's chair. If Leigh's mouth hadn't been so dry and her throat so tight, she would've refused the drink too, but she needed to finish her business and get out of there fast. "Jack, we don't have anything for you yet. We need your help to narrow the search. How old was your dad when he died?"

Jack put his fork down and took a swig of tea. He blinked several times and swallowed hard before answering. "For—forty. He was only forty years old."

Susan squeezed his shoulders as if offering comfort, and Leigh cringed. She recalled being sick and asking to stay home from school, but Susan insisted she go so Hedy wouldn't be alone. Susan had plied her with cold medicine and sent her off without the one thing she needed most, her mother's nurturing and understanding. She couldn't remember a time when Susan had touched her in the reassuring fashion she'd just shown Jack. She and Hedy had never seemed to matter that much. Refocusing on the case, she said, "This would be a lot easier if you'd just tell us who you are. We could locate his family quicker and get you back home, which is where again?"

Jack shook his head. "Nice try, but not until I find my father's relatives. Sorry, Detective. Guess I'm stuck here with this nice lady who cooks great meals. Poor me."

For a moment she stared at him, trying to reconcile his glowing opinion of Susan with her less flattering one. He was just a kid who didn't know anything about her life. Villains and monsters came in all guises, shapes, and walks of life. She had no doubt Susan's true colors would float to the surface, and when they did, CFS would take her off the approved-parent list.

Jack and Nate shoveled spaghetti into their mouths like they were in a competition and then asked for seconds. She considered grabbing Nate by the collar and dragging him out but didn't want to make a scene in front of Jack. When they finally finished, she stood and nodded toward the door, hoping Nate would take the hint.

"Hey, Jack, want to play a few hoops to settle that huge lunch?" Nate looked back and forth between her and Susan in his not-so-subtle way of saying they should talk.

"Sure." Jack started out but turned to Susan. "Thanks, that was really great."

She wasn't about to be left alone with Susan Bryce, not for one second. She stood and started toward the front of the house. "Nate, we really don't have time for—"

"Sure we do. It's my lunch hour, and you got nothing better to do. A growing boy needs exercise. Won't be long." He gave her his dimple-faced smile and almost ran out behind Jack.

She stood in the archway between the kitchen and the living room, unable to be in the same room with Susan. Unwilling to look at her, Leigh stared out the window to where Nate and Jack played, wishing she was there or anywhere other than here. *What's stopping you? You're not a kid anymore.* She headed out.

"Leigh, please wait."

The voice was her mother's, but she'd never used that pleading tone before. If she'd heard it from anyone else, Leigh would've been compelled to uncover the problem and remedy it. She was a fixer, but this was her mother, and she'd stopped trying to fix her years ago. "Why are you here, Susan?"

"Greensboro is my home…and…"

Typical. It's all about her.

"I wanted to be closer to Hedy…and you."

"Is that why you left us alone all the time when we were growing up?" She hated the bitterness in her voice, that she couldn't control it and that Susan could see her pain.

"I know that's what you think, Leigh, but—"

"What I *think*? Evidence to the contrary, Mother dear. If you check the police records, you'll find more than one call to our apartment when you were absent." She didn't want to have this conversation, not here, not now, not ever. Anger welled inside, making it hard to breathe, and then burst into pain begging to come out. She choked down a sob. "Why are you doing this…whatever you're doing?"

"You mean the foster-parent thing or living here?"

"Both."

"I lived in Virginia for years until my husband died." Her bottom lip trembled, and she leaned back against the kitchen sink as if needing support.

"Which husband, number four or five?" Low even for her. Hurt or not, she wasn't an intentionally cruel person. "I'm sorry, that was unkind and unnecessary." In another life, Leigh might've liked this intelligent, articulate woman with red hair and eyes that mirrored her own, but not in this life. She was an opportunist who married men for their money and resented having children who got in the way of what she wanted.

"I worked with CFS in Virginia for several years, and it sort of followed me."

She tried to imagine Susan taking care of other people's children the way she hadn't taken care of her own, and another wave of pain roiled inside. Did Susan have any idea how upsetting it was to see her parenting Jack? She and Hedy would've given anything for that kind of attention. Now it was too late. She wanted to forgive, for Hedy's sake and her own sanity, but she couldn't look at Susan without remembering what never was.

"Leigh, I'd really like to talk to you about everything, whenever you're ready."

"I can't do this. Tell Nate I'll be outside."

Chapter Ten

Macy sat on the front porch sipping an afternoon coffee, unable to bear the confinement of the small cottage. She'd woken up several times during the night, and when she checked this morning, Leigh's car was gone. Had she left early or simply not been home all night? Home? The irony wasn't lost on her. Why would Leigh stay in a place she obviously wasn't welcome and had been told to leave?

She'd accused Leigh of lying, when she was doing the same thing, pretending to take a break from work and painting while she withdrew more every day. Why were events from her childhood still dictating her life? Was she weak, had she held on for a reason, refused to move forward purposely, or maybe used them as an excuse to avoid relationships? None of those options suited the image of who she wanted to be. She flung the remnants of her coffee into the yard and reached for the doorknob as Leigh's vehicle pulled into the drive.

Removing boxes and a bag of Cheetos from her car, Leigh started toward the dock without acknowledging her. "Could I talk with you for a second?" Leigh kept walking. "Please?"

Leigh dropped everything and shuffled toward her. Hands in her pockets and shoulders hunched forward, she stared at the ground. The lively energy that usually surrounded her had turned dull and listless. Macy envisioned shadowy colors blanketing her and weighing her down. "What happened?"

"Nothing that would interest you." Leigh raised her head and stared at her with puffy, bloodshot eyes.

She extended her hand but Leigh leaned out of reach. She'd never seen her so dejected, and the pang in her chest burrowed deep. "Is this my fault, because I asked you to leave?"

"No. Now, if you don't mind, I need to pack."

"Wait, please. I'd like to talk about yesterday. Actually, I'd like you to talk and I'd like to listen for a change."

Leigh's eyes dug into her soul. "Why would you want to hear about my problems? Yesterday you wanted me to leave. I'm getting whiplash from your drastic mood swings. What's changed?"

"I went off half-cocked, without knowing the facts. And it's really none of my business what you do for a living, as long as you pay the rent. I'm sorry. I want to understand, if you want to tell me what happened."

"That might not be a good idea. You couldn't tell anyone, and that puts you in an awkward position if you're ever asked."

"Did you do something criminal?"

"No, but I did violate departmental policy, and I didn't tell the Internal Affairs detectives everything. So you're right, I lied, to them and to you. Not my proudest moments."

The admission caught Macy off guard. She'd expected an explanation that didn't include Leigh being a liar. It didn't fit her picture of the generous woman who'd mothered her baby sister for years and chopped wood for strangers. "I'm still willing to listen if you want to talk."

Leigh seemed to consider the offer. "I'd like to finally tell the whole story, if you promise not to repeat it—not for me, but because it might get an innocent third party in trouble."

Macy nodded and exhaled like she was blowing up a balloon, as some of the tension drained from her body. She loosened the grip on her coffee mug as the possibility that Leigh might refuse to talk to her evaporated. She wanted to know about Leigh's life, especially the buried parts that hurt or caused her concern. The easy parts flowed effortlessly. "Come in. I'll get us some coffee. Looks like you could use a cup."

"You have no idea. I'd ask for something stronger, but I don't think it'd help."

Leigh shucked off her leather jacket as casually as if she lived there and dropped it on the floor beside the sofa. Macy poured two cups of coffee and handed one to Leigh. Then she picked up Leigh's jacket and hung it by the door as she waited.

"Pam, my best friend who works at Children and Family Services, and I had a case involving an eleven-year-old girl, Lily. She was a very bright kid. How she managed to keep up with her schoolwork with everything going on in her life was a miracle. Her mother was an addict who died of an overdose, so Lily was about to be thrown into the system." Leigh took a sip of coffee and swallowed visibly.

"Her mother's boyfriend, also an addict with no job, lived in the apartment with them. When the mother died, he offered to take care of Lily, thought he'd be able to collect the money from Social Services. Lily didn't want to live with him." She dug into the side of her forefinger with her thumbnail, and her eyes turned cold. "Said he sexually abused her. Kids make up stuff, but Pam and I talked with Lily several times, and her story never changed. We both believed she was telling the truth."

"Oh, my God, what happened? Tell me you didn't take her back to him."

"Pam and I drove Lily to the funeral. The boyfriend wasn't even there, real classy. Afterward, we asked if she had any other relatives we could call, anybody who might be willing to look after her. She had a grandmother in Detroit, Pam called, and she was thrilled to have Lily live with her. However, she couldn't get to Greensboro for three days."

Macy's heartbeat accelerated and some of her anxiety melted away. "I'm beginning to see the problem."

"Pam and I agreed not to put her back in her home environment. She told us about an elderly woman who lived in a house behind the apartment complex. The neighbor had often let her sleep over and gave her food when her mother was gone for days. Lily thought she might step in until her grandmother arrived."

"So, you called the neighbor?" She inched closer to Leigh on the sofa, eager for the rest of the story.

"Couldn't do that."

Leigh smiled at her for the first time, and Macy's insides felt gooey, like chocolate in the hot sun. Her green eyes sparkled, and she looked like the Leigh of two days ago. "So?"

"I explained to Lily why *we* couldn't ask her neighbor for help, but if *she* did without our knowledge…"

"You sly devil. And she understood that cryptic cop double-talk?"

"Like I said, a very smart girl. She contacted her grandmother, told her where she'd be, and on day four she was in Detroit safe and sound."

"How do you know?"

"Her grandmother called to thank us. I think Lily will have a good life now."

"Wait, you got in trouble for getting a child out of an abusive situation and keeping her out of the system? Isn't that what the police and family services are supposed to do?"

"Pam and I were suspended a month for violating policy and procedure. We agreed not to involve the neighbor since she wasn't a relative, and we weren't sure if the boyfriend would try to retaliate. The police department and CFS wanted to know where Lily was for three days. Made them look bad, especially when the boyfriend started talking to the papers."

"Something's wrong with a system that punishes you for taking care of a child."

"A society is only as good as its laws, and some of ours are messed up. They protect the wrong people."

She smiled at Leigh, trying to relay her respect and admiration through the simple gesture. "Wow, the paper sure doesn't tell that story. You both showed a lot of courage."

"But I lied to the investigators and to you about being a cop. That wasn't very courageous. When I came here, I needed to escape from the publicity, get my head together, and decide what to do with my life. I was still living in Gayle, my ex's, condo, after nine months, and felt stuck. I hoped if you got to know me you might not kick me out when you heard how chaotic my life is. That one really backfired. I planned to tell you everything, but you beat me to it. Sorry." Leigh reached for her hand but pulled back.

She wanted Leigh to touch her but couldn't imagine why Leigh would want to. She'd been horrible to her. "Now that I know the whole story, I feel like an ass for the way I acted. I'm hardly one to judge. I've been hiding out for six months, pretending to launch my painting career. So far I haven't started the first piece. The closest I've come to returning to my craft and to feeling remotely human is when I manage an occasional nude sketch. You accidentally stumbled into my little patch of purgatory by accident."

"It's a beautiful place and you're not bad either, when you let your guard down."

Macy let the quasi-compliment pass, glad for the banter but afraid to push her luck. "What about Jack? How does he figure in? Another kid you're protecting?"

"Sort of, but I don't know what to do about his situation yet." Leigh told her about the search for his father's family, and then the look in her eyes became distant, as if she was recalling something more unpleasant.

"What else has happened? Is it your girlfriend, or sister, or…if that's too personal, you don't have to answer.

"Mother."

"Oh."

For the next thirty minutes, Leigh filled her in on Jack's foster mother, who just happened to be her real mother, and the talk they almost had. The worry lines across Leigh's forehead deepened, and sadness swirled in her eyes like sediment in a murky lake. Macy didn't have anything to say. Her advice on effectively dealing with parents would fill a thimble.

"And you couldn't talk to her at all? It sounds like you have some things to work through." Like her own life, in which she'd closed off everything and everyone. But Leigh lived her feelings in real time and vivid color. Macy doubted if she'd recognize an honest emotion if she had one.

Leigh shook her head. "It's not that I hate her. And I'm not hiding my feelings, believe me. I just can't look at her without remembering all the times she wasn't around for us. How could a mother do that to her children?"

"Don't you think you should hear her side of the story? Maybe more was going on than you knew at the time. When we're children we attach meaning to our parents' actions that isn't necessarily accurate."

"Sounds like you're speaking from experience."

"Nothing like what you've been through." She twisted her hands in her lap and avoided Leigh's stare. She'd only meant to offer encouragement, not talk about her own issues, again.

"If you could tell me, it might help—in the understanding-parents department. But only if you're comfortable."

She should retreat to the comfort of distance and the landlord-tenant relationship, but something in Leigh's eyes urged her to continue. "When I was a teenager, I told my parents I wanted to be an artist. They were dead set against it, refusing to pay my college tuition unless I took pre-approved courses. I was allowed to study art as a minor but had to keep my other grades up. I thought they were just being cruel, trying to bend my rebellion to their will. Now I realize they were only trying to do what was best for me—steer me in the direction of a useful education with the possibility of a job at the end of it. Things become clearer with the passage of time and the experiences of life. I'm just saying, your mother might have had another reason for her actions."

"Is that why you're not close to your parents, because they didn't support your passion?"

Leigh seemed to be able to discern things about her life she'd never meant to reveal. Maybe that's what made her a good detective. Would those same attributes serve her in a personal relationship, make her more compassionate and understanding? The question brought her back to the conversation, and she blushed at the intimate detour she'd taken.

"Yes, I suppose it is…and the fact that they have more money than God and choose to piss it away on vacations and toys instead of doing anything meaningful. We've talked about my art since, and they're more supportive. But it was hard to broach the subject after so many years, and it will be with your mother as well." Leigh smiled at her and she suddenly felt self-conscious. "What's that grin about?"

"I just like seeing this side of you. It's very attractive. You should show it more often."

She flashed back to the exchanges they'd had and realized she'd been in avoid-and-deflect mode since Leigh arrived. "I haven't exactly been the most helpful and welcoming landlord, have I?"

"You're enjoying the solitude of this fantastic place…and protecting yourself."

Leigh's green eyes bored into her and she felt exposed. "What do you mean?" Her chest ached like someone had suddenly pressed a weight there. Leigh had scratched her tender underbelly, the part no one was allowed to touch. She pulled her sweater tighter and leaned back on the sofa.

"I'm sorry. I've made you uncomfortable." Leigh gently took her hand and entwined their fingers just as she had when they admired her paintings. The sensation was just as strong, the combination of light, color, and texture. Closing her eyes, she breathed it in—rich, bold, and soothing. When she looked up, Leigh was staring at their joined hands.

"It's just…I'm not…how do you know…"

"You seem sad…almost wounded, like you've lost something precious." She traced the jagged scar on Macy's wrist with the tip of her finger, her eyes full of apology for dredging up the pain. "Have you lost someone? Is that what *this* is about?"

The simple questions were like arrows to her heart, summoning the grief and unleashing the emotion trapped for so long. For the first time in years, she wanted to purge, to open the box where all the loss for Jesse lived and set it free. Tears burned her eyes and she struggled to contain them. "I…can't…"

"It's okay." Leigh pulled her close and cradled her head against her shoulder. "You don't have to say anything."

When Leigh wrapped her arms around her, she wanted the pain to stop but sensed the only relief for such deep sorrow was more time and tears. She clung to Leigh, uncertain why but positive she had to, as sunlight drained from the room. The silence between them occasionally cracked as she breathed a deep sigh or shifted against Leigh's chest to listen to the comforting beat of her heart.

"You're safe." Leigh's words were almost a whisper, soothing in their sincerity.

She'd never allowed anyone close enough to comfort her, perhaps because she didn't deserve to be comforted. Her pain and a single toothed scar seemed just punishment for losing her best friend on what should've been a simple night out. How did Leigh know what she needed? It was as if she opened her heart and saw the image of Jesse filling every space.

As Leigh held her, rocking back and forth, whispering reassurances, Macy imagined how loved and protected Hedy must've felt when they were children. Leigh oozed affection and compassion, and it soaked into the raw places in her soul. She wanted to tell Leigh about Jesse, but she didn't have the courage, the strength to relive it.

"Why are you so nice? I've been horrible to you." Her voice was almost inaudible and timid with uncertainty.

"Because I'm a nice person and I really like you. I have since the minute we met and you threatened not to rent to me after only two seconds. Maybe I'm a hopeless romantic."

"Or maybe you're just a sucker for lost causes."

When Leigh looked into her eyes, Macy was drawn toward her like Earth in the sun's gravitational force. Only a breath away from Leigh's parted lips, she licked hers, whether from anxiety or desire, she wasn't sure. She'd never wanted to kiss anyone so badly, to taste her. "Oh, God."

"Sorry, didn't mean to crowd you," Leigh said, and started to pull away.

She caged Leigh so quickly and so closely she could barely breathe and, without allowing herself time to think, kissed her.

"Macy?"

"I want this." She'd barely spoken the words when Leigh teased her lips with the tip of her tongue. Heat scorched through her like a wildfire in the dry season. Leigh's lips closed over hers and she fell into a vat of liquid velvet, softness inside and out. She opened her mouth and Leigh's delicate tongue strokes claimed her, sparking desire in her core. "Umm." Her response released a flood, an urge to wrap Leigh between her legs and ride her until she collapsed. "Yes."

Leigh caressed the side of her face with such tenderness that she leaned into it like a purring kitten. Leigh's hand skimmed over her shoulder and down, coming to rest in the small of her back—a touch so gentle and possessive. How she craved this woman's touch, like a drug to her starved system. Her clit throbbed with an ache so powerful she'd almost forgotten such passion existed.

She hadn't needed anyone in so long—not physically and certainly not emotionally—the possibility was immediately sobering. She stopped with her lips a breath away from another scorching kiss. "Stop. *Stop!*"

"What? Did I do something wrong?"

Macy stood and moved away from Leigh, not trusting herself in arm's reach. "I'm so sorry. I don't know where that came from. It's just…you're so…I'm really sorry."

Leigh's gaze, hungry and pleading, followed her as she paced. "I'm the one who should apologize. You were upset and I took advantage of your vulnerability."

"What? No, no, you didn't. It was my fault. I can't really explain."

"Why do you need to? We're attracted to each other. Isn't that enough?"

If only it was. How did Leigh manage to boil everything down to the simplest terms? "Not for me. I had no right to kiss you…or to lead you on."

"I'm not complaining."

Leigh reached for her, but she moved away, afraid that if they touched again the same thing, or something more, might happen. "Maybe you better go."

"I'm sorry if I upset you, but I'm not sorry about the kiss. I've wanted to do that for a while now." She retrieved her jacket, slung it over her shoulder, and walked toward the door. "Thank you for talking to me. I know that wasn't easy."

"Leigh, wait." She was desperate to keep Leigh close but had no valid reason beyond the desire threatening to consume her. She glanced around the room, searching for an excuse. "I…" Her gaze fell on the painting they'd admired together, and she took it off the wall. "I want you to have this, for the apartment. I painted it from the balcony, so it sort of belongs there."

"Are you sure?" She nodded. "I know just the spot. Thanks. Does this mean you're not kicking me out?"

"Not yet…and don't worry about what happened. I wanted that kiss as much as you did. I'm just not ready to deal with what it means. Now, if I could get you to stop exposing yourself on the dock, you'd be a perfect tenant. After what just happened, I understand how you must've felt that night when you left—makes us sort of even."

"I'll work on my exhibitionism, if you'll stop being so damn tempting. But remember, well-behaved women seldom make history."

"Jeez, you and your bumper stickers. I don't want to make history, Monroe. I just want to live a full, honest life." As she closed the door behind Leigh, she realized she hadn't spoken truer words in quite some time.

❖

Leigh's jeans irritated and chafed as she walked, making each step excruciatingly pleasurable. Her body was like a circuit board with all components firing at once. Not even a cold shower would stop the subcutaneous itch. But her needs surpassed sex. She craved the discovery of everything Macy Sheridan—her dreams and nightmares, her likes and dislikes, what turned her on, her deepest secrets and most private thoughts. What prevented Macy from accepting the comfort of human touch? And what had caused that classic suicide-like scar on her left wrist? The image of it flashed through Leigh's mind, and she almost dropped the painting she was hauling up the stairs to the apartment.

Macy's kiss had reminded her of the need for passion that fueled her body and the connection to another woman that fed her soul. She'd bonded with Gayle but been dismissed like a cheap pair of shoes. Seldom in their three-year relationship had Gayle shared a vulnerable moment or shed a tear about anything. She'd always been the initiator with Gayle, asking for affection, bargaining for sex, and pleading for intimacy. Gayle never kissed her like Macy just did, uninhibited and hungry, like nothing and no one in the world mattered more in that moment.

How had she gotten to this place with Macy? Two days ago she'd been on the verge of homelessness, vilified by an angry, unsympathetic woman hell-bent on maintaining her privacy and autonomy. Today

Macy had apologized, showing a sensitive side Leigh had only glimpsed before. They'd talked about parents and misunderstandings and the sadness Macy wore like a garment. She'd wanted to get to know Macy better, not bring up a painful past. What caused her so much turmoil and grief?

She rubbed the fabric on her shoulder and inhaled Macy's fragrance, like rosemary on the dunes. Reaching out to her had seemed the most natural thing she'd ever done. Her heart had shattered as Macy crumpled against her, and she was powerless to do anything but listen. It seemed so little for someone in so much pain.

Whatever was bothering Macy was the reason she'd reached out to her and the reason she'd withdrawn. Macy had admitted she wanted the kiss as much as Leigh did, so what was powerful enough to override her innate sexual urge?

If she wanted a relationship, she'd have to wait until Macy was ready. It wouldn't be easy to stay away now that she'd glimpsed Macy's underlying passion. But something strong and unrelenting haunted Macy. Until it was resolved, Leigh didn't stand a chance of being a part of her life, much less a priority.

CHAPTER ELEVEN

As Leigh jogged her morning route along Egret Lane, the trees seemed fuller, the flowers brighter, and her mood significantly improved. She'd maintained her workout routine for almost two weeks and was beginning to feel like her old self again. Today she was even more energized and horny as hell. She'd developed a definite case of Macy-lust that pulsated like a transformer about to overload. She made the final sprint to the top of the driveway in record time, and her breathing was hardly labored. If her hormones didn't calm down, she'd have to chop another cord of wood or bat down Macy's door with the ax.

She was leaning against the mailbox, stretching her hamstrings when her cell phone rang. Checking the caller ID, she groaned. Nate was normally not this early. "Hello."

"Do you ever check your messages, Monroe?" His tone was flat and tight. "I've left three. This living-in-the-boonies shit isn't working for me."

"What's wrong?"

"We've got a problem."

"I hate it when you start a conversation that way. Which particular one are you referring to? We have choices."

"Don't want to get into details on the phone. Never know who's listening. But it's about our most recent venture. How soon can you meet me?"

"About an hour. Just finished my jog so I'd like a shower."

"An hour. Dunkin'." He didn't need to say which one, and he didn't bother with good-bye.

She wasn't even in the city anymore. What could've gone wrong now? How could she screw things up remotely? As she trotted toward the apartment, she told herself she hadn't done anything wrong.

"Leigh?"

Macy stood on the porch watching her with eyes that raked her soul. Her lips were full and the deep red of burning embers. She remembered their softness against hers, the sweet-salty taste of her tongue, and stumbled forward. "Yeah?" It was the only thing that came out around the pounding in her throat that mimicked the throbbing between her legs.

"Want a cup of coffee or some breakfast? I could make blueberry pancakes."

And she cooks too. "Uh…I'd love both, but I have to meet Nate. Could I get a to-go mug, after I shower?" She started to add, *and a piece of you for the road.* Macy's right leg peek-a-booed from the closure of her burgundy bathrobe, and her creamy cleavage was highlighted by the plunging neckline. She couldn't decide which was the better view. Both made her ache.

"Sure. I'll have it ready on your way out. Do you like what you see, Detective?"

Busted. "Very much." She forced herself to turn and walk in the opposite direction. If that hadn't been an invitation, she was losing her ability to read women. But it would take more than a flash of flesh and a subtle comment to convince her that Macy was ready to take her on. "See you in a few."

Leigh's shower left her clean and dirty. The sweat and grime from her run disappeared, but the sheets of water trailing down her body tantalized like she imagined Macy's hands and mouth would, causing a flood of another kind. After several attempts to shake Macy's image, she turned the water off and stepped out of the shower. The thought of putting clothes on her sensitive skin was not appealing; sandpaper on sunburn came to mind.

As she dressed, she glanced at the stack of reports on the coffee table. The cold case Captain Howard had entrusted her to review was still unfinished. One unpleasant task at a time. First, she'd figure out what Nate was on about, and tonight she'd dive back in. She slid down the stair railing to the dock below, lucky she didn't pick up an ass load of splinters. Macy sat on the porch, fully dressed, sipping a mug of coffee with another by her chair.

"You certainly look refreshed."

She laughed, unable to ignore the pulsing in her center and her unsuccessful attempts to shower effectively while thinking about Macy.

"Did I say something funny?"

"No, I just…it's me. Strange morning. Is that mine?"

Macy offered her the mug but held on to it when she tried to take it. "Are you all right, about yesterday? I didn't mean to complicate things…any more than they already are."

"I'm fine. Maybe a little keyed up, but otherwise, okay. How about you?"

"The same, I guess. I shouldn't advertise things that aren't for sale."

Leigh nearly spat out her sip of coffee. "I beg your pardon?"

"It's an old saying my dad used when I was a teenager, a warning about boys. If you tease them with the goods, they'll expect you to put out. Come to think of it, some of the women I've dated had that same philosophy."

"Yeah, lesbians can be like that. Sex is a big deal, at least in the beginning. Don't worry. I won't give you the bum's rush. I'm a patient woman, especially when it comes to something that's worth waiting for. Thanks for the coffee. Gotta dash."

On her way into town, she replayed her parting conversation with Macy. Their exchange had been easy and uncomplicated in spite of the kiss last night. She'd expected some discomfiture, but Macy seemed fine, even a little flirtatious. Maybe their honesty had allowed them both to relax a bit. She certainly felt emotionally closer to Macy, but she'd have to be careful. One conversation didn't make a relationship, and Macy Sheridan wasn't the kind of woman to leap easily or often.

When she pulled into the Dunkin' Donuts lot, Nate was sitting on the hood of his car with two cups of coffee and a donut. "Is that chocolate-glazed custard-filled, and is it for me? Please say yes." She snagged the fried-dough confection before he could answer. "Too late." She bit into the warm treat and custard oozed out the sides. "This is heaven."

"It looks like something diseased or—"

"Stop. If you ever want my help again, let me eat this in peace." She'd regretted not having Macy's blueberry pancakes on the drive and was ravenous. Three monster bites later the donut was gone, and she licked her sticky fingers clean.

"Am I free to speak now that you've gorged yourself on that disgusting thing?"

"What's going on? Spit it out before you bust a gut."

"We've been waved off the search for Steven Temple."

"By whom?"

"The feds. They stormed into the office this morning, before any of the detectives arrived, and grilled the admin assistant about running information on the guy. They told her, in no uncertain terms, that we were all to steer clear of Temple and any of his relatives past, present, and future. When she told us, you can imagine she was scared shitless, didn't even know what branch of the feds."

"Sounds like we've stumbled into a big pile of crap. Feds could be the Department of Agriculture, Army, Homeland Security, Border Patrol, Post Office. The list goes on. Any idea what it's all about?"

"Nope, and we aren't likely to find out either." Nate cocked his head to the side and gave her a mischievous grin. "Are we, partner?"

"We most certainly are not," she said as she nodded. "I expect you to do exactly what the feds said and stay out of this. I mean it, Nate."

"Jack is my responsibility now that he's officially in the system, in case you forgot. I'd say they're the ones stepping out of bounds."

"Don't stick your neck out too far. Let me do that since mine's already on the block."

"I'm going to do my job, like you would. If anything goes tits up, I'll just blame it on you, all right?" He grinned and nudged her in the side. "Let's talk to the kid again and see if he'll cough up anything else. He's our only shot."

"Anything from missing persons?"

He shook his head.

"I'm surprised someone hasn't filed a report. He's a good kid. Somebody's bound to be looking for him," Leigh said.

"You'd think, but I check every day."

"If he doesn't give us anything, maybe we should post his picture and see if anything pops."

"I think it's time, but we can't post on the Center for Missing and Exploited Children site until we have the documentation to back it up. You know the drill."

"Yeah, but I know somebody who works in the call center. Maybe I can cash in a favor. In the meantime, let's go chat with young Jack. See you at the foster home."

When they parked outside Susan's townhouse, Leigh felt as unprepared as she had the first day of recruit school—unsure if she'd measure up, afraid of the challenges. They had to find another way to help this boy that didn't involve constantly encountering her mother. She summoned her courage and met Nate on the doorstep. "Let me talk to Jack alone. I think he'll be more likely to open up one-on-one."

Nate nodded. "Great. I'll see if Susan made breakfast. That spaghetti the other day was to die for."

She gave him an evil glare and knocked on the door. When Susan answered, she acknowledged her with a slight nod. "Is Jack awake?"

"Good morning, Detectives," Susan said. "He's upstairs getting dressed, but you probably shouldn't go up yet."

Leigh stopped halfway up the stairs. "And why not?"

"He's a young man who needs his privacy."

"Yeah," Nate said, "you definitely don't want to barge in on a guy when he's getting dressed, especially not first thing in the morning."

"Like you have a clue," Leigh said as she sat down on the last step.

"I was young once." He beamed at Susan. "Is that bacon I smell?"

"Sure is. Can I offer you both some breakfast?"

"No."

"Yes, I'd love some. Thank you, Susan."

Nate sounded like he was auditioning for the world's most cordial male, and Leigh was about to be sick. Sucking up to Susan Bryce wouldn't win him any points in her book. But he had charm. The man could score a free meal anywhere with his dimpled grin and slick compliments. No wonder women flocked to him like techies to a new smartphone giveaway.

"Leigh, would you like some coffee? I made a fresh pot."

"No, I'm good. I'll just wait here for Jack." As they disappeared into the kitchen, she thought how accommodating and polite Susan was. But polite and accommodating had never been Susan's problems; loyalty and compassion had. Hedy and Macy had suggested she listen to Susan, give her a chance to explain. It couldn't make things any worse.

"Hey, Detective Monroe, what're you doing here so early?" Jack bounded down the stairs two at a time and plopped onto the step beside her. "Good news?"

"Afraid not. Let's go outside." They stood at the railing overlooking the backyard, and neither spoke for several minutes. This young man would make a good FBI agent someday. He had patience, intelligence, and self-confidence that most kids his age hadn't yet mastered. "Jack, you have to give me more to go on. We've run into a roadblock, and without your help, we won't be able to find your dad's family."

"What kind of roadblock?"

Tell him the truth or lie? "The feds have ordered us off." If she expected honesty, she had to give it. "Do you have any idea why they'd be interested in your dad or his family?"

Jack's gray eyes were wide, his bottom lip trembling. "Do you think he was a criminal?"

"I honestly don't know. He could've been a suspect, a material witness, or just a person of interest in a case. But it doesn't make sense they'd want us to back off now that he's…passed."

"My dad wouldn't do anything illegal, wasn't his style. He'd work late so a coworker could go to his kid's basketball game. He gave an elderly lady in the neighborhood a ride to the grocery store once a week. Guys like that aren't crooks, are they?"

He looked at her with all the innocence and insecurity of his young years, and she wanted to help preserve the spotless image of his father. "Not usually, Jack. He sounds like a good man. Tell me again why you think his family is in this area." She watched the mental struggle play out on his smooth face as his eyes squinted in the morning sun and his lips straightened into a thin line of consternation.

"When I was younger, I heard him and my mom talk about a lake. I don't remember the name of it, but she said Greensboro, North Carolina. They didn't know I was listening, but I've never forgotten how sad their voices sounded, like that place was special."

"Greensboro has three lakes: Lake Brandt, Higgins, and Townsend, though some count Lake Jeannette as well. Guilford County has five additional lakes, so that doesn't really narrow it down much. What about your mother?"

"She's not a part of this."

"Do you mean she died, you never knew her, you lost faith in her, or something else?"

"Yeah."

If she weren't a patient woman, her hackles would be bristling. Dealing with children and teenagers was like waiting for the next eclipse. "Yeah what? Help me out here, Jack."

"She's just not part of the equation."

Jack wouldn't look her in the eyes, and that made her nervous. He was hiding more than the obvious, but she couldn't figure out what. A trickle of familiarity rolled down her spine. Her dad walked on water, partly because he was dead, and mother never quite made up for the loss. Is that what Jack was going through?

"Is your mother still alive?"

"Yes."

"Do you want me to contact her and let her know you're okay? Even if we don't get along with our parents, they always want to know we're alive and healthy." She tried not to think too deeply about what she'd just said. She didn't like the bitter taste of hypocrisy.

"Would you? Talk to your mother…if things weren't right between you anymore?"

Now Jack's gaze met hers and she couldn't look away or lie. Susan was just inside, and she couldn't be bothered to let her know anything about her life. "Things get more complicated as you get older. That's why it's best to stay on good terms when you're young, so they don't ever get complicated. Know what I mean?"

"Yeah. You don't talk to your mother either."

Too smart for his own good. At least she knew now that his mother was still alive. "Look, Jack, if you don't help me, I can't help you."

"Then we're at a stalemate, Detective. I'm content to stay here, go to school, eat *your* mother's excellent meals, and wait until you find my relatives."

"How did you know Susan's my mother?"

"I listen to what's said and to what isn't. Pretty good skill for a detective, right?" He smiled at her and walked back into the house.

She stood on the deck and stared out across the lawn toward the park. Susan had chosen a townhouse located in an historic area of town, close to walking trails and easy access to the downtown business district. She'd paid cash when she bought the unit a year ago. Leigh had checked out everything about Susan Bryce when she found out she'd moved back to Greensboro. None of it made sense based on her memory of life with her mother—where she got the money, why she came back, how she became a foster parent, and why she wanted contact with her children after all these years. She used to be so certain about her feelings for her mother, but things were starting to blur and she didn't like it.

When she walked back into the kitchen, Nate and Jack were scarfing down the remnants of breakfast. "Nate, why don't you give Jack a ride to school." She leaned down and whispered, "And see if he'll talk to you. I tanked."

He shoved a piece of toast in his mouth and herded Jack toward the front. "Let's go, kid."

A ticking clock, like a time bomb, was the only sound in the kitchen when the guys left. She sat down at the table, determined to make Susan open any conversation. Yes, she was being petty, but she couldn't bring herself to reach out first. She'd tried too many times as a child and been put off or relegated to the end of the priority list.

"Coffee?" Susan asked. She set a mug and the pot in front of Leigh and then sat across from her at the table. "It's true, what you told Jack about parents wanting to know their children are all right."

"Were you eavesdropping?" Her pulse accelerated. Not a good start.

Susan pointed toward the open kitchen window. "I like the fresh morning air before I have to turn on the air-conditioning."

"Oh." She felt like an overreactive child. "I was trying to get him to talk to me. Has he said anything to you about where he's from?"

"Not a word. He's very bright but also very guarded at the moment. Sort of like you."

"We're not talking about me. I'm trying to find this kid's family so he can go back home. I'm sure his mother's worried crazy."

"I know I would be, but he hasn't dropped any clues. He goes to school, comes home, has dinner, does his homework, and then we play Scrabble or some game-station thingy he has until bedtime. He hasn't had contact with anyone except me and the kids at school, that I'm aware of."

Leigh tried to imagine her mother playing Scrabble or gaming and drew a blank. She'd tied a length of braided packing twine to a bike rack so she and Hedy could jump rope because her mother was too busy to be bothered. Who was this woman?

"I wish I could be more helpful, Leigh, but he doesn't talk about his life or family."

"Just let me know if he does. I hate to think about the pain his mother is going through." The irony of her statement didn't escape Leigh. She couldn't look at Susan. "How about Hedy being pregnant? Can you believe it?" She had no idea where *that* came from. Was she actually offering an olive branch to her mother?

"I don't think I've ever seen Hedy so happy. I'm looking forward to spending more time with my grandchildren than I did with you girls."

Was Susan saying she realized she'd been basically an absentee mother and wanted to redeem herself with a grandchild? What had happened to make her miss out on watching her girls grow up? Did she seriously want to make amends? Leigh had never cared enough to even ask the question. Why was she interested all of a sudden? Maybe her talk with Hedy, maybe the baby, or perhaps Macy had something to do with her change of heart. "Susan, I think we—" Her cell phone rang and she pulled it off her belt. "Sorry. Hello?"

"Took our little charge to school, got nothing. He's more tight-lipped than the CIA. You still at Susan's?"

"Leaving now. Thanks for trying, Nate. See you." She took her last sip of coffee and stared into her mother's eyes for the first time in years. Eyes the same emerald color as hers but deeply troubled stared back. "I have to go. By the way, have you seen Jack with a cell phone?"

"No, come to think of it I haven't. That seems strange for a kid his age."

"Really strange. Watch your cell- and house-phone bills for any calls you didn't make. He might try to contact somebody and that could lead us to his family."

"Sure." Leigh started toward the front door. "Leigh, do you think we can have a talk sometime soon, a real talk?"

"Maybe." As she left, Leigh realized she was actually considering it.

❖

Macy donned her old lab coat as soon as Leigh left and headed for the studio. Her body teemed with energy, and she was anxious to start the artistic phase of the reconstruction. She hadn't been this focused since—three days ago, the last time Leigh touched her. No, she'd worked hard to regain some enthusiasm, and it had nothing to do with Leigh Monroe. Her work was finally beginning to feel like art again instead of a chore because she'd decided to move forward regardless of the results.

The emotional connection that usually accompanied her work emerged, and she sensed the irresistible pull of the creative force that drove her paintings. She sketched the contours of the skull, using the underlying photographs and tissue markers as guides. Slowly, she filled in the soft lines and shadows of the face that belonged to her current and final forensic task. This phase of the process was particularly challenging. She had to keep her ego in check and remain objective, careful not to project any of her wishes, hopes, or memories of Jesse onto the work.

An hour later, she was ready to work on the eyes, but the struggle between creating just an anatomically correct eye and one that actually conveyed substance was daunting, especially with the image of Jesse's always in the back of her mind. As she picked up her pencil and ruler to measure the location of the eye, she heard a knock at her door.

She considered ignoring it because she was making great progress and she wanted to finish the eyes before stopping. But the knocking persisted. Damn. Ruler and pencil in hand, she opened the front door to a smiling Leigh Monroe. She flushed with pleasure and embarrassment as she realized she was actually happy to see her. "Hi. I wasn't expecting you."

"I'm obviously interrupting. I'll go."

"No, no, please come in." She wasn't sure why she'd said that. Her mind was still on the sketch, and she was torn between her old familiar passion and a newer, equally stimulating one. "You can sit with me, while I finish one thing…if you don't mind."

Leigh's smile blossomed across her freckled face, and her eyes sparkled. "I'd love to, if I won't be distracting."

She turned back toward the studio with Leigh so close she imagined she could feel the heat of her body. The emotions she'd tamped down to work flashed, and her nerves jangled. Distracting indeed.

"So, this is your studio. It's different from the rest of the cottage."

"This is the one place I'm not totally anal about order. My art seems to defy structure and any attempts to contain it."

"That's probably a good thing, right? I imagine trying to control or suppress creative energy would be like trying to manage the natural elements." She glanced at the drawing and back at Macy. "Wow, that looks like something out of a sci-fi movie with all those little bits sticking out of the skull. How long does it take to do a total rebuild, or whatever you call it?"

"Depends. If the skull is intact and I concentrate, I can finish the sketch in a day and the clay reconstruction in a couple of days. But I haven't been particularly focused lately." Leigh was standing so near she imagined the hairs on their arms were touching, and her entire body ached. "Let me find you a place to sit." She pulled a rolling work chair from the corner and a brown plastic box slid off, scattering its contents across the floor.

Leigh knelt and scooped up a handful of the items. "What are these things?" She held one of the rectangular transparencies to the light. "Is that a nose?"

Leigh's expression was like that of a kid who'd picked up something icky, and she laughed. "Yes, it's a nose, and these are a mouth, chin, hair, and eyes." She pointed to some of the other slides. "It's an old Identi-Kit system of facial characteristics. They're superimposed on one another to create a description of a person."

"I've never seen one before. Some of the older guys talk about using these to make composites before computers. I had no idea they were actual transparencies you place on top of each other to make a whole. Interesting." Leigh sat down on the floor and began picking up the acetate pieces. "Don't let me interrupt your work. I'll amuse myself with these."

Macy looked from her drawing to Leigh camped out on the floor and felt a twinge of anxiety. She wasn't used to anyone besides a model being in the studio when she was working. She'd never trusted anyone enough to share her artistic process, and besides, people distracted her when she was in the zone. So why was Leigh in her studio, playing with her Identi-Kit? Maybe it was just one of those split-second decisions that happened and needed no explanation. She smiled at doing anything on the spur of the moment and returned to her drawing.

She measured each orbital cavity and drew the eyeballs, centering them within the openings. Conforming the lids to the contour of the eye, she drew them lightly onto the thin paper and angled the corners slightly higher. Next, she sketched the brows, careful not to place them too high and create a deer-in-the-headlights expression. She'd almost forgotten how satisfying this type of work could be. Hopefully, someone would be comforted by her efforts.

She glanced at Leigh sprawled across the floor like a kid with a box of Tinker Toys. She liked having her close, so comfortable in her space. Julia had asked numerous times to watch her work, but she couldn't allow her to share a process that touched her soul. Julia's materialistic values had too closely resembled her parents' for them to ever truly connect. She'd taken two years to figure that out, along with the fact she had no real passion for Julia.

Passion would never be a problem with Leigh Monroe. Though they were several feet apart, the chemistry between them sparked like lightning in the air. Easy-going, responsive, compassionate Leigh, who'd been so concerned she'd tried to take responsibility for their first kiss. As much as she'd wanted to deny her culpability at the time, Macy couldn't imagine letting Leigh think she hadn't wanted that kiss just as much as she had. And she wanted to kiss her again, right now, in this very spot.

"Why are you staring at me?" Leigh asked.

"Sorry. I was admiring how cozy you look decorating my studio floor." She glanced at the transparencies Leigh had compiled, desperate for a distraction from her physical desires. "You've created a composite of yourself. Cute."

Leigh's brows furrowed. "No, I didn't."

"Sure looks like you. Uh-oh…mother?"

"Yeah. Nate thinks we look alike. I don't." She scrambled the slides, stuffed them back in the box, and snapped the lid shut.

"If that composite is even remotely similar, you do—which is quite attractive, in case you haven't noticed."

Leigh stood and stuffed her hands into her jeans pockets. Macy envisioned Leigh as a child doing the same thing when she was upset or confused. She'd probably had another run-in with her mother, and by the looks of her scrunched-up face, it hadn't gone well.

"Let's get out of here. The sunsets are spectacular from the dock. What do you say?"

"Perfect," Leigh replied.

"I'll be right down. Grab a couple of chairs out of the boathouse, and I'll bring a bottle of wine. You do like wine, don't you?"

"As long as it doesn't come in a box."

A few minutes later they sat on the floater, feet dangling in the water, sipping wine. "Do you want to talk about it?" She was usually the one being prodded for information and her feelings. Was this cosmic payback for past relationships or were the scales just tipping to center, giving her an opportunity to grow and compromise?

"I don't want to bore you. Just more mama drama."

"I'm sufficiently fortified. This is my second glass. Did you have a disagreement?"

Leigh finished her wine, refilled the glass, and took another gulp before answering. "Not really. We talked about Jack mostly. It's hard to imagine, but she actually understands him. What makes it worse is he likes her."

"Let me make sure I've got this right. You're upset because Jack likes your mother, she's good with him, and that doesn't sync with your memories of her?" She understood why that would bother her, but Leigh needed to hear someone else say it. People didn't change their basic nature, no matter what our memories of them.

"When you put it like that, I sound childish and petty."

"Look at me." She waited until Leigh made eye contact. The hurt was evident in Leigh's eyes, and she wanted desperately to erase it. "All memories are hoaxes of a sort. They represent a picture that's faded and lost some of its color and definition."

"What are you saying, that I should forgive her?"

"I'm just asking if perhaps it's time to reexamine the work in a different light, in the present. Maybe you missed something before."

Leigh stared toward the lake. "I've been wondering that too. I like the way you see things through the lens of an artist. You make life seem richer and more interesting, definitely a perspective I don't see much in my line of work."

Simple words really, but so desperately needed they brought tears to her eyes. She'd never been validated for her art, much less for a unique viewpoint that offered anything valuable or worthwhile. Leigh seemed to divine the gaps in her and slowly fill the voids. She hoped to repay Leigh for the vitality she was pouring back into her life, maybe by encouraging her to consider her mother in another way.

"I wish I could capture this sunset on canvas, but I've never been able to come close. There's something elusive about nature that defies duplication even in photographs. Have you ever noticed?" When their gaze met, Leigh was staring at her mouth with the hungriest eyes she'd ever seen. "What?"

"Your lips are so sexy. I love watching you talk. And the things I want you to do with your mouth are painful to think about."

Heat flushed her face and neck, and she took another sip of wine. "Well, thank you, I think." If Leigh didn't stop looking at her like she could devour her, she'd jump her like a ninja.

"I forgot to tell you, wine makes me amorous. Can I kiss you right now?" Without waiting for an answer, Leigh leaned over, cupped the back of her head, and brought them together. "Please?"

She answered with a kiss so needy it took her breath with its urgency. Her lips crushed Leigh's and her tongue demanded entry. She searched the hot recesses of Leigh's mouth, memorizing the ridges and edges of her teeth, the texture of her cheeks, and the strength of her dueling tongue. Leigh tasted like wine and sunset, intoxicating and promising. Dropping her wineglass, she fisted Leigh's hair in both hands and held her in place. Her body was inflamed, and only Leigh, naked and sweaty on top of her, could quench it.

"Macy." Leigh pulled back just enough to speak. "Macy, shouldn't we go…somewhere?"

Panting, she reached for Leigh again but stopped when she realized what Leigh was saying. "Somewhere?"

"Yes. I have a strict landlord who doesn't like exhibitions on her dock." Her smile was a combination of teasing and tempting.

"Quite right." She felt she'd disintegrate if she moved too far from Leigh, but she managed to regain a single thread of control. "Jeez, what is it about you that makes me want to attack you every time we're within touching distance?"

"I have no idea, but I like it." Leigh skimmed her finger up Macy's arm to her neck and then circled her ear. "Don't you think we should go upstairs or to the cottage?"

She wanted exactly that but knew she couldn't have it. She had no idea if Leigh could handle a purely sexual relationship. The better question was, could she? Were physical encounters with no complications the answer to her relationship failures? "I think I better go home. We need to think this through before we do something we regret."

Leigh tried to kiss her again, but she pulled away and stood. "Trust me, I wouldn't regret kissing you or having sex with you… ever. And I won't hurt you."

How many times had Macy heard that line? As many times as she'd delivered it to have sex with a woman she had no intention of staying with? Did she want to believe she'd never be hurt again? Was that the stake grounding her to the past? When Leigh said those four words, she almost believed them.

Leigh slid her arm around Macy's waist and brought their bodies into full contact. Need flowed between her legs and she straddled Leigh's leg. "Oh, my…" She slid her aching crotch up Leigh's thigh as far as her tiptoed stance would allow. "You undo me. I have absolutely no self-control."

"I want you so much, Macy. Can't you feel it?"

The only thing she felt was sexual need and the certainty she'd never tire of Leigh's candor about her feelings. "I have to stop now or I never will. Please help me." She placed her hands in the center of Leigh's chest and gently pushed.

"I'll give you anything you want," Leigh said, and Macy totally believed her.

"I'm sorry." As she walked toward the cottage, she called back over her shoulder, "How about a drive around the lake tomorrow after I finish work?" She didn't hear Leigh's answer, but her insides quivered with the anticipation of being near her again. If she didn't regain a modicum of control, she wouldn't be able to resist her desire for Leigh much longer.

CHAPTER TWELVE

Leigh had finished the open bottle of wine Macy left on the dock before falling asleep, too tipsy to relieve her sexual frustration. When she woke on the sofa, the sun was blistering one side of her face, and the ache between her legs was just as painful as the night before. Toby stared at her like he used to when she came home after a party-hopping night in college.

"I know. I'm a romantic idiot who always goes for unavailable women. Is that what you were going to say?" His gaze didn't change. "You're just like her, you know, teasing, tormenting, but so freaking gorgeous I can't resist. What should I do?" Still no answer. "Thanks for that, as usual, no help at all."

While she showered, Leigh thought about Macy and how being with her somehow felt right. She'd never believed a lover accepted her just as she was, occasionally impulsive and often overly emotional. Macy's logical and orderly approach to life seemed more grounded and stable, something she missed in relationships. She sensed that Macy secretly craved an expressive woman with a touch of spontaneity. They'd be a good match, if she could only get Macy to consider it. But something or someone held her back.

Macy had kissed her twice, actually initiated the first, so maybe she was only interested in a physical relationship. Having sex with Macy would definitely be pleasurable, but she didn't like the idea it couldn't go further. Why was it so hard for Macy to open up? They'd had a couple of intimate conversations, but she'd stopped short of the deeper feelings that guided her life and held her hostage to the past.

How many times could Macy pull away from her without permanently damaging their connection? Every time she was with Macy, touching her, kissing her but unable to have her, she moved closer to her breaking point. Every link had its tensile strength. Susan had taught her that she could only be pushed away so many times before the damage became permanent. She prayed that wouldn't happen before she and Macy had a chance to test their power together.

Leigh dressed, combed her hair, grabbed the witness statements from the cold-case file along with a hot cup of coffee, and took them to the balcony overlooking the lake. Maybe concentrating on something besides Macy would dull the needy ache in her body. She didn't have a deadline on the case review, but she knew her former coach, and sooner was always better than later.

Flipping through the witnesses' statements, she stopped at the longest one and pulled it from the middle of the stack. Witness name, Macy Reynolds. She reread the name and checked the address. Macy wasn't a common name, but she would've remembered meeting Macy Sheridan even if it had been sixteen years ago. Macy would've been a teenager and Leigh had just turned twenty-two. This Macy was the victim's best friend and had reported her missing. She was certain she'd never actually seen this witness, Macy Reynolds, because she'd only conducted the neighborhood canvass at the crime scene, but the unsettled feeling remained.

She read the witness's statement and found nothing indicating the two Macys were connected. Still, she'd ask Macy Sheridan when she saw her later if she remembered the highly publicized case. Breathing a sigh of relief, she scanned the other accounts before moving on to the rest of the case notes. No one had seen anything of importance that night. Over the next four hours, she came up with the same unacceptable conclusion over and over. Jesse Quinn had simply vanished. She wondered if somewhere Jack's family was thinking the same thing.

If she hoped to find anything new about an old case, she'd have to go back to the beginning and do it the hard way. She folded the witnesses' statements and tucked them into the pocket of her jacket and headed for her car. On the way into town, she called Hedy, hoping she'd have time for a quick brunch. They agreed to meet at the deli in half an hour.

"Do you have my house staked out?" Hedy asked as she hugged Leigh and scooted into the booth across from her.

"What? No. Why?"

"You usually call when Bo's out of town. You still like him, right? Because he *is* the father of my child."

"Eww. I don't like to think about any guy putting it to my baby sister. Can we move on? How are you feeling?"

"Sick as a whore in church, but otherwise, not bad. When I don't have morning sickness, I'm eating everything in sight. What're we having?"

"Don't know about you, but I'm having the jumbo cheeseburger all the way with sweet-potato fries. And before you ask, no, I'm not pregnant."

"Are you at least having sex?"

"No."

When the waitress took Leigh's order, Hedy added, "Ditto," and waited until she left. "So why not?"

"If you count orgasms with nobody else in the room, I'm having lots of sex. Otherwise, it kind of requires a partner, which last time I checked, I don't have."

Hedy tried to suppress a grin. "What about your landlord?"

"What about her?"

"Pam says you have the hots for her and you two had a moment." She finger-quoted the last three words. "Any truth to the rumor, Detective? Would you care to comment?" She held the saltshaker toward her like a microphone.

"Since when do you and Pam talk about my nonexistent sex life behind my back?" She tried to sound stern, but Hedy was having too much fun to spoil it.

"Since she called with congratulations on the baby news and bought Bo and me a celebratory dinner. Sweet of her. The subject just came up because we care about you and want you to be happy."

"Thank you, I'm fine. We don't have a relationship, but I am attracted to her."

"What's stopping you?"

Leigh recalled the pained look on Macy's face when they'd kissed on the dock. "She has some things to work out, and I'm not jumping into anything where I have to play second or third fiddle again. Been there, done that, have the scars to prove it."

Hedy covered her hand where it rested on the table. "Good. You deserve better than, what did you call it, a vacationship?"

The waitress brought their food and they ate in silence for several minutes. When Leigh looked up, Hedy was staring into her plate like she'd seen something distasteful. "What's wrong? Yours no good?"

"It's not that." She stuffed a fry into her mouth, and Leigh remembered the young child who'd done the same thing when asked a question she didn't want to answer.

"Just tell me, Hedy. You don't look well."

"I'm worried." She was pale, and the corners of her mouth turned down like she was about to be sick.

"Do I need to call an ambulance? Take you to the hospital, right now?"

Hedy shook her head and tears filled her eyes. "No." Her voice had a scared-little-girl quiver.

She grabbed both of Hedy's hands and rubbed, trying to keep her own voice calm and soothing. "Honey, just take a breath and tell me what's going on."

"I had a miscarriage."

She wasn't sure she'd heard properly. "What? When? Are you all right?"

"Not *this* baby, Leigh. I was pregnant before."

What Hedy said didn't make sense. She would've known if something so significant happened to her sister, wouldn't she? They shared everything. "When was this?"

"You were working undercover. Bo and I hadn't been married long, and you were fairly new with the department. I didn't want to worry you, especially while you were working with a bunch of crazy drug dealers. I'm sorry."

"How did you get through it? Are you okay? How did I not know?" Then the lightbulb came on. "Susan?"

Hedy nodded, unable to meet her gaze.

"Is that why you didn't tell me, because Susan was helping you?"

Hedy nodded again.

"Oh, honey, I'm so sorry. You must think I'm a selfish, unreasonable brat."

Hedy finally looked up, tears streaking her face. "I don't think any of those things. You just weren't very receptive anytime I mentioned Susan. I needed help, Bo was a basket case, and you weren't available. I didn't have anywhere else to turn."

Suddenly her baby sister looked older. The laugh lines around her eyes and mouth seemed deeper, conveying more grief than joy. The pain of such a loss would never go away. Her heart ached for Hedy, and again she couldn't do a thing. "I'm sorry for putting you in that position. I wish I'd been there, and I'd like to think I would've put my feelings aside. Can you ever forgive me?"

"There's nothing to forgive, and I don't want you feeling guilty about this too. You've got enough old baggage."

"You haven't told me in all this time because of how I feel about Susan."

"It never seemed right, but now, with the new baby, maybe we can all move on. She was there for me when I needed her, Leigh. That counts for something."

She thought about what Hedy said and about the last two times she'd seen Susan. Something was different about her, but she hadn't given her the benefit of the doubt. Maybe now was the time to put old hurts behind her and look forward. New life, new possibilities. "You're probably right. I'll try harder. Does the miscarriage put you at greater risk with this pregnancy?"

"The doctor said I should be fine as long as I get lots of rest and avoid stress, but I still worry. We want this baby so bad."

"She'll be fine because she's my niece. And yes, I've already decided you're having a girl, so don't argue." She grabbed one of Hedy's fries and pointed it at her. "Now eat your lunch. That little track star needs nourishment."

An hour later, Leigh was walking the parking lot of the old bar where Jesse Quinn disappeared, reviewing witness statements, and waiting for a return call from her contact at the Center for Missing and Exploited Children. She'd placed herself in the position of witnesses, as much as possible, and read their stories from their perspective. Checking off the businesses and residences in the area, she made a list of those not contacted at the time. One of the buildings had been completely demolished and was now the parking lot of a dry cleaner.

When her phone rang, she answered immediately, anxious to make progress in at least one of her seemingly hopeless and unsanctioned cases. "Hello?"

"It's me." They never exchanged names over the phone, a little paranoid and overly cautious about some of their methods. "Sorry it took so long to call back. How can I help?"

"I need you to check for a missing boy, fourteen or fifteen, small build, whitish-blond hair, gray eyes, five-feet eight inches tall, about a hundred ten pounds. Don't have a name, and before you ask, I'm not sure if he's been reported missing. He showed up here looking for family, and we've run into a dead end."

"Any idea where he came from, possible name, or anything to narrow the search."

"He said his father's name was Steven Temple, but I'm not sure that's true. He's going by Jack, but I wouldn't count on that either. Nothing else. Give it a shot, that's all I can ask."

"I assume this is off book?"

"Yep, and one more thing…some branch of the feds warned us off the search for Steven Temple. Let me know if you run into resistance. I'll owe you one."

"You always do."

Leigh hung up and started knocking on doors around the club. Of the remaining witnesses, one had died, two moved, and one didn't remember anything new. It was mid-afternoon when she finally gave up for the day, leaving only four more places to check. As she drove back to the lake, she thought about her conversation with Hedy again and decided she'd make time to talk with Susan in the next few days. She couldn't postpone the inevitable forever.

❖

Macy shaded in the area of the sketch around the chin and dropped her pencil on the table. She'd concentrated on the details of the nose, mouth, and ears separately, careful to project only what was on the underlying skull photographs or indicated by the tissue-depth markers. She took a breath and, hoping for the best, stepped back from the drawing.

When she looked at the face she'd recreated, she knew immediately it wasn't Jesse's. The disappointment slammed into her. She reached for the table edge, feeling sick as her stomach churned. Jesse's crystal blue eyes had been so alive and so different from the sketch she'd just completed. She'd thought she was ready for this possibility, thought she'd remained objective and detached. But even with all her psychobabble and rigid control, she couldn't keep the feelings from ambushing her again. Tears clouded her vision and splattered to the floor. God, how she missed her friend, how she desperately needed to know what happened to her, even if the answer was the most horrible one imaginable.

She slid to the floor and buried her face in her hands, letting the tears fall. She'd promised herself this would be her last case, but maybe—"No." She said the words aloud, cementing them in her mind and making them permanent. "You…will not…do this…to yourself… again. I forbid it!" Even as she made the sobbing commitment, her lungs ached like she'd breathed in acid.

She had no idea how long she'd been crying or how long Leigh had been sitting beside her before she noticed. "Sorry."

"I didn't know if I should disturb you, leave you alone, or just wait. Are you hurt?"

Macy stopped crying and laughed. How could she answer the simple question that summed up her entire adult life? Of course she was hurt. She'd always been hurt and had no idea when or if it would ever end. But that wasn't really Leigh's question. She wanted to know if Macy was functional. "I'm fine." Isn't that what everyone wanted to hear?

"You're obviously not fine, but you don't want to talk either. So, what about that drive you promised me?" She stood and offered her hand.

She hadn't expected Leigh to be so perceptive or to know how desperately she needed a distraction. Wiping her eyes on the sleeve of her lab coat, she took Leigh's hand and stood. "That would be perfect. But don't get your hopes up. The pickings are slim at Belews Lake."

"I've been duly warned."

Leigh's steady gaze was like a caress, touching her soul and assuring her that whatever had upset her wouldn't last forever. She gave herself permission to believe the unspoken promise. At least her drawing proved this deceased person wasn't Jesse, and though the consolation wasn't absolute, a part of her felt lighter. As she discarded her coat and opened the front door, the evening sunlight cast a rainbow of colors like an omen in their direction.

Leigh grasped her hand as they walked to her car, as comfortably and naturally as if she'd done it hundreds of times. Macy intentionally focused on their connection. When Leigh's fingers entwined with hers and wrapped around her palm, she knew she'd follow her anywhere. The certainty of that feeling spiraled through her, and with it came the inspiration for a new painting—light, bright, and immense. She envisioned a canvas splattered with thick acrylic and finessed with her fingertips until the emotions of this moment breathed from the base. How long had it been since she'd wanted to paint, much less had an idea for an actual piece? As they walked, she looked down at their joined hands and the answer made her ache.

The afternoon sky was awash with twilight colors as she dropped the top on her convertible and maneuvered out of the driveway. She inhaled the fresh air, absorbed some of Leigh's obvious enthusiasm, and let the disappointment of her workday ebb. "I'm going to take you to a local hotspot. The place is renowned for its cuisine and entertainment."

"Seriously, out here in the great next-to-nothingness?" Leigh's smile was as crooked as the skeptical look she gave Macy.

"You'll see." As she drove, she pointed out Dean's Service Center gas station, Smith's Grocery and Grill, and the Riverside Golf Course. Leigh played along, expressing exaggerated enthusiasm for what passed as local landmarks. When she pulled into a gravel parking lot and stopped in front of a brown log building with a red tin roof and shutters, Leigh looked confused.

"And this is what, exactly? I'm guessing a livestock barn by the goat and farmer-milking-a-cow cutouts on the side. Am I close?" Her green eyes twinkled as if they shared a secret known only to them.

She laughed, and the confusion on Leigh's face deepened. "I promised you a dining and entertainment venue—voilà."

Leigh's head was like a tennis ball, back and forth from her to the building. "Really? This? You *are* kidding, right?"

"I most certainly am not. This is the famous Hillbilly Hide-A-Way. It's a true historical landmark in the area. They're open on weekends for dinner, or supper as it's called in these parts, and Sunday brunch. And there's live music on Saturday night—bluegrass, country, and gospel—for three hours, if you can stand it that long. Contain your enthusiasm, please."

"I'm just dying to hear about the menu."

"Well, I'm glad you asked. They offer the usual country delicacies family-style, like fried chicken, ribs, country ham, pinto beans, fresh taters, chicken gravy, hoecake, cornbread, and green beans. For breakfast on Sunday, you can choose from eggs, sliced tenderloin, sausage, country ham, grits, biscuits, and sawmill gravy. What more could you want?"

"A defibrillator close by. Have you ever actually eaten here? Please say no or my opinion of you will suffer badly."

She reached over and ruffled the tangled mass of copper curls on Leigh's head. "I've been here many times, but not of my own volition. My parents loved this place when I was growing up. I always felt like I'd been dropped into Mayberry hell without even a hotdog or hamburger stand. What they serve is what you get, and I didn't like any of it."

"Then I guess this place is out for our first date." Leigh cocked her head and grinned. "That is, if you accept."

Leigh's gaze was like fuel in the pit of her gut, swirling and burning a path lower. Part of her wanted to say yes, but what exactly was Leigh asking for—one date, a full courtship, sex, or a commitment? She couldn't take the chance Leigh wanted more when she wasn't prepared to give it. "I'm not sure that's such a good idea, the dating thing. I'm not really in a position to—"

"I know. You have things to figure out."

"You *do* know I'm attracted to you, right?"

"Yeah, so we're attracted to each other. What's wrong with exploring? We don't have to make an exclusive, total commitment, if that's what you're worried about. I promise not to cramp your style."

"It'd more likely be the other way around. I just don't want to give you the wrong idea or mislead you. I'm absolutely horrible at any kind of relationship. Just ask my exes."

Leigh took her hand, raised it to her lips, and gently kissed her palm. "If I promise not to fall in love with you, would you consider dating me a little, or maybe a lot?"

Her heart pounded like a wild mustang stamping at the corral enclosure. Again she struggled with saying yes immediately, but the practical, orderly part of her won. Caution was her touchstone, but she'd learned that extremes produce the same result. If she gave too little or too much, she'd end up in the same place she was now, alone and in denial. "Maybe." It was as if someone else had spoken, but with Leigh kissing her palm again, it seemed the only answer she was capable of uttering.

"Excellent. I'm a patient woman, but will you give me some indication if or when you decide? I'm more the blurting type. You're subtler. I might not catch your delicate subtext."

"Let's keep it loose. I can't believe I said that. I'm the queen of schedules and timelines. And I really can't explain my lack of control lately. It seems every time you see me I'm in tears or on the verge of a breakdown." She wondered again how long Leigh had been by her side this afternoon as she cried, waiting patiently, completely silent, providing the support she needed.

"Maybe you just need to let some things out. Can't keep the past bottled up forever."

"Sounds like you've been thinking about that subject a bit yourself."

"Could be." Leigh smiled and ran her hand along the back of her neck, before kissing her on the ear.

Macy needed to change the subject before she said or did something more foolish. "Let's get out of here before the Clan Hillbilly comes out and runs us off with shotguns."

"I'm at your service, pretty much kidnapped."

"Good, because I have another treasure to show you."

"I'm riveted."

Leigh trailed a finger down her arm and rested her hand on her thigh as she drove. With each touch, her fuse burned shorter and her passion hotter. She floored the accelerator, hoping the evening air would blow away the naked images of Leigh swirling through her mind. By the time she pulled into the Pine Hall Boating Access area, her crotch was soaked.

"Where are we?" Leigh asked.

"Duke Energy substation. Close your eyes." Leigh complied without question, and she parked between the trees facing the lake. "Keep them shut until I say." She backed up, repositioned the car, and turned off the engine. "Now, open."

"What am I looking for?" As Leigh asked the question, her gaze landed on the surprise—a huge white water tower shaped like an upside-down lightbulb with painted red eyes and mouth, red lightning bolts on its head, red electrical sockets for ears, and a yellow lightbulb nose.

"What the heck is that?"

"It's Reddy Kilowatt, the power company's mascot. Isn't he fantastic? I smile every time I see him. Sorry, he's like a person to me. We came here when I was a kid. My parents fished, but I drew pictures of Reddy and imagined him in front of our dock."

"That's something you don't expect to see, a giant lightbulb with a face sticking out of the lake."

"And we're just in time for the show." She nodded toward the sunset and Leigh's gaze followed. "Isn't it magnificent? It's one of my favorite places to watch the colors, worth the trip. I used to come here often."

"I can see why."

Leigh's fingers stroked the top of her hand as they watched the array of light and shadow that made sunset on the lake so spectacular. In her mind, she expanded the painting she'd imagined when they left the cottage and let the beauty and enormity of it wash over her. She was almost ready to start working again.

"You okay?" Leigh asked.

"Yeah, but we should probably go. The ranger will be around shortly to close the gate." She wanted to stay in this place with Leigh until they were bathed in moonlight and the ambience of a romantic evening, but she had to do one more thing first—tell her about Jesse.

As she drove back to the cottage, their conversation was light, and the atmosphere around them crackled with electricity. Macy tried to remember the last time she'd visited any of the local sites but drew a blank. One thing was certain: she'd never enjoyed them so much. Leigh looked at everything with fresh eyes, and her enthusiasm was contagious. Macy now viewed the area and the quirky locations with the appreciation and enthusiasm of an artist instead of a bored teenager or a jaded adult.

When they pulled into the driveway, Leigh insisted on helping put the top up on the car, thanked her for a great evening, and then scuffed her shoes in the gravel as if waiting for something.

"If you aren't totally bored with me yet, come in for a while," Macy said.

"I've really enjoyed being with you, and I'm not quite ready for it to be over." Her tone sparked with innuendo and promise, and Macy loved her ability to just put her feelings out there.

They walked inside the cottage and she motioned toward the kitchen. "There's chilled wine in the fridge, if you want to grab it. I need to put some things away in the studio, and then I'll be right back."

As she tidied up the tools left scattered across the table, she replayed the afternoon with Leigh. She hadn't watched the sunset at the boating ramp with anyone since Jesse. Maybe this was the perfect moment to let go of the painful memories, maybe Jesse was sending her a sign, and maybe the drawing was confirmation it was time to move on. When had she started thinking about a future with Leigh? Is that what she wanted? The realization opened a floodgate of possibility, and this time she didn't want to stop it.

When she walked back into the den, Leigh handed her a glass of wine. "A toast to a wonderful afternoon with a beautiful woman."

"I'll drink to that." They clinked glasses, and the look Leigh gave her made her legs tremble. "Let's sit. I want to talk to you about something."

The laugh lines around Leigh's mouth disappeared, and Macy felt like she'd been robbed. "It's not bad. Relax." When they were settled on the sofa, she set their wineglasses on the table and took Leigh's hand in hers.

"I'm sorry about earlier. The drawing, my sketch of the missing person, wasn't what I expected." Leigh didn't respond. She seemed to know Macy needed to get through this all at once. "I've been trying to find someone, a friend, for a long time. When I do a reconstruction, I always fear and hope it's her…but it never is. I promised myself this would be the last one, so it was especially hard. Guess I lost it."

"You don't owe me an apology. Must've been very painful, but isn't that really what you want—not to find her in circumstances like this?"

"Yes and no. Wondering is a steady drain of energy you can never completely turn off."

"But you still want to know what happened. I understand. Can I hold you?" When she nodded, Leigh urged her closer and hugged her.

Her emotions were like a naked electrical wire seeking connection. Leigh's gesture touched her, but the turmoil about Jesse raged. Was she doing the right thing, telling Leigh about Jesse? Before she could process the question completely, she started talking again. "We were teenagers, and every guy at school was in love with her. I wanted to beat them off when they hovered around her like dogs in heat. She had long blond hair and eyes the color of blue crystals. Guess I was more than a little in love with her. We told our parents we were spending that night at the other's house, like kids do, but we went to a bar not far from her place, walked along the tracks."

The ominous weight of that night closed around her as she recalled what happened next. "I didn't really want to go, but I'd never been good at denying her anything. She disappeared in the crowd the minute we walked in. Guys were lined up three deep to dance with her, each with a drink in his hand. She was in her element, and I was in hell. All I wanted was to be alone with her."

Leigh brushed a strand of Macy's wavy brown hair off her gorgeous face. Her insides were at war with the story she was hearing and the feelings for Macy blossoming from her heartbreaking revelation. She wanted to comfort Macy, but she also wanted to stop her from repeating the story she already knew so well. The stories were too similar to be a coincidence—Macy's tale and the case she'd wondered about her entire career and that now sat on her table awaiting a final review. She had to tell her…but what? Captain

Howard had instructed her to tell no one about her efforts, and what if she was wrong and the two weren't connected. "Macy—"

"Leigh, please let me finish. The rest of that night was a blur. I saw her when she danced by a couple of times or on her way to the restroom. And then she was gone. The bar closed and I couldn't find her. I searched inside and out, almost assaulted a couple of the guys she'd danced with. No one had seen her leave. I walked back along the railroad track hoping to find her passed out or maybe back at the house. She was…gone…I never saw her again. It was my fault. I was older and should've taken better care of her."

"No, Macy, it wasn't. None of it was your fault."

Macy buried her face in Leigh's shoulder and shook with the soul-wrenching sobs of a tortured woman. Now Leigh understood why. Macy felt guilty for her best friend's disappearance and had carried the guilt for years. Leigh already knew the answer to her next question but had to ask. "What was her name?"

"Jesse…Jesse Quinn." Macy muffled another strangled cry as she covered her face. "And the cops, I'm sorry, the police, didn't make much of an effort to find her. Who closes a missing person case in two weeks, especially one involving an innocent teenager?"

A tremble of something akin to fear skittered up Leigh's spine. The case Captain Howard had given her suddenly took on greater significance. Macy Sheridan *was* Macy Reynolds, but why the name difference? She would find out what happened to Jesse Quinn if only to bring Macy some peace. Sixteen years was a long time to wait for answers, for all of them. But first, she had to tell Macy about the case and her involvement in it. "Macy…"

"I'm sorry," her voice was tight and distant, "it's just so hard to say all this aloud after so long. I've never told anyone before." When she looked up, her brown eyes were black and bottomless with grief. "I feel so, I don't know, empty, I guess."

"Oh, Macy."

"Kiss me." The request was a soft and pleading whisper. The look in Macy's eyes turned serious and then dangerous, pulling her farther in.

"But I need to tell you—"

"Whatever it is, don't. Not right now."

"Are you sure?"

"Please just kiss me, before I think myself out of it."

Macy's lips were urgent and firm against hers as they met. When Macy licked her lips and slid her tongue inside Leigh's mouth, her body felt molten at the core, her bones brittle, muscles loose, and her heart pounded with the exertion of a hard run. The salty taste of tears clung to the corners of Macy's mouth, and she licked them away. "So good." She fell deeper into this woman who kissed as if this were her last embrace.

Macy slid sideways across her lap and Leigh pulled them closer. The kiss intensified, and Macy rubbed her breasts against Leigh's until she felt their skin would combust.

"Make love to me, Leigh."

"Are you sure?"

"Please stop asking me that."

"Would you like me to take you into the bedroom?"

"Just take me. Don't treat me like a girlfriend." Macy rose, unbuttoned her blouse, and dropped it on the floor, followed by her jeans. Before Leigh adjusted to the fact Macy was serious, she wore only a pair of bikinis and a bra. "Are you going to make me beg?"

The image of Macy Sheridan begging for her touch was all the encouragement she needed. She shucked off her clothes and stood before Macy completely nude. "The only thing I want you begging for is more."

Macy kissed her again and the room grew smaller, the air suddenly thick with the scents and vibrancy of sex. She skimmed Macy's curved hips and gently pressed their pelvises together. She locked her knees to remain upright when Macy cupped her ass and the heat and moisture of Macy's arousal slicked her leg.

"Sit." Macy placed a hand on her chest and guided her back down on the sofa. "You are so damn hot, long and lanky with breasts the perfect size for sucking and an ass I can't wait to come all over."

Was this the same reserved woman she'd met two weeks ago? It was as if she'd flipped a switch and a she-devil emerged. "This is so unbelievable, but I really need to let you know—"

"Don't talk. I'll tell you exactly what I want. Can you do that for me tonight, Leigh?"

"Yes." In her heart and mind she'd just committed to more than tonight.

Macy straddled Leigh's lap and rubbed their breasts together. Macy's balconette bra pushed her firm breasts up, creating an exposure Leigh wanted to lick. The fabric was sheer lace, and the frilly trim scraped her nipples like delicate teeth.

"Suck my breasts." Leigh started to pull the fabric down. "Leave it on. I like the heat and moisture from your mouth trapped in the fabric, just like it is in my crotch right now." Macy shifted sideways and rubbed her center up Leigh's thigh. "Feel that?"

"Macy, you're killing me." Her clit twitched, and she clenched her muscles to stop the urge to hump.

"You don't like sexy talk?"

"Oh yeah, but I won't last long if you keep it up."

"My mission is to make you come without touching you below the waist. Now suck."

Leigh cupped Macy's breasts and kneaded the soft flesh until her nipples were tight and her areoles dimpled. She lowered her mouth and breathed on the thin fabric. Two could play Macy's little torture game.

"Please, Leigh, I need your mouth."

She licked the protruding nipple first with very light pressure, the result just as she'd intended. Macy bucked toward her, and their centers collided with just enough force to make Leigh moan. When she clamped her mouth over Macy's tender flesh and sucked, she got exactly what she wanted, several enthusiastic rubs that almost took her over the edge.

"Faster." Macy grabbed Leigh's breasts and tweaked her nipples between her thumb and forefinger until Leigh complied. "Yes, that's it. You have a great mouth. Use it."

"Macyyyy, please." Leigh didn't know if it was because she hadn't had sex in so long or because Macy was so hot, but she was about to explode—exactly as Macy predicted.

"Are you getting all wet and horny?"

"Not getting."

"I want to show you what I was doing the night I saw you on the dock, naked and playing with yourself. This is what you drove me to. Give me your hand." Macy guided her fingers to the sweet spot between her legs. "Right there." She rocked against Leigh. "I need you, right there. Did you hear me come that night?"

"Yes." Leigh remembered the primal scream she'd heard echoing across the lake. Macy's need had been as urgent as hers. "I wanted you so much that night. I couldn't stop."

"You were so beautiful standing in the moonlight, pleasuring yourself because of me."

"Because of you and for you. I could live right here, between your hips."

"Touch me, but don't go inside the bikinis or stop until we both come. Promise."

"Promise, baby." Leigh wedged her hand between Macy's body and hers for optimal contact. She captured Macy's other breast in her mouth, sucking and teasing with her tongue while massaging her clit through the gauzy bikini fabric. The edge of her palm rubbed her own clit in a painful rhythm that wouldn't last long.

Macy was exquisite, head thrown back, dark eyes open and staring into hers, lips red and constantly licked by her hungry tongue, and her mouth open and ready to scream the instant Leigh brought her to climax. The sight of her was too much. Leigh couldn't look away as the heat between her thighs burned.

"That's right. Faster. I see that look in your eyes now. Couldn't see it on the dock. Too far away. Aww, yeah. You want this, don't you?"

"I need you, Macy. Come with me. I'm so close."

Macy rocked up and down on her knees as if Leigh was pumping inside her. "Harder, right now. I'm coming. Oh. God. Yes."

The orgasm curled from Leigh's center and spiraled out to the frazzled nerves in her body. As she watched Macy flush bright red and her eyes widen, she came. Macy claimed her with her mouth, and their bodies jerked in unison as spasms milked them dry.

"Thank you," Macy whispered. "Thank you so much."

CHAPTER THIRTEEN

Macy woke eyeball to nipple with a rosy-tipped breast and smiled remembering last night's marathon sex session. Her arms and legs were entwined with Leigh's long ones in a postcoital clutch, and her hair fanned across Leigh's stomach like a protective shroud. The air was pungent with their mingled scents, and her mouth tasted like Leigh. She licked her lips and a shiver of arousal rose from the base of her clit. Every erogenous zone on her body throbbed from overuse, but she was still unsatisfied.

She tried to keep her breathing even as she heated up again. Last night she'd done two things she hadn't imagined possible—told another person about Jesse and had sex with a woman she hardly knew. And not just everyday run-of-the-mill sex, but hot, raw, I-gotta-be-fucked-now sex. She'd never been sexually assertive with a lover until last night, and Leigh complied exquisitely.

When Leigh tried to be gallant and take her to bed, she'd asked not to be treated like a girlfriend. What did she want to be treated like, a slut? Quite honestly, yes. The answer didn't suit her carefully polished self-image, but she'd wanted nothing to do with her former life. With the truth about Jesse finally released, she needed to feel totally different and free. And she'd succeeded.

She looked at Leigh's sleeping face sprinkled with freckles, a glimpse of white teeth through recently sucked lips, and copper lashes resting on her cheeks. This woman fulfilled every sexual request she had without question and made her feel like the most desirable and important person in the world. Leigh had worshipped and feasted on her body until she begged for mercy. And still she hungered. Now what?

Was her desire to escape into sex and emotionally uncharted territory only temporary or the beginning of something more? Her track record with women sucked. She couldn't ask Leigh to sign on for that. But she was making a huge assumption Leigh would even be interested in more than sex. She'd told herself she could handle a purely physical encounter. Now was the time to prove it. While she agreed with the premise, the possibility didn't settle well in her gut.

"Leigh, you awake?"

"Could be. What did you have in mind?"

"Sorry, but I need to get to work. Want some coffee before you leave?" She couldn't look at Leigh as she retrieved her wrinkled shirt from the floor and pulled it on.

Leigh reached for her but she moved out of range. "What, no morning-after nooky, snuggle, kiss, nothing? I must've been way off my game last night." Her pouty lips spread into the most kissable smile Macy had ever seen.

"You were fantastic, but real life calls. Coffee or no?" The playfulness drained from Leigh's face, and she realized she'd probably been too matter-of-fact. "Sorry, I didn't mean—"

"You don't have to explain. I get the message." Leigh pulled on her jeans, slung her shirt and briefs over her shoulder, and a few steps later closed the door softly behind her.

Macy slumped onto the sofa. "Shit. Shit. Shit." No wonder she couldn't hold on to a relationship. She had no idea what to do in those awkward, intimate moments. Actors made it look easy in the sappy romances she liked, but the right words weren't scripted and never came naturally to her. When some of the sting wore off, Leigh would realize keeping things real was the best way. Sex was sex, and that was all they were ever going to have.

After a quick shower, Macy dressed in only her soft, worn lab coat and headed to the studio. She was too sensitive for clothing that rubbed her body in spots still aching for Leigh's touch. With the memories of last night too fresh in her mind, she needed to busy herself with the clay reconstruction of the skull. Working would redirect some of her frenetic energy into other parts of her body besides her breasts and genitalia.

She faxed a copy of the completed facial drawing to Sergeant Rickard and put it aside. He could start on comparisons with missing persons while she finished the model. She gathered her materials and placed them on the table beside the skull: sculpture tools, spatula, pointed stick, millimeter gauge, plastic roller, X-acto knife, oil-based clay, cotton balls, sandpaper, and flexible mesh.

The next step of the process involved setting the prosthetic eye, or the plastic eye cap she preferred. When she considered eye color for this model, she didn't see the cool blue of Jesse's crystal orbs as usual but the mesmerizing green of Leigh's staring at her with so much hunger her hand trembled. *Concentrate.* As if. Her censure couldn't erase what had been indelibly tattooed on her body and branded in her mind.

She chose a basic brown color and positioned the eye in the center of the orbit, protruding slightly if viewed from the side, and fixed it in place with a lump of modeling clay. She rolled some blocks of clay into uniform thickness, cut several strips, and laid them neatly within reach. The connection of the tissue-depth markers that protruded from the skull would provide the general shape of the face. Starting at the number-one marker high on the forehead and proceeding down between the eyes, she set the first strip in place, followed by the second and third over the eye orbits, and the fourth and fifth down the side of the eyes. Time suspended as she positioned the disconnected layers of clay around the skull.

As she slowly worked the strips into the proper depth to coincide with the markers around the mandible, she remembered Leigh's sensitivity along her sexy jawline. A simple lick or nibble made her as pliable as this modeling clay. She squirmed in her chair as the memory trickled down her body. *Damn it. Stay focused.* Next, she covered the top of the head with long strips of clay to keep the shape of the forehead and cranium. When she finished rolling the clay bands to the appropriate depth, they resembled the wire frame of a catcher's mask.

She stood back and examined her progress, not bad for a day's work. The application of clay, rolling to depth, and checking for consistency was time consuming. She'd worked through breakfast and lunch and suddenly realized she was hungry, in more ways than one. The detailed task hadn't completely vanquished the memory of Leigh or their night together. When she'd thought about her, passion jolted through her as stimulating and frightening as a shot of pure adrenaline.

But something else had happened to her yesterday. When she retold Jesse's story, she'd released the cage around her creativity. Ideas for new paintings floated to the surface and she was anxious to commit them to canvas, but images of Leigh bled over. She pulled a blank canvas from the stack under the table and placed it on an easel near the window. Dusting the surface with her hand, she enjoyed the dimpled texture of the fabric and her energy surged again. As soon as she finished her final reconstruction, she'd begin her new life as a painter.

She was about to prep the canvas by applying an ochre ground color when she heard the distinctive crunch of a vehicle pulling into the drive. Her pulse quickened. Leigh. They hadn't spoken since she practically pushed her out this morning. She was anxious to explain her behavior, if she could figure out how. As she took off her lab coat, she realized she still hadn't dressed for the day. Rushing to her room, she pulled on jeans and a shirt with no underwear and reached the door just as Leigh knocked.

"I'm glad you came—" The woman standing on her threshold was definitely not Leigh. She was Leigh's height with blond hair that cascaded in waves to the top of her ample breasts and eyes the color of milk chocolate. Her lips blossomed with a mixture of amber and caramel coloring. Macy followed her curves, highlighted by snug skinny jeans and a red body-hugging T-shirt that made her look like a flame. Macy tugged on her shirt, very happy she'd chosen a baggy one that covered the top of her thighs. When she realized she'd been blatantly staring for several seconds, she spoke. "Can I help you?"

"Good afternoon. I'm looking for Leigh Monroe. Is she here?" The woman tilted her head to glance around her into the cottage.

"No, she isn't. May I ask who you are?"

The woman extended her hand. "Sorry, I'm Gayle."

Gayle, the ex. A knot the size of Texas settled in Macy's stomach. The only thing she'd heard about Gayle was her name—not that she was a drop-dead gorgeous blonde who exuded sexuality with every breath. An image of Leigh and Gayle kissing flashed through her mind, and she shook her head to dislodge it.

"And you are?" Gayle asked.

"Macy. Sheridan. Leigh's...landlord." She wanted to sound more substantial in Leigh's life, to stake a claim however tenuous, but she had no right. One evening of spontaneous sex didn't qualify her as a lover, and she'd rarely treated her like a friend.

"I'm sorry to drop in like this, but I've just flown in from Toronto and really need to see her. It's important."

"Did you try her cell phone? She *does* have one, you know." She sounded snarky, like a jealous girlfriend, but she wanted to get rid of this woman, preferably before Leigh returned.

"I didn't want to leave a message. This is too important."

"So you've said." Again with the attitude.

"Do you mind if I wait? Does Leigh stay here, with you?" She looked past her again as if trying to suss out the living arrangements.

"She's renting the apartment over the dock." She pointed toward the lake and could've sworn Gayle sighed with relief. The least she could do was make the woman comfortable, because she obviously wasn't leaving. "You can wait if you want, but I have no idea when she's getting back." *Perfect. Now she knows you have no significant relationship.* "Would you like something to drink—soda, wine, water?"

"I'd love a glass of white wine. Something tells me I'm going to need it." Gayle's smile dazzled with its sincerity and a touch of sadness. If she hadn't been here, looking so damn hot and wanting to talk with Leigh, Macy might've liked her, just a little.

"Why don't we sit on the porch? There's a beautiful view of the lake. I'll get the wine." While she poured, she considered changing clothes, but no matter what she chose she wouldn't come close to the tantalizing ex-girlfriend's style. She had no idea how to compete with someone like Gayle. She'd had sex with Leigh, not bonded for life or discussed their future. If this was the kind of woman Leigh preferred, she was doomed.

As she handed Gayle a glass, she wondered what had brought her from Canada after a nine-month separation. The scenarios bouncing around in her head could cause serious damage if she dwelled on them. She could simply ask, but she should really let them work it out. *Damn the coulds and shoulds.* "Why are you here?"

Gayle glanced at the lake, took another sip of wine, and finally focused those deep-brown eyes on her. "Are you and Leigh having sex?"

They stared at each other like competitors vying for psychological advantage, but the stakes were much higher. Both were willing to ask the difficult questions. The real issue was, were they willing to answer them?

❖

Leigh walked out of the cottage that morning without her shirt on purpose, hoping the cool morning air would slap some sense into her, remind her of the reality of her and Macy's situation. Macy had told her about Jesse, a revelation that couldn't have been easy. The anguish was etched across her features as clearly as if on a movie screen. Her heart ached for Macy as she cried and told the story that had emotionally bound her for years.

As some of the pain subsided, she'd seen the potential in Macy, a free woman capable of fully living again. But she couldn't have imagined the sexual scene that played out in Macy's living room. Their interaction had been more assertive, more playful, and much sexier than anyone she'd been with. She'd lost count of how many times they pleasured each other with hands, fingers, mouths, toys, and nothing except full-body contact. She'd imagined Macy would be different as she released her hold on the past, but this went beyond transformation.

She'd loved everything about their time together, until this morning when Macy sent her away like a call girl. The sting of dismissal cut much deeper than the soreness from their lovemaking. Perhaps it was for the best. When she told Macy about her involvement in Jesse's case, she'd probably reject her for good. The right thing to do was tell her, now. But she needed distance from what they'd shared last night. Their connection had been too perfect and the aftermath too unexpected for her to face so soon.

She relived their night together as she showered, dressed, and drove to the station. With each memory, she became more attached to the woman and their potential, though she had no idea what came next. She pushed the distracting thoughts aside and headed to Captain Howard's office to check in.

When she tapped on the door, the voice from the other side sounded tired and a little annoyed. "Yes, come in."

"Bad time?"

"Not for you. As a matter of fact, I needed to see you. Have a seat. Coffee?"

She shook her head. "Here for my weekly check-in, and before you ask, I don't have anything new to add to my suspension case."

Captain Howard smiled at her, but something else was obviously on her mind. "I'm not surprised, but any progress on the other matter?"

She debated telling the captain about her accidental reconnection with the primary witness in the case but decided it might lead to the revelation of their recent sexual liaison. "Nothing yet, just a review."

"And a recanvass of the neighborhood and follow-up with witnesses?"

"How did you know about that? I was discreet."

"One of the original investigating officers, who's now a lieutenant, got a call from a witness. He stormed into my office this morning demanding to know why a suspended detective was snooping around in a closed cold case."

"I'm sorry, Boss."

"I told him to get the hell out of my office. Before he left, he more or less threatened me with censure from 'above my pay grade.' I'm not sure what he meant and he wouldn't explain. Have you had any problems or uncovered anything unusual?"

"No, ma'am. This case would be a lot easier if everybody back then had had mobile phones and CCTV was on every corner. But as the saying goes, the key that works will always be the last one you try. I'll keep at it." She considered again revealing her connection to Macy. Captain Howard might consider sleeping with a material witness as significant, but since it wasn't likely to happen again, Leigh kept quiet.

"All right. Keep me posted and let me know if anybody tries to sidetrack you. I'll manage the fallout. That's why they pay me the big bucks."

She stood and started toward the door. "Captain, thanks for trusting me with this."

"We've both wondered about it for years. Who else would I trust?"

Leigh stopped by the Youth Division office, but Nate was out with another detective. She wasn't ready to go back to the lake and face Macy. What would she say, thanks for the sex, and by the way, I helped screw up your best friend's case? If one of those comments didn't get her permanently evicted, the other certainly would. She had to admit her involvement in the case and the sooner the better. She couldn't afford for Macy to think she'd intentionally kept something else from her.

She was on the way back to her car when her cell rang. "Hello?"

"Leigh, it's Susan."

For a second she couldn't place the voice. *Mother.* How did she get her cell number? *Hedy.* "Yes, Susan, how can I help you?"

"Actually, I might be able to help you for a change."

"Okay." She was always cautious where her mother was concerned. Experience had been a harsh and expensive teacher.

"When I went to school to pick Jack up yesterday, he was on the emergency pay phone by the basketball court. I pretended I hadn't seen him, and he didn't mention making a call. I just thought you might want to know. Is it helpful at all?"

"Maybe. What time was that?"

"About three thirty."

"I'll look into it." Susan didn't have to pass along the information. It must've been hard to choose between keeping Jack's confidence and possibly helping Leigh find his family. "And thanks. I won't tell him."

"I appreciate that. He'd see it as a betrayal, and that wouldn't help anybody."

Leigh started to disconnect but remembered her last conversation with Hedy. "Susan, I want to thank you for helping Hedy, with the miscarriage. She finally told me."

After a short pause Susan answered. "You don't need to thank me. I wanted to help. Sorry she wouldn't call you, but she can be just as stubborn as you sometimes."

"You tried to get her to call me?" Leigh heard the disbelief in her voice and her throat tightened.

"I knew you'd want to be there for her."

"Well…thank you for that too." Tears stung her eyes, something that had never happened where her mother was concerned. "I'll talk to you later." She hung up without waiting for a response and leaned against the side of her car. Her mother had actually tried to do something good for her.

When her breathing returned to normal, she went back inside to track down Nate. He was at his desk and she motioned him into the hallway. "Canteen coffee?"

"Sure, my stomach is cast iron, why not? You all right? Look a little green."

"My mother has that effect on me." When they were out of hearing range of the other detectives, she passed along Susan's information. "Can you have your contact with the phone company check it out? This could get Jack together with his mother again pretty quickly."

He gave her one of his you're-kidding-me smiles. "This is the phone company you're talking about. Quick is relative."

"It's all we've got right now, unless you've uncovered something I don't know about."

"Afraid not."

"I don't understand this kid. We told him we've hit a dead end with his father's family, but he still won't go home. Who stays in foster care when he doesn't have to? Maybe he's in some kind of trouble or it's an abusive environment," she said.

"I don't get that feeling from him. He seems pretty well adjusted and brainiac smart."

"Yeah, I know what you mean. I should be going. Don't want to make your new partner jealous. Let me know if you come up with anything."

"Will do. Hurry back. You're my entertainment. I'm bored with these guys."

"Thanks, smart-ass." She winked and blew him a kiss. "See you soon."

On the way back to Belews Lake, she stopped by a gas station and picked up a real-estate magazine. She'd gotten back into her workout routine, had a quasi-conversation with her mother, and was going to be an aunt. The occasional pangs of disappointment from her breakup with Gayle seemed less and less frequent. She was reclaiming her life again. Now she needed to consider what to do about housing after the inevitable eviction from Macy's apartment. When she pulled into the driveway at the cottage, she almost rammed into another car parked in her space—Gayle's car. Macy and her ex sat on the front porch, sipping wine and looking toward the lake like long-time acquaintances. Trouble had come to the burbs.

Several greetings flashed through Leigh's mind as she walked toward Macy and Gayle, but none of them expressed exactly what she was feeling—an entrée of disbelief and a side of fear. Disbelief that Gayle had gone to the trouble of finding her, taken time off work, and come to the end of civilization to talk to her. The fear was all about Macy. What was she thinking? What had Gayle told her? Was it already too late to salvage what they'd started? Neither of their faces gave anything away as she moved toward them. She poked her finger with her thumbnail, trying to remain calm, and chose the stunned-beyond-words approach, merely nodding at them when she stopped at the steps.

"Leigh, darling." Gayle placed her wineglass beside the chair and rose with the poise of royalty receiving her subjects. "Your landlord has been gracious enough to entertain me until you returned."

She faced Macy, willing her to see the apology in her eyes. "That's very kind of you."

"No problem. It's been enlightening." Macy retrieved their wineglasses and headed inside. "Now, if you'll excuse me. You have things to discuss and you don't need an audience."

"Thank you, Macy," Gayle said, and gave her arm a light squeeze.

When Gayle turned back to her, Leigh remembered why she'd fallen so completely in love with her the first time they met. Those potent brown eyes violated her soul with their vulnerability, but Gayle was capable of turning it off and on at will. She felt herself being dragged back into the abyss buried beneath her gorgeous shell.

"Why are you here, Gayle?"

"Your *landlord* asked the same question." The emphasis indicated she either knew or strongly suspected she and Macy shared more than a financial arrangement.

Panic rose in her throat as she grappled for a response that revealed nothing. "I'd be interested in your answer."

"Let's go somewhere more private." She took Leigh's arm, kissed her lightly on the lips, and guided her toward the dock. "Are you just a little bit happy to see me?"

"Surprised is more like it. You made it clear when I moved out we didn't have anything else to talk about." She tried to recall the pain she'd felt when their relationship ended, but Gayle's body was distracting next to hers, their long strides matching perfectly as they made the short walk to the lake. So many things about their life together were good. She could almost hear Pam saying *not*.

"You put me in an untenable position with your ultimatum."

Typical Gayle. She sounded more like she was giving a presentation in court than talking with an ex-lover. Leigh struggled with the disbelief screaming for release. This was not going to be one of those conversations Gayle won by default because she became too emotional to continue. "Ultimatum? Is that what you call a request for a commitment? I'm surprised you didn't recognize the difference, Counselor."

When they got to the bottom of the apartment steps, Gayle slid her arms around Leigh's waist and pulled her close. Those eyes again, imploring her to remember, to succumb to the promises and the pleasures Gayle would gladly give. She licked her lips without the slightest thought for what it would signal to Gayle. When it occurred to her, it was too late.

Gayle's lips closed over hers, and the gentle tug on her bottom lip made her weak. She didn't want to kiss Gayle, didn't want to want her, but she had to know if she still did. Opening her mouth, she welcomed Gayle's tongue and waited for the burn that always started in her gut. Instead of the hungry longing she expected, an image of her and Macy emerged, standing in this very spot, kissing for the second time. She instantly cooled and pushed Gayle away. "Stop."

"Yes, let's go up." She ascended the steps and took Leigh's hand. "Come with me."

She had no intention of coming the way Gayle proposed, but they did need to talk. She followed her up and closed the stairway after them.

"Quaint little place." Gayle's tone reminded her of what a materialistic house snob she could be. If it showed the slightest wear, Gayle turned it in for this year's model, size, or color. She believed her years of education, experience, and now status came with certain benefits, usually the ones with dollar signs attached.

"I like traditional, and the size suits me perfectly at the moment."

Gayle shrugged and reached for her. "Let me hold you, Leigh. I've missed you so much." Gayle pulled her to the sofa, tossed Toby in the corner, and took Leigh into her arms. She caressed Leigh's face, her arm, occasionally stroking the side of her breast or the curve of her hip. "My God, you feel fantastic. Tell me you haven't been with anyone else."

"What?"

"I asked Macy if you were having sex."

"You did *what*? You had no right. We haven't been together in nine months, in case you haven't been counting." She knew exactly how Macy would've felt under the scrutiny of those eyes and the pointed questions. "What did she say?"

"I interpret anything except a flat denial as an affirmative response. So, I guess you've had sex with her. Am I right?"

"This isn't about Macy or anyone else I might or might not have slept with. It's about us. Isn't that why you flew here from Toronto?" She could almost see Gayle's mental wheels turning. She never just spoke from the heart. Her responses were always calculated for maximum benefit, hers.

"You're exactly right, darling. I've got some great news." She kissed Leigh's forehead and fingered the hair around her ears. "You're not going to believe it."

Leigh's warning system flashed red and the nerves along her spine tingled. "What is it, Gayle? Just tell me."

"I've taken a job in the States so we can be together." The expectant look on her face was almost comical. Her perfectly plucked brows arched slightly, and her eyes opened wide. It was obvious Gayle thought she'd scored a major coup d'état. "Isn't that fantastic?"

She'd learned not to accept anything at face value with Gayle. "I didn't realize the Canadian Citizenship and Immigration Service had a satellite office in the United States. How does that work exactly?"

"Can't you just be happy? It's what you wanted, us together. I've made it happen."

She moved out of Gayle's arms and put her knees between them on the sofa. Touching was not a good thing at this point. She needed all her energy focused in the intellectual parts of her body. "Tell me, Gayle."

She couldn't meet Leigh's stare, focused instead on the view of the lake. "Most of our attorneys work a stint in another country periodically."

"So, let me see if I've got this straight. You'll be working here temporarily? What happens at the end of your assignment?" The look of discomfort on Gayle's face told the whole story. But Leigh needed to hear her say it.

"Leigh, darling, I know it's not perfect, but it's a start. In the meantime, we'll work something else out. I've missed you." She tried to pull Leigh back into her arms, but she resisted.

"You still don't get it, do you?"

"I thought this would make you happy."

"Seriously? After nine months, no contact, I move out of your condo, without any help from you, and now you show up offering me the same thing we had before? How is that supposed to make me feel? What I've always wanted is someone who loves me enough to make me a priority in her life, the same as I would for her. You never understood that."

"How can I do that when we live in different countries?"

"It's not about where we live. It's about how we choose to live together. We're very intelligent and resourceful women who solve problems for a living. We get to create our life. It would be unconventional, granted, but it could work for us if we wanted it badly enough. I just want more than a vacationship. We're separated by something much worse than distance."

"What do you mean?"

"Apparently we want different things. You always thought you had to choose between your career and me. I was willing to do whatever it took to be with you, including changing jobs. If you think the only answer to a question is *either/or*, you're wrong."

Gayle bowed her head and stared at her hands, resting limply in her lap. For the first time, she looked defeated. "I know I didn't give you what you needed, Leigh, and I'm sorry. I just don't see another way around this at the moment."

"And that's why I ended it. Right now your career comes first. I get that, but I also get to choose not to be second with the woman I love. Do you understand?"

She nodded. "I believe I finally do, but I can still be unhappy about it."

"Absolutely." She started to add, *because I have been,* but she chose not to intentionally hurt Gayle. Her dad used to say, if it's not a gift, don't give it.

Gayle reached across the sofa and took her hand. "Would it be all right if I stayed the night? I came straight from the airport and haven't made a hotel reservation. If it wouldn't be too much of an imposition and wouldn't upset your landlord."

"Sure, you take the bed and I'll be here." She retrieved some blankets and a pillow, made her bed, and rescued Toby from the corner. "If you need anything, let me know."

"You won't sleep with me, one last time?"

"If by sleep you mean have sex, the answer is no. It's best if we don't complicate things."

She loved Gayle, but the dynamic between them had shifted. She'd tried to mold their relationship into something Gayle would want as much as she did, but their priorities weren't the same. Everything she wanted in a relationship was still the same, but she no longer wanted it with Gayle.

Chapter Fourteen

Macy watched Gayle hook her arm through Leigh's, reclaiming what was hers as they walked toward the lake. The image was branded in her mind and flashed on an infinite loop. She didn't want to look, but the scene worsened like a major disaster, compelling her attention. Gayle kissed Leigh with the passion of a starved lover, fingers entangled in her hair, their bodies fused at hot places. She cursed under her breath, willing them to disappear, and when they climbed the steps and Leigh closed the hatch, she almost collapsed. An aching like the deepest shade of black swallowed her.

She waited, certain Leigh would emerge momentarily, rush to her and…what, deny Gayle and declare her love? Something akin to anger bubbled inside. What the hell was she thinking? Leigh Monroe didn't care for her, much less love her. They'd shared one night of sex, nothing more. Leigh had confirmed that when she returned Gayle's kiss on the dock, another display obviously intended for her. Leigh didn't have to worry; she wasn't the type to get attached either. The only way to stay safe in relationships was to stay out of them. Her logic was sound but her feelings were not. She retreated from her vigil at the window and forced herself back into her routine.

Gathering her lab coat around her, she rubbed her sweaty palms down the front and opened the studio door. The skull seemed to stare at her through vacant eyes, and the intermittent clay strips against bone looked as if a wild animal had shredded it. She felt the same way inside, like she'd been ripped into pieces with remnants left hanging. How had she gotten so deeply involved with Leigh that it bothered her to see her with another woman? *Work. Focus.*

She'd completed the technical phase of the reconstruction, and now the artistic phase could begin. She loved creating a face by rolling clay, carving details, and sculpting the finishing touches with her fingers. She picked up the Boley gauge and measured the height of the enamel of the upper and lower teeth, which would provide the vertical thickness of the mouth. A measurement of the front six teeth gave her the width. She transferred the measurements to a strip of clay, cut it, and placed it on the lower lip margin. When the strip was positioned properly, she incised it at the halfway point to create the parting line of the lips.

She remembered the touch of Leigh's lips against hers the first time they kissed. She'd been instantly aroused. Nothing was more sensuous than a woman's lips—soft, hot, wet, and wanting. As she spread the clay lips with a flat wooden tool, her memories tormented her—her fingers sliding tenuously into the slick folds between Leigh's legs, her tongue urgently traveling the same path, and Leigh's total surrender. She dropped the tool and it skidded across the floor. Her body was sticky, perspiration and desire pooling uncomfortably.

Stooping to pick up the instrument, she envisioned Leigh nude, spread-eagled offering herself—to Gayle. This time Gayle's fingers teased Leigh's breasts, Gayle's mouth sucked her clit, and Gayle's tongue drove her to climax. Leigh screamed Gayle's name, not hers, as she orgasmed. Macy flung the small wooden blade against the wall. *Shit.*

She paced circles around her work desk, repeating her calming mantra over and over. "I'm fine. Everything is under control. I'm fine." The familiar words should've been reassuring, but they sounded hollow and filled with desperation as she tried to convince herself of a lie. She washed the clay off her hands, and her fragile control trickled through her fingers and down the drain. She'd never been an irrational drama queen, but now she couldn't stop the random bouts of emotion. She was in big trouble and her normal escape avenue failed. But if she stopped working, she didn't know where she would end up—maybe knocking on the apartment door.

It was four o'clock in the morning when she finished detailing the clay mouth and was satisfied with the results. She stretched her aching shoulders and went into the kitchen for a cup of tea. Caffeine wouldn't hurt. She couldn't sleep anyway as long as Gayle's car was in her driveway and Gayle's body in Leigh's bed.

The apartment was dark like her mood. She didn't know what to do with the petty comments rambling through her mind like a parade of stray cats. Part of her wanted to open the window and yell, "I bet she's not as good in bed as I am." Another part of her was afraid of Leigh's possible responses. "At least she admits she loves me. She came back to me. We have history. I love her." Macy couldn't argue with any of it.

What could be worse than the woman she cared about making love to someone else only a few yards away? *Having to watch.* After having sex with Leigh and seeing Gayle, she could imagine vividly the two of them entwined. If she could just close her eyes and have the images disappear, but it only made them worse. She swallowed the last sip of tea, and it settled in a nest of tangled nerves in her stomach. How could she be so confused after only one sexual encounter? If she couldn't handle this, anything else was doomed. The worst part was, she didn't know what to do about it.

She returned to the studio and started developing the area around the eyes. The sex, race, and probable age of the subject taken into consideration, she laid thin strips of clay under and over the eye and manipulated them with the flat wooden stick she used for detailed work. She paid particular attention to the location of the eyelids inside the bony orbits, their thickness and angled corners. The slightest miscalculation or deviation would change the entire appearance of the face. As she added the final touches to the tissue around the eyes, the sun was rising through the trees behind the house.

Stepping away from the table, she evaluated her work and nodded. She expected to see some aspect of Leigh Monroe staring back at her. She'd spent the night re-creating a face she'd never seen while trying to block one she couldn't erase. The reconstruction resembled neither of the women who now haunted her sleeping and waking hours.

As she cleaned up at the kitchen sink, Leigh lowered the apartment steps and came down. She held her hand and helped Gayle descend in her heels and tight jeans. Macy tried not to stare, but she scoured both of them for telltale signs of postcoital bliss. Did Leigh have the same satisfied look she'd had after sex with her only a day ago? Did their bodies seem magnetized, unable to bear any distance? Were their eyes blazing secret messages no one else could read? *How ridiculous you are, Sheridan.*

She dried her hands and moved away from the window as they walked toward Gayle's vehicle. She refused to be seen pining like some love-struck puppy. If Leigh wanted a near-perfect model-type blonde, who could blame her, but she didn't have to watch.

❖

Leigh purposely looked away from the cottage as she walked Gayle to her car. Her ex didn't need any more ammunition to speculate about her friendship with Macy. She just wanted Gayle on her way back to Toronto as soon as possible. She'd grieved the loss of their relationship and saw no point in belaboring the obvious. It had been over long before she ended it nine months ago. Now they both knew it.

"You're sure about this?" Gayle leaned against the side of the car and reached for her, but Leigh sidestepped.

"Yes, I am. It's best for both of us, don't you think?"

"You're probably right, but I had to ask. Will you keep in touch?"

"If you want, but not right away. I need a bit more time." She gave her a quick straight-girl type hug and opened the car door. "Thanks for taking the time to come and talk with me. It means a lot."

"You won't hate me, will you?" Gayle asked as she cranked the car.

"I promise. We're not bad people, we just want different things. Take care." She waved as Gayle pulled out of the drive and then started back to the apartment when her cell rang.

"Hello?"

"It's me," her contact at the Center for Missing and Exploited Children said.

"Yeah, what do you have?"

"You're not going to like this but nothing really concrete about the child. I haven't found anyone resembling your kid in the database, anywhere in the country."

"Why do I sense a but?"

"I think I've narrowed down which of the alphabet agencies is blocking your inquiries. The Marshals."

"I'd have guessed DEA, FBI, maybe even IRS, but never Marshals. How did you come up with that?"

"They contacted me when I searched the last name Temple, just like you did. Since I'm not law enforcement, they weren't threatened but still told me to back off. Sounds like your guy might've been a witness or a turned informant, but that's just my guess. Nothing they said specifically."

"Did you mention why you were checking the missing kid?"

"They wanted the whole story. I tried to keep it vague. They'd already figured out GPD was involved. Their focus seemed to be primarily Steven Temple. Sorry I couldn't do more."

The information didn't help and didn't really make sense. Why would the marshals still be interested in a dead witness? She retrieved her notes on the Jesse Quinn case from the apartment and drove into town, still no closer to finding Jack's family. Maybe she'd have more luck with Jesse's case, or maybe she was just doing busy work to avoid telling Macy about her involvement in the original investigation and to keep from discussing Gayle's unannounced visit.

She'd been doing a lot of conversation avoidance with Macy, and the discomfort settled inside her like an extra organ, squeezing and jostling for room. She preferred the open approach, but life was complicated…more so where Macy Sheridan was concerned. She certainly didn't want to hurt Macy further, especially when she'd just started dealing with her feelings about Jesse's loss. But she couldn't keep hiding things from her. She had to make time to tell her the truth, and soon.

She parked in the club parking lot and flipped through the four remaining residences she needed to check. A twentyish girl answered at the first location and had no idea what Leigh was talking about. She'd inherited the apartment from a distant aunt and moved in only two years ago. The second and third locations produced similar results, both college-aged kids with no interest in or knowledge of an old missing-person case.

Her energy and enthusiasm waned as she knocked on the last door and waited for an answer. She heard a distant murmur from inside, knocked again, and waited again, but still no response. As she turned to walk away, she heard a voice from inside.

"I *said* wait a damn minute. I don't move as fast as I used to."

A few seconds later the door opened but she didn't see anyone, until she looked down. A man in his mid-forties, shaved head, broad shoulders, and sitting in a wheelchair stared up at her. If he'd been standing, he would have been at attention or at least parade rest. He gave off a strong soldier vibe with the short haircut, posture, and direct eye contact. "I'm sorry to disturb you, sir, but do you have a minute?"

"Does it look like I'm going anywhere in a hurry? Who are you and what do you want?"

"I'm Detective Leigh Monroe, Greensboro Police Department." She flashed her credentials and gave him time to check their authenticity. "I'm doing an old-case review."

He rolled the chair back and waved her inside. "Excuse me for not standing, but I didn't have time to strap on my prosthesis with you pounding on the door." From the contour of the blanket across his lap, she saw his right leg was missing below the knee.

"I'm sorry."

"For knocking, for being so damn impatient, or for not knowing I'm a cripple?"

She searched for an answer this obviously proud man might not find offensive. "All of it, I guess. War injury?"

He shook his head. "Should've been so lucky. An *actual* goddamn training accident."

He struck her as the sort of man who'd rather have been killed in war than injured in some simulation. "Can I ask your name, sir?"

"Sorry." He offered his hand. "Bradley Duncan, Brad. Have a seat, Detective."

The meager apartment appeared to be a one-bedroom with kitchenette and bath but was meticulously tended. If she looked under the sofa, she'd expect it to be as spotless as the kitchen countertops. "As I said, I'm looking into an old missing-person case."

"Little fucking late, aren't you?"

"I beg your pardon?"

"I've been waiting for you people to contact me for years. Is this about the shooting in the alley outside the club, too?"

The hairs on the back of her neck saluted. "What shooting?"

"Damn, don't you fucking people talk to each other? A guy was shot outside that hellhole the same night the girl went missing. I saw it from the window right there." He pointed to the small kitchen window facing the alley. "Nobody came by to ask me questions, and the next day I shipped out for maneuvers—and got this." He waved a hand over the remaining portion of his leg. "Fucking nightmare for the next six months in a goddamn foreign country. The injury didn't sever the leg cleanly so I had multiple surgeries to remove shrapnel and debris, and then I had a reaction to almost every medication they gave me for pain and infection. Fucking wonder I didn't die in that godforsaken place."

"So, you weren't here when they did the initial investigation." The comment was more for her clarification than an actual question.

"I was here the damn night the guy got capped, but they didn't bother then. And they dropped the ball, I guess." His statement made her cringe because it confirmed what she'd suspected but didn't want to believe. "I had more pressing matters to deal with when I came back, and I rationalized you'd probably already found the girl anyway."

"What did the shooting have to do with the missing girl?"

"Aren't you listening? The fucking killer took her."

"He *took* her? The killer?" She was almost dizzy as fragmented pieces of different puzzles swirled in her head. Jesse was kidnapped? By a killer? Why would he take her? If she'd seen something, the killer would have certainly disposed of her. The initial officers hadn't conducted a proper investigation, and they hadn't connected the two cases or even considered the possibility they might be connected. Maybe she was grasping at straws. "Jesus H. Christ."

"Pretty much what I said too, with a *fuck* thrown in here or there for good measure."

"Did you call that night and report what you'd seen?"

"Yeah, but the dispatcher said the shooting had already been reported. Guess they didn't need my details. They didn't even find the body until almost dawn."

"Witnesses are often contacted later in the investigation, after the scene is cleared. But why didn't you call and check when you returned?" The minute she asked the question she regretted it. His face was etched with the pain and guilt of loss and failure.

"I know I should've, but when I got back I was fucked up on drugs for a while, then in rehab, and finally working my way out of that. You don't understand. I had my whole life planned—a distinguished military career, family, kids, and a comfortable pension when I retired. Instead, I got an abbreviated stint in the service, a disability retirement, a fake leg, drug addiction, and no wife or children. The last thing on my mind was playing do-gooder for the local police who couldn't find their fucking asses with both hands. No disrespect intended."

"I understand, and you're right. It's not your job to fix our mess. I just wish someone had followed up." What would they have uncovered if they had? Was the homicide case cleared? If so, she might uncover something in the file to help her find out what happened to Jesse Quinn. "Do you mind if I record your statement? Sorry to ask you to repeat it, but I had no idea what I was going to hear."

"Sure, go ahead." For the next thirty minutes, he recounted the story of that night and what he'd seen as she recorded it on her phone. When he finished, she thanked him and drove directly to the police station.

The detectives were leaving lineup when she opened the back door and stepped into the hallway. "Nate, got a minute?" He didn't ask any questions but took her by the arm and guided her to his car in the parking lot.

"I'd know that look anywhere. This is serious."

"Can you get me a copy of a homicide case that happened sixteen years ago outside the club on Patterson Street?"

"Probably. Rickard owes me after getting Macy to do his reconstruction. Why do you need it?"

"I can't really say right now. Just trust me, it's important. Think you can get the file on the QT? I really don't want Rickard or anyone else to know about this yet."

He gave her a skeptical look, wrinkling his eyebrows in an exaggerated fashion for show. "Seriously? You're talking to the King of Smooth. Besides, one of the girls in records and I have been out a couple of times. Shouldn't be a problem. How's ten minutes?"

"Great." She replayed Brad Duncan's statement again while she waited. The circumstances of his life and the time lapse between the homicide and the report of Jesse Quinn's disappearance had collided in a sequence of events that made the two cases seem unrelated. Now it was obvious they were. The uneasy feeling in Leigh's gut told her the possibility of Jesse Quinn being alive had just gone from miniscule to nonexistent.

Nate walked across the parking lot like a man who'd just gotten laid, all smiles and self-assurance. "Here you go. Don't clap. Just throw money." He offered her the file like a present. "You've got twenty-four hours before I have to slip this back where it came from. Even my considerable charm has its limits."

"I'm shocked. Thanks, Nate." She started to leave but turned back. "Anything from the phone company yet?"

"They're slower than a wet week. I'll call as soon as I hear anything. And if you need help with that," he pointed to the file, "just let me know."

"Thanks, but I've got a feeling the further you stay away from this, the better. I'm going to the diner to look it over. I'll call if I need anything else." She couldn't explain why she needed the homicide file without telling him about the Quinn case, which Captain Howard wanted kept quiet. Another secret she'd have to keep to protect someone she cared about.

She left her car in the lot, tucked the file under her arm, and walked next door to the diner. She'd missed dinner thanks to Gayle's unannounced visit and had rushed out before breakfast to get an early start. Her stomach growled as she entered the small establishment filled with the scents of bacon, toast, and coffee. She felt like she'd been transported back to the fifties in the retro-clad diner, but it was one of her favorite places to eat. Their gifted cooks could make anything from eggs and grits to pasta with pesto sauce or a perfectly grilled steak.

She settled into a booth in the back and spread the file out on the old laminate tabletop. When the waitress passed, she placed her order for the breakfast special and lots of coffee. She was so engrossed in the details of the report she didn't notice the woman standing next to her until she cleared her throat.

"Mind if I join you?" Macy asked. Her dark eyes shielded any emotion that might've clued Leigh in to her mood.

"Of course. I mean no…join me." When Macy sat down, Leigh noticed the discoloration under her eyes and the rigid set of her jaw. She looked exhausted. Had she spent another sleepless night with dreams about Jesse? "Are you all right?"

"Of course, why wouldn't I be?" Her tone was more curt than normal, and Leigh felt the distance between them. "I didn't know you were here. I wouldn't have bothered you, but the place is packed and I'm starving."

"I'm happy to share a table. What are you doing in town so early?"

"Ran out of modeling clay and had to make a supply run." Macy glanced at the papers scattered across the table. "I thought you were suspended."

She swept the pages back into the file. "I am. My partner's afraid I'll get rusty so he gave me something to keep me busy." She'd been staring at Macy, trying to figure out what was so different about her. What had happened? *Gayle happened.* "Sorry I didn't stop by on the way out this morning. I was in a rush."

"You purposely avoiding me?" Her eyes were suddenly sharp and probing, more intimidating than any interrogator Leigh had ever faced.

"I'm sorry about Gayle showing up out of the blue. She didn't call. I mean I wasn't expecting her." Why was it so difficult to just say what she wanted to say—it was over with Gayle and they'd finally put it to rest?

"Did you enjoy your reunion?"

"Yes…no."

"Which is it? You've never had trouble with your words before, Detective. What's wrong?"

"It wasn't a reunion."

Macy leaned back in the booth, and her hot gaze seemed to skim every inch of her flesh as if searching for fingerprints or some telltale sign of her evening with Gayle. "She traveled all the way from Toronto to see you. It sure looked a reunion from where I stood. Another tantalizing display on the dock."

Was Macy actually jealous, or was she getting ready to launch into another sermon about inappropriate behavior in public? She reached for Macy's hand but she pulled away. "Is that what you're upset about? You think we got back together?"

"I'm not upset." She straightened in her seat and cocked her head to one side. "But if an ex-lover spends the night in your bed, I'd say there's a pretty good chance of a joining of some kind…but that's none of my business. If she's what you want, I—"

"Macy."

"I'm just saying—"

"Macy, stop." She reached, palm up, toward Macy. "Take my hand, please."

"We're in a public place."

"I don't care. I have something important to say, and I need to touch you." Macy sighed and took her hand, diffusing the angry air around her. "Gayle and I did not get back together. That's what she wanted, but I don't. And we certainly didn't have sex. I slept on the sofa."

Macy's grasp on her fingers tightened, and she stroked the back of her hand with her thumb. "I totally *suck* at this emotional stuff. I have no right to question anything you do with anyone. I'm certainly not offering you a happily ever after. I'm not even sure such a thing exists. I'm sorry, Leigh."

If they'd been alone, she would've kissed Macy. She seemed so vulnerable and Leigh wanted to reassure her. "You don't have to make promises. I know you're going through a hard time. But if you want, maybe we could spend some time together and see what happens."

The shocked look on Macy's face was almost comical. "You mean you still want to? You know I'm a basket case, right?"

"I like what I see, very much, and I want to get to know you better…if you'll stop pushing me away." She smiled and squeezed Macy's hand.

"I'll try."

Now was the perfect time to tell Macy about her involvement in Jesse's case, while they were being so honest. Maybe she was a coward because she knew it would create a rift between them, but they'd need more privacy for this particular discussion. No matter which way it went, Macy was going to be upset. Might as well get it over with. Just as she started to speak, the waitress returned.

"Sorry to break this up," she nodded to their joined hands, "but I got hots coming through." She set their plates down and sloshed more coffee into their cups. "As you were." She gave Macy a wink and swished off.

"What was that?" Leigh asked.

"Nothing. She sat for me a couple of times."

"Maybe I'm the one who needs to be jealous, with all these young college students posing nude for you in the boonies."

"At least they don't fly in from another country to see me."

Leigh held up her hands in surrender. "Let's call a cease-fire and eat breakfast. Tell me about your evening."

"I worked on the reconstruction all night and made pretty good progress."

"All night?"

Macy kept her head down and pushed a piece of bacon around on her plate. "Most of it, when I wasn't imagining you and Gayle rutting like rabbits. I'm awful, I know. I've never given a damn what another woman does or with whom, until you."

"I'm really glad you do." Leigh wasn't aware anyone had ever been jealous of her before, and she liked the warm feeling it gave her. Macy was admitting she cared. That was good enough, for now.

When they finished breakfast, Leigh paid the check and walked Macy to her car. "I'll see you back at the house. I've got some work to do, but if you're not busy, how about dinner later?"

"I'll cook and bring it over to the apartment. I haven't eaten out there in ages. Tonight is supposed to be perfect weather." Macy pulled

Leigh toward her through the open driver's window and kissed her. "Don't make me wait too long."

"Ms. Sheridan, I do believe that was a PDA right here beside the police department."

"Where you're concerned, I don't really care about public displays of affection. I can't seem to keep my hands off you."

Her eyes burned into Leigh. "You better stop looking at me like that or they'll see more than a chaste kiss."

"Promises, promises." Macy laughed as she pulled out of the lot, waving until she was out of sight.

CHAPTER FIFTEEN

After breakfast with Leigh, stomach full and emotions soothed, Macy returned home and went to bed. Her all-nighter had finally caught up with her and she slept until early afternoon. She woke energized and ready to finish the facial reconstruction. She couldn't wait to return to her art.

The nose was one of the most difficult facial features to reconstruct because the underlying bone was limited and the possibility of variation extensive. She measured the width of the nasal aperture and the nasal spine and applied the appropriate calculation to yield the approximate nose length. Next, she examined the direction of the nasal spine to determine the pitch of the nose, in this case a slightly upturned one. She mounted a block of clay in place and filled the remaining nasal tissue, using the surrounding markers as a guide for the bridge of the nose. Her fingers slid along the clay, fashioning and smoothing the remaining muscles, building up the tissue until the thickness markers were covered and the final characteristics of the face etched.

As the face became more defined, a story about this unfortunate girl emerged in her mind and with it the feelings she always tried to suppress. Friends and family would never smile upon this child again. She'd never kiss a lover, never bear children, raise a family, or be a grandmother. Macy skimmed the clay with her finger and felt a rush of sadness and resignation. Tears blurred her vision and she wiped at them with the sleeve of her smock. It was difficult to accept the immortality of youth when combined with the finality of death.

While working, she resisted the temptation to add her own artistic flare to the reconstruction or to individualize the face in any way. She wanted to make this child's final viewing her most beautiful and memorable, but she had to rebuild, not interpret. As she cleaned her hands, she sobbed, purging the remaining emotions and saying good-bye to the young girl.

She photographed the final product using a digital camera and slipped the card into an envelope. With her other reconstructions, she'd immediately stripped the skull back to its original condition after photographing it and repackaged it for return to the police. But she left this one, as a last nod to the forensics work she'd done for seven years and maybe as an apology to Jesse for leaving her case unsolved. Though she would never truly forget, she had to move on.

It seemed appropriate to finish the case today after she and Leigh had agreed to explore their feelings. But building a relationship wasn't the same as reconstructing a face. The skull provided a map of sorts for her to follow. She didn't have a guide for navigating the subtleties and nuance of intimate interactions with another woman. And whether she wanted to admit it or not, she had feelings for Leigh Monroe. No matter how things turned out for them, she owed Leigh a great debt for helping loosen the grip of the past and rekindling her artistic passion.

Time crept as she tidied up the studio, showered, and began preparations for dinner. She stole frequent glimpses at the clock, telling herself she was just timing the meal with Leigh's arrival. She'd decided on a grilled-salmon salad: simple to make, hard to mess up, quick to eat, and not heavy on the stomach. How long had it been since she'd planned a meal with sex as dessert? She rubbed a hand across her quivering abdomen as she heard Leigh's vehicle pull into the driveway.

Crunching footsteps on gravel and a light tap on her door. She stared at the wooden structure between her and Leigh, willing it to open so she could watch her lover cross to her. Another knock. She was rooted in place, unable to take the first step. "Come in."

When Leigh opened the door and walked toward her, she felt as if she'd been cast in a sappy lesbequin romance. Leigh, green eyes blazing, red hair a portent of the passion underneath, and lips slightly parted, strode toward her like an archetypal hero come to claim her.

"I thought this evening would *never* get here," Leigh said, grabbing her in a hug that forced her to breathe again. "How is it possible to miss someone I barely know so much?"

Leigh's lips pressed against hers and all rational thought vanished, replaced by a wanting so immediate she struggled to stand. Their tongues clashed and searched and soothed until she had to pull back. "I...don't...know. Me too."

She wasn't used to being so enamored with someone, so hungry for her that time crawled and everything else dimmed. Could she handle that kind of need? Did she want to? Her body said yes, but her mind cast a shadow. Years of hands-on death and hands-off emotions had anesthetized her, and she'd found a degree of comfort in the belief that she couldn't be hurt again. She stepped out of Leigh's embrace and nodded toward the refrigerator. "If you don't stop, we'll never eat. Get the wine while I finish up."

Leigh looked as if she'd stolen something precious from her. "Are you sure you want to eat at the apartment? This is awfully cozy." She slowly moved away, retrieved the wine, and placed it on the counter.

"I haven't spent much time out there recently, and I always enjoyed it as a kid, so yes." She wouldn't admit she also wanted to erase the image of Leigh with Gayle in that space and replace it with their memories.

"I like being with you in a place you feel so comfortable. You look different. Has something happened?"

"I completed the reconstruction. How could you tell?"

"You just look more relaxed. You've decided to return to your art, haven't you?"

"Yes, but how did you know? You're a little spooky."

"Good spooky or bad spooky?" Leigh pressed close behind her and encircled her waist.

"Not sure yet. Now back off before I totally lose concentration and slice a finger." She playfully waved the knife she held and pointed toward the kitchen table. "Would you mind putting the salads on that tray after I add the toppings?"

"I don't really want to take my hands off you, but I guess I could manage."

Her words sent another shudder of desire through Macy, and she fought the urge to take her right there on the table. Leigh provoked urges that hadn't surfaced in her for years, and she itched to dominate this woman who seemed so willing to please. "If you don't stop, we won't have a meal. Let's get to the apartment before I completely lose control."

"Losing control can be a very good thing. Want me to show you?" Leigh reached for her again, but she spun in a circle and started toward the door, tray in hand. "Killjoy."

"You'll pay for those words, later. I promise." Macy heard an anguished moan from Leigh as she headed toward the dock. Teasing was fun, but it wasn't nearly enough. This meal couldn't be over fast enough.

While she sprinkled seasonings on the salad, Leigh moved the small settee from the living area onto the balcony overlooking the lake. The air was a perfect blend of late-winter cool and early spring warmth, with no hint of humidity or bugs. They settled with their feet on the rungs of the balcony and lap trays full of food and wine. Neither spoke as they savored the ambiance of the setting and their food.

Leigh lifted Macy's hand to her lips and covered the backside with light kisses. "I adore you for this. Spending time with someone I care about is the most important thing to me. I'd much rather sit quietly or just talk than do mindless activities. When it comes down to it, these are the moments of real connection, when important things are said and done. This is true intimacy."

"I never knew you were such a romantic, Detective." She kissed Leigh's cheek, careful not to start the real kiss they both wanted. "Now finish your dinner. I have plans for you, and the longer you talk, the more I ache."

"Yes, ma'am." Leigh stuffed an oversized forkful of salad into her mouth.

What had come over her? The first time they'd made love she was like a wild animal during mating season. She'd orchestrated every move to tease Leigh and bring her to multiple orgasms as quickly as possible. Tonight she'd wanted to take it slow, savor the deliciousness that was Leigh, just in case she didn't get another opportunity. But the longer she waited, the more certain she became that extended foreplay was not in her immediate future. She wanted the throbbing in her to stop, and only quick, raw sex would satisfy. Something this enjoyable and uninhibited didn't happen to her often, and the possibility that it might be short-lived made her crave it more.

"Done, and that was delicious. Is it a special recipe or specific seasonings?" Leigh moved the dishes to the kitchen, returned with the wine bottle, and topped up their glasses.

"Something my mother used to serve. I'm glad you liked it."

"That's an understatement." Leigh swung her legs onto the sofa and tucked them under her in the relaxed pose Macy had come to expect. "Do we need to talk about yesterday? Gayle?"

She blushed as she remembered her vehement response to Leigh's ex and the intimate exchange she'd seen between them at the dock. "I've already said too much about that, and I apologize. I really had no right."

"I liked how honest you were. I believe it was your first emotional response toward me that wasn't anger."

"Sorry, I can be a bit stiff. I'm just glad you're finished with her." She sought Leigh's gaze. "You *are*, right?"

"Absolutely, no doubt. I think I was the first moment I saw you."

The words seeped into her pores like a potent aphrodisiac. She edged closer, pulled Leigh's legs out straight on the sofa, and lay with her back against Leigh's chest. "Do you mind?"

"Never." Leigh wrapped her arms around her and periodically stroked down her sides and across the top of her shoulders.

She absorbed the steady cadence of Leigh's heartbeat and the warm brush of her breath on the back of her neck. She usually equated physical intimacy with sex, but with Leigh, this closeness was enough. "What have you done to me, Leigh Monroe?"

"What'd you mean?"

"When I'm with you I feel completely dismantled."

"Is that a good thing?"

"I believe it is, but I need to test my theory. Will you make love with me, please?"

"I'd be honored." Leigh rose and offered her hand. "Come with me."

"Right here, in the open, under the stars."

"I'll give you whatever you want."

"Take your clothes off, slowly, and talk to me as you undress."

"You do like to be in charge, don't you?" Leigh didn't hesitate for an instant. She moved to the balcony in front of Macy, kicked her shoes into the room behind them, and unbuttoned her polo. "I've imagined being with you every day since we met, feeling your hands all over me. Every night is another wet dream of you." Leigh slid her hand under her shirt, her nipple immediately puckering and making Macy's mouth water. "I'm imagining your hand squeezing my breast, twisting my nipple, so good it hurts. Oh, Macy. Do you see what you do to me?"

She tried to answer but her mouth had gone dry, all fluids racing to her crotch. Leigh shucked off her shirt and it fell to the floor. Her pale skin glowed in the moonlight like a beacon stirring Macy's blood.

Leigh worked her breasts between her thumb and forefinger from the base to the tip. "Oh, I love the way you're watching me. You want to touch me. I see it in your eyes. Do it, Macy."

She shifted uncomfortably on the sofa, trying to scratch the itch growing stronger by the second. "Not yet."

Leigh continued the breast massage with one hand and trailed the other down her waist to the buttons of her jeans. Instead of opening the fly, she grabbed a fistful of fabric and yanked, pulling the seam tight against her center. "Aww, I could come just like this." She writhed into the seam like a belly dancer. "Do you want to watch me come right now?"

"Don't you dare." Macy wedged her hand between her legs and cupped her sex. "Strip."

"But this feels so good. I need to come."

"No. I want you naked and hurting." She'd never imagined a woman in physical pain from wanting her, but the evidence stood before her in the form of gorgeous Leigh Monroe—the flush of her face, her rapid breathing, and the tightly bunched muscles running the length of her body. How beautiful and what an agonizing turn-on. "You're exquisite. I've never wanted anyone more. Hurry."

Leigh made quick work of the buttons on her jeans. She pushed them to the floor and stood before her in all her splendid nudity. Leigh skimmed her hands slowly down to her thighs and into the join of her legs, avoiding the center.

"Go ahead. You need to," she said. Leigh obeyed every directive without question, and her openness and vulnerability tugged at Macy's heart.

Leigh slid a finger over her own clit. "Oh, jeez." Her knees trembled, and she raised her hand helplessly. "See what you've done?" The tip of her fingers glistened in the moonlight. Macy was hungry to taste her, to feel Leigh's heated skin against hers, and to smell their mingled fragrances again. "If you don't touch me soon, I'm going to lose it."

Macy unbuttoned her blouse, peeling out of the sleeves but leaving the fabric draped over her shoulders. Leigh reached for her. "No. You can touch yourself but not me, not yet."

"I'm dying here." Leigh's moans ratcheted up the pounding between her legs. She unzipped her slacks, kicked them off, and stood on the balcony in her underwear while Leigh was completely nude. Desire surged as Leigh pawed herself as she'd done that night on the dock.

Macy had dominated the first time they had sex and had intended to let Leigh take charge tonight, but something inside her wouldn't let go. Did it really matter who was in control as long as they were both satisfied? She chose not to examine the question too closely. "On your knees."

Leigh knelt in front of her, eyes glazed. The control Macy wielded rode her like an impatient mistress, and her arousal spiked. "Lick me."

Burying her face in Macy's crotch, Leigh gripped her ass and inhaled deeply. "You're so hot, and you smell delicious."

"I need your mouth on me." Sliding Macy's bikinis off, Leigh spread her labia with her fingers and licked from the base of her clit to the tip, then flicked back and forth. "Stop."

"Mmm, but it's so good," Leigh said.

She clutched Leigh's shoulders to remain upright. "Too much… have to lie down." Leigh eased her down on the sofa, settling between her legs, and blew a hot breath between her lips that registered like physical touch. She pulled Leigh's hands to her breasts, entwined their fingers, and kneaded her hungry flesh. Her hips pumped to meet Leigh's mouth as she claimed her. "Now."

But Leigh slowed, circling her clit with the tip of her tongue, teasing and refusing the hard, consistent contact she needed. Leigh was trying to control the pace. "More…" She refused to beg. Her other commands stuck against the dry walls of her throat. Long, torturous foreplay wouldn't be possible tonight. She needed to come. Trying to convey her needs to Leigh, she arched toward her and moaned. "Ohhh…"

"You don't like being teased, do you?"

"No, I—" Leigh's tongue found the perfect spot. "Right there." A swell of urgency rushed her as the hands at her breasts and the tongue at her clit synchronized. "Oh…yes." They rocked in unison. "Don't stop." When Leigh's finger slipped inside her, all sensation coalesced between her legs and oozed out. "That…is…so…good." She cupped the back of Leigh's head and held her in place as she rode her mouth through a wave of powerful orgasms.

As her body slowed, she felt Leigh's insistent pace against her lower leg. "What do you need?"

Leigh crouched over her and straddled her upper thigh. "Give me your hand." Leigh guided Macy's hand between her legs and pressed her fingers against her rigid flesh. "Rub right here, but don't go inside."

She centered her middle finger along the length of Leigh's clit, her own twitching in response. "You are so hard."

"Need you, Macy." She stroked slowly, pressing firmly at the base and withdrawing before reaching the tip, balancing Leigh's climax on the end of her finger. "Please…"

She rolled Leigh over. She had to watch Leigh's face. "How badly do you want this?"

Leigh's nails dug into her ass. "Hurts…"

"I love teasing you and seeing how much you want me. You do want *me*, don't you, Leigh?" She stalled, her finger poised for the next stroke.

"Oh, God, yes. Don't stop touching me."

"Say my name. Tell me who you want."

"Macy. I want *you*, Macy."

"Good girl." She tweezed Leigh's clit between her fingers and rocked back and forth. "I promise to let you come soon." She kissed Leigh, sucking her tongue hard as she simultaneously pulled at the base of her sex. The throbbing between her legs mirrored their pace.

"Umm…" Leigh moaned deep in her throat and bucked against Macy's hand.

"Open your eyes, Leigh. Look at me."

When Leigh opened her eyes, they were wide and wild, and the pleading Macy saw encouraged her to relieve the pain. She stroked faster and watched as Leigh's tongue repeatedly licked her dry lips and her chest rose and fell with labored pants. Leigh teased the nipple of one breast with her forefinger while massaging the other breast with her open hand. Macy touched only one spot but memorized every self-inflicted action that heightened Leigh's arousal. "Are you ready to come, my darling?"

"Please." Their gaze locked as Macy's frenzied rubbing brought her repeatedly off the bed to meet her. "Oh, yes. Harder." The concentration on Leigh's face froze and suddenly drained away as her body arched one final time and collapsed beneath her. "Ohhh, yes! Oh, Macy, so good."

Macy slid her hand down between Leigh's folds and reveled in the flood she'd released. She draped herself across Leigh's body and squirmed until they were touching in the most intimate places. Rubbing her center against Leigh's, one pass, then two, she felt another tiny orgasm seep from her body and spill over her lover. *Perfect.* She drifted off.

CHAPTER SIXTEEN

The warmth surrounding Macy evaporated as her backside chilled, then her arms and legs, and finally the side of her face. She opened her eyes and looked past Leigh's chin to the morning sky above the apartment balcony. It was going to be a beautiful spring day. The front of her body was hot, still pressed against Leigh. She nuzzled closer and pulled the blanket from the back of the sofa over their bodies. She hadn't slept so comfortably since their last encounter.

Leigh shifted under her. "Good morning, gorgeous. I thought maybe I dreamed you. What a perfect night."

"It was, wasn't it?" She prayed her agreement wouldn't break the spell. If there was a way to jinx a relationship, she'd find it. The last time she'd woken in Leigh's arms, she'd panicked and rushed her out of the cottage like a cheap trick. She wouldn't make that mistake again. "Thank you for that, by the way."

"No, thank you." Leigh raised her left hand and kissed each knuckle before turning it over and kissing her palm and then the faded scar across her radial bone. She didn't ask, but the pain in her eyes was enough.

"I couldn't take losing Jesse. I blamed myself and went into a severe depression for months. The guilt was unbearable. Thought I had nothing to live for, but I was a teenager." She snuggled closer to Leigh. "Fortunately, I was wrong."

"I'm sorry you lost your best friend. That would be hard at any age, but especially so when you're young."

The comfort of Leigh's arms kept the usual wave of sadness to tropical-storm instead of tsunami level. She kissed Leigh, tenderly at first in appreciation for her understanding, but as heat rose between them, her body fired to life again. "God, you make me so horny."

"I'm glad," Leigh said.

"I just haven't felt this way in a very long time, and I don't want what we have to just be about sex." She paused. "I'm sorry. Not sure where that came from."

Leigh hugged her closer. "Don't be sorry. I'd love to know what you want."

"I'm not sure yet."

"You know what they say, appreciate the power of *yet*. Would you try, for me?"

Was it possible to verbalize something she'd never clearly formulated? "From the time I was old enough to know about feelings and sex, I wanted only Jesse. When that was no longer possible, I didn't want anyone. But I went through the motions because I couldn't just give up. You're the first person I've ever told about Jesse. With everyone else, I couldn't get past that block. I couldn't share my greatest loss with them, so how could I share my deepest fears or desires? My exes can attest to the fact I wasn't very good at pretending."

"And now?"

"Now I don't know what this," she waggled her finger between them, "means."

"Maybe you don't have to. You're doing a great job with the intimacy part right now. It's a process."

Was she capable of caring so deeply that she *wanted* to be patient, to share everything, to discuss the minute details of their lives ad nauseum? She smiled at the thought of lying naked in bed with Leigh every morning while they drank coffee and talked about Leigh's latest case or her new painting. "Maybe, I don't know." The idea made her uncomfortable. "I should get up." She stretched out of Leigh's embrace and reached for her clothes.

"Why?"

She continued to dress but then remembered the hurt on Leigh's face the first time they'd had sex and she'd pulled away so abruptly.

"This isn't like before, promise. I was just going to get us some coffee. Then we can enjoy the sunrise and have a bit of quality time."

"Macy, wait." Leigh caught her arm as she headed for the kitchen. "I need to tell you something important."

"Then it'll definitely have to wait. Too much serious talk already without coffee. Hold that thought." She leaned down, kissed Leigh's forehead, and thumbed the worry lines between her eyes. "And stop looking so solemn. I'll be right back."

She tucked the blanket around Leigh and padded barefoot into the kitchenette. The stainless coffee canister was exactly where it had been for years, but a new four-cup pot sat nearby. She measured the coffee, poured the water, and pushed the button.

"I was thinking maybe we could—" The words died on her lips as she focused on the folder on the corner of the table. *Jesse Quinn.* She picked it up and looked closer, sure she'd misread. *Jesse Quinn.* Opening the file, she stared at the witness statement on top of the stack—her statement. Then she couldn't see anything as tears blurred her vision and then created dark circles as they fell onto the pages.

"Wh—what is *this*?" When she turned, Leigh was standing within arm's distance, nude, with a look of horror. "Strike that. I know what it is. Why do you have it?"

"That's what I wanted to tell you. I've been trying to talk to you about this since—"

She held up her hand, "Wait. Was it before or after we had sex the first time?" Her stomach roiled, and she breathed through the nausea.

"Before, right after you told me about Jesse. Remember, I tried to tell you that night, but—"

"So you're really going to blame me? Shit, how could I have been so stupid? You've been hiding this from me all along? Is this why you're here? Are you people still trying to cover up the truth about Jesse? Or maybe you think it was my fault too."

Her thoughts were tight knots of confusion. She wasn't sure what she was asking or what all this meant, but she was interrogating a naked woman—a woman whose beautiful body she'd devoured in every conceivable fashion only a few hours earlier. If the situation wasn't so horrific, it would be laughable. "Put some clothes on. It's hard to have a dignified conversation when you're nude."

"I don't care about being dignified. You have to listen to me."
Leigh reached for her but stopped when Macy stared.

"No, I don't…and I can't. Do you remember our discussion
when I found out you were a cop?"

"Of course I do, and I haven't lied. Don't you want to know why
I have the file? I can explain."

"You do know this case is why I became a forensic artist. You
also know I've lived and breathed this nightmare for sixteen years.
And it's also why I quit doing forensics work six months ago, because
Rickard flatly refused to review it for me. You're the only one I've
ever told about the pain and guilt I've carried over this. I just can't
believe you'd keep this from me."

Leigh's body was flushed a light shade of pink as she gestured
desperately. Macy was torn between wanting to hold her and pretend
she'd never seen the damn file and pushing her over the balcony into
the cold lake.

"Don't you want me to explain?"

"I'm not sure I'd believe you. I'll find out for myself."

"Really, Macy, I've been waiting for the right time. I didn't want
you to misunderstand and be hurt again. You have to trust me."

"Wrong." The coffee machine chimed as Macy headed for the
steps. "Get your own coffee, and you should probably leave."

❖

Leigh watched Macy descend the stairs, and the room
immediately became too cold and empty to endure. She grabbed the
blanket from the sofa and wrapped it around her. Macy's rosemary
fragrance wafted from the fibers, making her ache for what suddenly
seemed so far away. She clung to the balcony railing and flipped
through the scene that had just played out.

Everything that had seemed so perfect had just vanished on the
morning breeze, as if it never existed—and it probably hadn't. She'd
disregarded the caution signs, ignored Macy's warnings that she
wasn't relationship material. Maybe she'd also purposely withheld
the truth about the case review because she wanted to prove Jesse was
dead, so Macy could move on. But now she needed to face the fact

she could never replace Jesse in Macy's heart, never be that one true love she still craved.

As she stared over the lake, the pain settling in her heart had no equal. She'd fallen in love with Macy Sheridan and in trying so desperately to make everything perfect had destroyed it all.

She turned from the balcony toward the room that had seemed like a real home for such a short but wonderful time. She'd imagined herself here with Macy, learning about each other, testing the waters of a new life, molding it into what they needed and wanted. Those images faded.

Packing wouldn't take but a few minutes, so she sat and drank her last cup of coffee in this place, which had lost most of its rich flavor. She couldn't bring herself to shower off the remnants of her night with Macy, so she pulled on yesterday's clothes. In less than two hours, she'd packed everything into the raggedy boxes she'd brought and lowered them to the deck below. One by one she hauled them to her car, casting a glance at the cottage with each pass, hoping Macy would stop her or at least be willing to talk.

She climbed the apartment steps one final time and checked for anything she'd left behind. Toby sat on the kitchen counter as if refusing to leave. His knit face looked as unhappy as hers felt. "Sorry, buddy, we're homeless again. I promise we'll have a place of our own. Maybe not with a view like this, but something nobody can throw us out of."

Scribbling a quick note to Macy, she folded it around the key and tucked Toby under her arm. She knocked on the cottage door several times but got no answer. Circling the house, she called out, but Macy wouldn't respond. She wedged the note under the door and drove into town.

It was eight thirty when she knocked on Pam's door, and it took her awhile to answer. Several neighbors gave her annoyed looks out their windows before the front door opened and Pam hustled her inside.

"This better be good." She waved a hand in front of her nose as Leigh passed. "You smell like pussy. Anybody I know? Wait, I detect a whiff of paint and clay—forensic artist?"

"Not funny."

"Uh-oh. Trouble in paradise so soon?"

Leigh shrugged out of her leather jacket, dropped it on the floor, and slumped into Pam's sofa. "I'm glad one of us can be humorous this morning. Got any coffee?"

"Does a wild bear shit in the woods? Be right back." Pam returned with two travel mugs and joined her on the sofa. "So, what brings you out so freaking early without a shower after a great night of sex?"

"What makes you think—"

Pam wiggled her index finger at her with way too much energy. "Don't even try it. We roomed together in college. I'd know your fresh-fucked look anywhere. You had sex with the artist and the morning-after bombed? Let me guess. She made commitment demands? Wanted you to move in? Never mind, you're already there. Wanted to have your babies or wanted you to have her babies? Started feeling like a cling-on?"

She shook her head with each inane suggestion.

"Well, I give up. Tell me already. Daylight's burning."

She recapped the details of Jesse's missing-person case, the possible connection with a murder, and that she'd kept her review of the case a secret from Macy.

"What the fuck? For somebody who's so damn emotionally expressive and tuned into other people's feelings, you can be thick as a brick sometimes. She already went ballistic about the cop thing. Didn't you think for just a minute this might rattle her cage even worse? This is about her best friend's case. This is serious shit."

The sip of coffee she'd taken suddenly tasted like poison. "I wanted to tell her, but every time I tried, she'd stop me or we'd…"

"You'd end up having sex—not good, my friend. Now she thinks you withheld the truth so you could keep fucking her."

"Don't say that." She wasn't going to let anyone talk about Macy in an unflattering way, not even her best friend.

"It's true and you know it."

"I meant the fucking part. It's not like that with her."

Pam lowered her coffee cup and stared at her for several seconds. "Oh, shit, are you in love with her?"

"I think so."

"Fuck. Fuck. Fuck. We've got to figure something out and fast."

"Did you miss the part about her wanting me to leave?"

"She's just upset right now and not seeing things clearly. It's amazing how easily the truth can become convoluted beyond recognition, isn't it?"

"I've got a feeling we're not talking about Macy any more."

"If the shoe fits," Pam said.

"Please don't start about Susan, not now."

"Fine, just drawing an obvious parallel. And don't give up on Macy. She'll calm down, and then the two of you can talk. And when that day comes, you better tell her *everything* down to the most minute detail—like the fact that you masturbate to images of Sigourney Weaver in *Alien*."

"Hey, don't ever say that aloud again."

Pam crossed her heart. "I swear. Do you need a place to stay?" She nodded. "Let's get you settled."

They unpacked the boxes that had been in her car for less than an hour and stashed them in Pam's spare bedroom. "I really appreciate this."

"What are best friends for? Besides, it's not like I'm nesting with the woman of my dreams at the moment, so you're not interrupting anything. Stay as long as you need or until I get a girlfriend, whichever comes first."

"What happened to the nurse you were seeing?"

"She already had a girlfriend but didn't bother to tell me."

"Ouch. Sorry, pal."

"Easy come, easy go. Now go shower before I start humping your leg."

Being in Pam's place felt more like home than anywhere else she'd been, until the lake, so she adjusted quickly. After a hot shower, she dressed and headed back to the den. When she walked in, Nate had claimed her spot on the sofa and was drinking coffee and eating donuts he'd obviously brought in.

"How did you find me?" she asked.

He wiped the powdered sugar off his lips. "Didn't. Was on my way to work and saw your shiny little red car in Pam's driveway.

Thought she might let me in, since I had a fresh box of Dunkin'. I won't ask why you're not at the lake with Ms. Short, Dark, and Sexy."

"Good idea." She refilled her coffee mug and joined them, declining the offer of her favorite chocolate-glazed custard-filled pastry. "So, what's up?"

"Got a call this morning from my phone-company contact. Pay dirt on the number Jack called from school." He grinned and stuffed half a donut into his mouth.

She rolled her eyes. "Really? Where is it? Chew fast or I'll choke it out of you." Pam shook her head. They both loved Nate, but he could be a pain in the ass.

"The number is listed to a resident of Windsor, Colorado, population around twenty thousand, home of mostly nothing, in the middle of mainly nowhere."

She gave him an exaggerated stare, as if that made one ounce of difference when he held a tidbit of information she desperately wanted. He clearly savored making her wait. "Who is it?"

"The number is registered to our dead guy, Steven Temple."

She and Pam high-fived each other. "Yes!"

"So the little scoundrel was telling the truth about his father's name," Pam said.

Nate nodded. "He was also telling the truth about him being dead. According to the local newspaper, Steven Temple died six months ago of a massive heart attack. He's survived by his wife, Karla Temple, and son, Ryan Jackson Temple. And it turns out little Jackie boy has called this number every day he's been here. So, not really missing at all."

"I'll be damned," Pam said.

"He could still be missing. Just because he's been checking in doesn't mean his mother knows where he is. Do we have any idea about the connection to Greensboro?" Leigh asked.

"Nope, that part is still a mystery, but at least we have a place to start." Nate took a swig of coffee and reached for another donut. "What now?"

"Obviously our first priority is reuniting Jack with his mother, but if we tell him we know who he is, he might leave before that can happen. I say we contact Karla Temple ASAP. Pam?"

"Agreed. Do you want me to take care of that from CFS?"

"Would you mind if I handled it?" She looked from Pam to Nate and they shook their heads. "I know you've been working on this too, but I feel a connection with him, maybe because we've both lost our fathers." Maybe also because he could relate to her mother, something she'd never been able to do, and she wanted to understand how. "I need to check in with Captain Howard this morning, and then I'll make some calls. Thanks, guys. And, Nate, I'll drop that item I borrowed from you yesterday off on your desk. Will that work?"

"Sure." She saw the light dawn when he realized she was referring to the old homicide file he'd secured from records.

By the time she pulled into the station parking lot, she'd decided to call Karla Temple right away. She wouldn't make her wait another minute to know where her son was. If Karla needed to make flight arrangements, she could get started. She dialed the number she'd memorized and waited.

Several rings later a recorded message announced: *The number you have dialed has been disconnected or is no longer in service. If you feel you have reached this number in error, hang up and dial your number again.* She did and got the same response. What the hell? Why would Karla Temple disconnect her phone when she'd been getting daily calls from her missing son? Something was definitely off. It looked like a trip to Windsor, Colorado was in her future.

As she entered the back door to the Detective Division, Leigh met Anita Howard in the hallway returning from the canteen. "Good morning, Leigh. Please tell me you're on your way to my office and I can offer you a decent cup of coffee instead of that rotgut from the canteen."

"Yes, ma'am, to both."

When they'd settled in the two leather swivel chairs in front of Howard's desk, Leigh got to the point. Anita Howard didn't mince words and didn't like stall tactics or evasions. "There's been a development in Jesse Quinn's case."

Captain Howard's left eyebrow arched slightly over her deep-brown eye, the only indication that Leigh's news was unexpected. "Oh?"

"In my recanvass of the area, I found a witness who'd never been interviewed about the missing-person case. He was a soldier who lived in the apartment building behind the club."

"How did the investigators miss him initially?"

"He was deployed on a training exercise out of the country the day after and didn't return for months. So even if they'd followed up later, they could've missed him."

"Nice try, Leigh, but I'm not buying it. They should've been more diligent. What else? You're holding something back. Come on. We'll sort it out together." One of Howard's strong suits had always been her willingness to listen to all theories and suggestions.

"There was a homicide at the club the same night Jesse Quinn went missing. We never considered the two were connected because of the big time lapse between the reports. And why would we assume a missing teenager could be involved in a murder?"

"Are you saying the two incidents *are* connected?"

Leigh nodded.

"How?"

"I think Jesse Quinn witnessed the murder. This new witness, who also saw the shooting, said the killer took her."

"Jesus." Anita Howard seldom showed emotion, but she pursed her lips and the muscles along her jawline tensed. "It's our job to look at all possible scenarios. If the suspect took this girl, he most likely killed her too. And if that's the case, we've got another very cold murder on our hands instead of a missing teenager." Leigh was quiet as she allowed Captain Howard to process this latest information. "I assume you've reviewed the homicide case? Anything?"

"No, ma'am. Nothing that connects the two, other than the location. The case is still open but inactive."

Howard placed her coffee mug on the corner of the desk. "So we're no closer to finding out what really happened to this girl than we were." Leigh shook her head. "And don't you dare blame yourself. We didn't create this mess, but one way or another, we're going to clean it up, even if it takes the rest of my career."

"Is there anything else you want me to do, Captain?"

"Have you talked with her family at all?"

"Apparently they moved shortly after Jesse disappeared. I couldn't find a record of them anywhere."

"We're in a holding pattern at the moment. In a few months, I'll have Crime Stoppers run both cases again and see if anything shakes loose. Thanks for all you've done." She stood, shook Leigh's hand, and escorted her to the door. "And only a couple more weeks until you're back at work. You're missed around here."

"Thank you, ma'am. And by the way, I'm going out of town for a few days. If you need me, call my mobile."

On the way back to her car, she phoned Pam and filled her in on her plan. She declined Pam's offer to accompany her to Colorado and asked her to update Nate. She hadn't bothered asking the department to fund the trip. No supervisor would authorize a home visit sixteen hundred miles away, especially for a suspended officer who shouldn't be working cases.

She should just call the local authorities and have them contact Karla, but a personal visit would answer a lot of questions and ease her mind about sending Jack home. She had to do it, and if that meant springing for her own plane ticket, so be it.

CHAPTER SEVENTEEN

Macy was still reeling from disbelief the next morning as she repacked the skull in the evidence box, taped it, and wrote her initials over the seal. She'd watched Leigh move out yesterday from the safety of her cottage, ignoring her knocks and calls, unwilling to expose herself to any further hope, disappointment, or pain. She was angry with herself more than Leigh, because she'd opened up to her emotionally and sexually. Hell, she'd even shared her fledgling relationship dreams with her. And Leigh had rewarded her vulnerability with more betrayal. Today she was going straight to the source, or as close as she could get.

She drove to the police station and followed the familiar route to the Crimes Against Persons squad. When she deposited the box on the first detective's desk with a body attached, she felt relief and an odd sense of joy.

"Give this to Rickard and tell him it's my last one. The photos of my reconstruction are in here." She handed him the envelope containing the camera card and turned to leave.

"Hey, I can't take this," the young detective said.

"If you want to break the chain of evidence, that's on you. It's not my problem any more." She was finally free. The vacant spot in the center of her studio table now represented something more hopeful and enjoyable. Leigh had opened that possibility, and even without her, Macy would never have to go back to the darkness of forensics work.

She asked a records clerk how to find Leigh Monroe's supervisor and followed the directions to a reception area decorated with the latest furnishings from the seventies. She was glad the city didn't waste taxpayers' money on interior decorating, and the petty side of her was happy police officers didn't luxuriate in style.

When the receptionist ushered her into a private office, a very attractive African-American woman with intense brown eyes, silver-gray hair, dressed in a flattering business suit, greeted her. "Good morning, Ms. Sheridan. I'm Anita Howard."

She'd expected a gruff, overweight man whom she would immediately detest, just like the one who'd dismissed Jesse's case all those years ago.

"Please have a seat." Captain Howard motioned toward the chairs in front of her large desk. "Would you like something to drink?"

"No, thank you."

"That'll be all, Barbara." She dismissed the young assistant with a genuine smile that made her eyes sparkle. "It's a pleasure to meet you, Ms. Sheridan. I've heard about your forensics work with the Crimes Against Persons squad for years. How may I help you today?"

Macy didn't want to like this woman, but her professionalism and attentiveness inspired respect. "I'd like a progress report on the Jesse Quinn case." Anita Howard's eyebrow arched slightly, but otherwise her facial expression didn't change. "It's been a very long time, and I don't want you people to think she's been forgotten."

"Ms. Sheridan, I assure you *we people* have not forgotten any of our unsolved cases, especially not Jesse's."

The response wasn't what Macy expected. She was prepared to launch into a diatribe about the incompetence of the police department and the insensitivity of closing a missing teenager's case too quickly. Howard's assurance took her off guard. "So, what can you tell me?"

"Nothing new, I'm afraid."

"Is anyone actively working her case?" This was Howard's opportunity for full disclosure, to admit that Leigh was somehow currently involved.

"I'm not at liberty to say, at the moment, and I apologize for that. I can see you're very passionate about this."

"Passionate doesn't begin to cover how I feel. This case has been a significant part of my life for sixteen years, and I won't rest until I know what happened to my best friend. Now, I repeat, is anyone currently working on her case? I *need* to know."

Anita Howard leaned forward. "Forgive me for prying, but what's happened recently to elicit this poignant plea? I know cases remain quite emotional to family and friends, but few hold on to such strong feelings for so long. Do you know something that could help us?"

When she looked into Howard's eyes, she saw Leigh's emerald ones staring back at her, beseeching her to listen, to understand, but she hadn't. Her pride and ego had gotten in the way again—just like the first misunderstanding they'd had. All the feelings Leigh had resurrected in her erupted and she wanted to cry. She stared down at her hands, clenching them into fists to control herself. "No." Her voice sounded like a choking whisper. "I don't."

Captain Howard took her hands and forced Macy to look at her. "I'm going to tell you a story. But before I do, you must promise you won't draw any hasty conclusions from what I say, and you won't repeat it to anyone. Can you do that, Ms. Sheridan?"

She nodded. "Macy, call me Macy."

"Very well, Macy." She sat back in her chair, took a deep breath, and glanced at a photo on her credenza of a slightly older woman, seeming to draw strength from it. "Sixteen years ago we had a young female training officer on patrol with a feisty new female recruit. They were dispatched to assist detectives on a missing-person case. Their jobs were to help with a grid search for the body and evidence and to do a preliminary canvass for witnesses. They did their part and were dismissed by the detectives. But something about the case bothered the coach and trainee that night and for years to come."

"What are you telling me?"

Anita Howard held up her hand. "I'm just telling you a story, remember? Do you want to hear the rest or should I stop now?"

"Please go on."

"The detectives who handled, and subsequently closed that case two weeks later, rose through the ranks in the police department to become respected and highly decorated lieutenants, sergeants, and investigators. The training coach was eventually the first African-American woman promoted to captain, and she was assigned to the Youth Division. And the trainee, a very bright and committed woman, became the best detective in that division.

"When this captain took control of the Youth Division, she was finally in a position to order a review of any incident under her command. But if she chose to review this particular case, she'd have to be discreet, because these same men could cause her, and whoever assisted her, a great deal of trouble."

"Oh, my God. Leigh." The words were out before Macy could edit them.

"I beg your pardon?"

"Sorry, please continue."

"That's about it. But *if* this captain and detective were conducting any kind of follow-up investigation on a case like this, it would be essential that it be done quietly. You understand that, right?"

She nodded.

"The detective would be forbidden from discussing it with *anyone*." She glanced at the woman's picture on her credenza again. "And trust me, I know how difficult it is to hide things in this profession from the ones we love."

Anita Howard rose and started toward the door, the meeting obviously over, but Macy wasn't leaving until she knew how to get in touch with Leigh. "I appreciate this, really, but I have to talk to her."

"Who are you talking about, Ms. Sheridan? We were speaking hypothetically." Howard's eyes narrowed as she stared at her, as if willing her to understand her point.

"Thank you for that enlightening story. Now let me tell you a true story you might be able to help bring to a happy ending. A withdrawn, socially challenged woman developed feelings for a certain detective. But the detective withheld information about a case very close to the woman's heart. This woman took the detective's silence as a sign she didn't care for her and had intentionally lied to her, not that she was duty bound to keep quiet. This woman acted very badly and wants desperately to make amends, because, you see, she's in love with the detective. Where do you suppose that woman might find Detective Leigh Monroe?"

A wide smile brightened Captain Howard's face and her shoulders relaxed. "I'm afraid I don't know. She told me yesterday that she was going out of town."

"Any idea where?"

"None."

"Do you think her friend, Pam Wilkinson, might know?"

"If anyone would, it'd be Pam."

Gayle is out of town. Macy didn't want to believe Leigh would go back to her, regardless of their status. "Thanks for your time and for that interesting story, Captain."

"My pleasure, Macy, and good luck."

She didn't think she could possibly leave the police station feeling any worse than when she arrived, but she did. Leigh had tried to tell her the truth, in spite of being professionally bound to remain silent. For that she felt better. And she was certain Captain Howard and Leigh were reviewing Jesse's case. That was also good news. But Leigh was gone, probably out of the country with Gayle. She'd been terribly unfair, and now she had to live with it…and without Leigh.

❖

The residence Leigh was watching could've been any ranch-style house in the world. The beige siding and deep-green shutters appeared recently painted, and the grass was freshly mowed. She'd imagined her and Macy in a place like this, living a normal life—another dream that would never come true. She'd rented a car and driven the fifty-five miles from the Cheyenne, Wyoming airport to Windsor, Colorado, arriving down the street from Karla Temple's house two hours ago. She didn't usually conduct surveillance when delivering good news, but something about this case didn't feel right. So far, she hadn't seen anyone leave or enter the residence, but the same nondescript sedan had passed three times.

The rest of the afternoon, Leigh circulated in the neighborhood to keep from being reported to the local police. She'd walked within two car lengths of the sedan, close enough to determine it was a government-issued vehicle and the occupants were feds. Why would they still be interested in Steven Temple? Maybe he'd been in the Mafia and they were keeping tabs on the wife, in case she had knowledge of or access to illegal assets. Whatever the federal scenario, she wasn't interested in getting involved.

She waited until nightfall, weaved her way through backyards to Karla Temple's door, and knocked. The woman who answered didn't seem at all surprised to see a stranger at her back door after ten o'clock. She waved Leigh in as if they were neighbors preparing for a late cup of coffee. The small kitchen and den were as tidy as the outside of the house, with a warm, lived-in feeling. Karla was an attractive woman with blond hair just beginning to prematurely gray, brilliant blue eyes ringed by dark circles, and a figure any housewife would envy. She looked like she hadn't slept recently, and her gaze was distant and unfocused.

"Little late for a house call, isn't it? Coffee?" She waved toward the pot that was already on and topped up her cup.

"No, thanks." Who did Karla Temple think she was, one of the feds from the sedan? Leigh planned to play this out. Maybe she'd get some answers.

"Is this about the phone? The company came yesterday and changed the number." Her lips were tight and her jaw muscles clenched. "You want to check?" If Karla's tone could've registered on a thermometer, it would've been below freezing.

"That won't be necessary. You understand why we had to do that." She was playing a hunch and prayed Karla Temple was either too distracted, tired, or worried to be overly cautious.

"You're afraid the local police will track his calls. Have you found him yet? The only reason I agreed to stay here is because you promised you'd find my son. *Where is he*? Now that you've cut off my only means of contact, you have to know I won't stay put long."

Leigh retrieved her credentials and pushed them across the counter toward Karla. "Mrs. Temple, I'm Detective Leigh Monroe with the Greensboro Police Department."

Karla's face blanched and she closed her eyes, breathing in tiny puffs through her mouth. "Oh my God. No. Please." When she opened her eyes, the color so similar to Jack's, tears flooded her cheeks, but she made no other sound.

"Let me help you." She wrapped her arm around Karla's waist and guided her to a chair. "Can I get you a glass of water?" She nodded. "I didn't mean to upset you. I just needed to clarify that I'm not with them." She inclined her head toward the front of the house where the sedan was parked.

Karla's hand shook as she took the water glass and brought it to her lips. As she sipped, Leigh saw the fear and panic in her eyes. The question Karla so desperately wanted to ask clearly choked her and she couldn't speak.

"Jack is okay, Mrs. Temple. He's safe."

She slowly placed the glass on the table. "Thank God. Where is he?"

"Greensboro, North Carolina."

"Greensboro." She repeated the name as if she'd never heard it before, testing the sound of it out loud. "What's he doing there?"

"Trying to find his father's family. At least that's what he told me."

"Thank you for taking care of him and for finding me…how did you?"

"Well, Jack wasn't much help." She smiled to let Karla know she wasn't really upset.

"He can be headstrong, like his mother. You traced his phone calls?"

Leigh nodded.

"They won't like that."

"Who are *they*, Mrs. Temple, and why are they watching you? I mean, your husband is dead now. I assume he was a material witness, maybe a mob case or major fraud. Why the continued interest?"

"Look, I don't care about any of that. I just want to see my son." Karla silently paced in front of the stove. The way she cocked her head to one side as she moved reminded Leigh of Jack. She clenched and unclenched her fists at her side, her face a mask of concentration. Maybe she was considering how much to tell her, maybe she was devising a lie, but Leigh gave her time. She'd spent nine days wondering where her son was; she deserved a break.

"They're U.S. Marshals."

Leigh had expected more. "What was your husband into?"

"Nothing."

She considered dropping into badass cop mode, but Karla was a distraught mother, and upsetting her further wouldn't help. "Then why are the marshals outside your house?"

"You'd have to ask them that question, Detective."

Karla was as frustrating as Jack. Maybe on the plane she'd get more information. "I have a flight back to Greensboro at six in the morning. Shall I book a ticket in your name?"

Karla's eyes sparkled as if she'd been given the Holy Grail. "Yes, please, but what about the guys outside?"

"I'll tell them I've found your son and we're going to pick him up." She started toward the front door. Interagency cooperation usually worked between local and federal agencies, so an honest conversation should produce the desired results.

"No!" Karla practically vaulted across the floor toward her. "You can't."

Her reaction seemed a bit over the top. "Why? They're federal agents. They might help facilitate this mother-child reunion."

"I don't trust them, completely. I can't explain it. Can't you just help me get my son back…and leave them out of it?"

It was an unusual request. If the marshals knew Jack had been located, they'd probably fly him back to Colorado at no cost. That seemed like a win-win, but Karla was adamant, maybe even a little frightened about involving them. Leigh considered the possible downsides: paying for Karla's, and maybe Jack's, tickets herself, pissing off the feds if they found out, complicating or compromising a federal investigation, and delaying this reunion because the federal bureaucracy was notoriously slow. On the positive side, she'd make Karla Temple happy. Maybe seeing the love Karla had for Jack made her nostalgic for something she'd never had. Please Karla or the feds. No-brainer.

"Do they have a usual shift-change time?"

"Around six."

"Perfect. If you don't mind, I'll sleep on your sofa, and in the morning we'll sneak out before daybreak. Get everything you need ready and put it by the back door. My car is parked one street over. We'll be at the airport before they've had their first cup of coffee."

"Really?" Karla hugged her and stepped back. "Thank you, so much." Her gratitude seemed genuine, but Leigh had more questions than answers. Why had she let her son go across the country alone? Why hadn't she simply explained about his father? Why was she still the subject of government scrutiny? And why the hell hadn't the marshals brought Jack home if they knew where he was? She vowed to find the answers once mother and son had been reunited, government restrictions be damned.

Chapter Eighteen

Macy was up before dawn, drinking coffee, pacing, and looking toward the lake like she'd been beached by the last wave. She'd called Leigh's mobile several times since yesterday, but the image of her wrapped in Gayle's arms prevented her from leaving a message. She reached for her mug but stopped when she noticed her hands shaking from too much caffeine.

What was going on with her? The answer, swift and certain, wasn't what she expected. She was in love with Leigh. And she'd driven her away. Their liaison had been a series of awkward encounters, not because she didn't care, but because she had no clue how to handle her feelings or Leigh's. She'd resorted to anger and vented at Leigh, unable to verbalize what she so desperately wanted to say. She'd been wildly jealous of Gayle, acting like a teenager with her first crush. And when she and Leigh had sex, she'd controlled everything, unable to surrender. In spite of her ineptitude and uncertainty, she'd give anything for another chance. She'd never felt like this, and the possibility of never feeling it again weakened her like an all-consuming disease.

She poured her cold coffee down the drain and went into the studio. Her discolored old lab coat hung on the peg by the door, and the spot where she'd worked on the skull was now an empty space. Reconstruction tools littered the tabletop, and remnants of clay made it look like a miniature obstacle course. She'd finished her last forensics job, and it was time to make way for other things.

She delicately removed the coat from the hook, fingered the frayed neck and sleeves, and ran her hand down the stained trail on the front. She'd clung to this garment like an old friend, trying to protect herself from the energy of the dead that seeped into her. Like any physical barrier, her friend had become permeable and ineffective as her pain mirrored that in the faces she built. "We have to say good-bye now." She tossed the lab coat in the trash and retrieved a clean one from under the counter. This one would represent her new career, her new life, filled with light and color, and the kind of art that made her heart sing.

By the time the sun had risen, she'd transformed her studio from a place that worshipped the dead to a place that celebrated the living. She'd packed all her reconstruction tools and pulled out her paints, brushes, palettes, and canvases. The image she'd carried in her head for days, the one Leigh had inspired, came to life. This would be the centerpiece of her show. She looked around the room and smiled. She was finally home again…but one thing was missing. She'd given Jesse years of her life with no possibility of fulfillment. Leigh, alive and filled with potential, deserved no less. An hour later she stood on Pam Wilkinson's stoop, pressing the doorbell like it was a gaming button.

"What the hell?" Pam opened the door in a pair of boxers and a tank top, her short hair plastered down like a helmet. "It's not even eight o'clock yet. This better be—" Her eyes focused on Macy and then scanned the area behind her. "I'm not sure who you are, but I'd guess the forensic artist."

"Just the artist from now on." She offered her hand because she'd only seen Pam on the dock the day she helped Leigh move in. "I'm Macy Sheridan, and I need to find Leigh."

"Couldn't you hold the heavy stuff until after I've had coffee? Come in." Pam closed the door behind her, led the way into the kitchen, and pointed to a bar stool at the counter. She flipped the coffeepot on and a few seconds later put her cup under the drip to catch the strongest pour. "I don't know exactly where she is at the moment." Pam took a sip. "Want some?"

She shook her head.

"Wait…I thought you never wanted to see her again. Brain cells are waking up."

"Never claimed I was perfect. Actually, I suck at emotional stuff, but I love her."

Pam almost choked on a sip of hot coffee. "Why didn't you say so? Does she know?"

"I seriously doubt it. I haven't exactly been forthcoming. That's why I'm here. I really need to talk to her. Is she in Toronto…with Gayle?" The words were painful to imagine and harder to say.

"With Gayle? Where did you get that idea?"

"Her captain mentioned she was out of town. When I factored in the last thing I said to her, guess I jumped to the conclusion she'd go back to Gayle."

Pam shook her head emphatically. "Then you don't know Leigh very well."

"I just assumed. What happened between them? Why did they break up?"

"I think you should ask Leigh those questions."

"I just don't want to make the same mistake. I've made so many already, and if I can avoid even one, it would be helpful." She looked out the kitchen window and visualized her future with Leigh evaporating like fog at sunrise.

"Bottom line, Leigh was never a priority in Gayle's life, and that reminded her of childhood and her mother—has she told you about Susan?"

"A little. If Leigh needs to feel important to her lover, I've already failed her too. I've been obsessed with a case to the exclusion of everything and everyone else." Why hadn't she seen what Leigh needed before?

She stood slowly and started toward the front door. "Sorry I bothered you, Pam."

"Hey, where you going? I haven't answered your question yet. Don't you want to know where Leigh is?"

"It probably wouldn't matter."

"If you intend to give up that easily, keep walking. My best friend's worth a lot more effort than you've put in."

Macy spun on her heel as anger raged. "I love her, but I can't give her what she needs."

Pam had followed her to the door and they stood toe-to-toe. "You don't get to make that decision for her. If you love her, tell her, and then work it out. Trust me, Leigh's worth it. Nobody said love was easy. If easy is what you're looking for, go find another sixteen-year project and crawl back in your hole."

"*What?*" It took a second for Pam's statement to sink in. "She told you about that?"

"She had to talk to somebody. You two weren't communicating."

Pam was exactly right. She'd hidden behind the memory of a wonderful girl for too long. Jesse would've been appalled at the way she'd lived her life shackled to the past. She sighed, and some of the tension in her body eased. "You're right."

"Of course I am. Everything happens for a reason."

She rolled her eyes. "God, now you sound like her with your clichés."

"Sorry, must've rubbed off."

"So, where is Leigh?"

"On her way back from Colorado. We found Jack's mother."

"That's fantastic." She should be ashamed for suspecting Leigh of running back to Gayle when she'd been doing what she always did, taking care of others. "Does he know yet? Is he excited?"

"I'm not sure about that, but his mother is ecstatic. Why don't you wait here while I get dressed? Leigh will call when she gets back. I'm meeting her at the foster home with some paperwork to start the process for Jack's release. You can go with me, and you two can talk."

"Thanks, I appreciate it."

❖

When Leigh stopped in front of Susan's condo, the light wrinkles across Karla Temple's forehead deepened. "Is this the right place?"

"Yes, it's a temporary foster home. Why do you ask?"

"It's just not what I expected." During the flight Karla had been on edge, asking questions about Greensboro, the population, crime statistics, and the local art scene. She sounded more like a woman shopping for a house than picking up her missing son. Karla's blue eyes were bloodshot from lack of sleep, but she resisted Leigh's suggestion to get some rest. She'd hoped to chat with Karla about her situation with the marshals and about Jack and his father, but every time she broached the subject, Karla deflected. Leigh wrote it off as a mother too concerned about her son to think about anything else.

"Can we go in?"

"Before we do, I'd really like to know why your son came here alone looking for his father's family. Why didn't you just tell him what he wanted to know?"

"He gets an idea in his head and no one can talk him out of it." She continued to look at the house. "I'd really like to see him now." She opened the car door before Leigh could ask any more questions.

She'd called Susan to let her know they were on their way, and she greeted them at the front door. She held out her hand to Karla. "I'm Susan Bryce. I'm so glad you're here." She nodded to Leigh as they entered. "Nice to see you again, Leigh."

"Where's Jack?" Karla asked.

"He should be home from school any minute. He caught a ride with a friend." She guided them toward the kitchen that overlooked the small backyard. "Would either of you care for coffee, tea, or anything?" They both declined. "That son of yours is quite the little man. He's very intelligent and quite mature for a fifteen-year-old."

"Fifteen?" Karla looked from Leigh to Susan. "Jack just turned sixteen recently. Why did you think he was only fifteen?"

"That's what he told us," Leigh said. "He volunteered to go into foster care, gave us minimal details about his father, and let us do the work. Unfortunately, we weren't able to find any of Steven's relatives. The marshals blocked our inquiries, which brings me to my earlier question. Why wouldn't he have just asked you? And why weren't you looking for him?" The last one was the real question Leigh wanted answered. Why would a mother not look for her missing son, regardless of his age?

Before she had the chance to ask again, the front door opened and Jack called out, "Susan, you home? It's me, checking in." When he got to the kitchen, he stopped, his eyes fixed on Karla Temple. "Mom!"

"Oh, Jack!" Karla rushed to him and they hugged, dancing in a small circle around the kitchen. "Are you all right? Have they been good to you? I've missed you so much. Oh, my darling, please don't ever leave me again. Promise." She held him at arm's length and assessed him up and down.

"I'm fine. Susan has been wonderful. I've missed you too. And I promise not to leave again if you'll tell me the truth." The machine-gun responses seemed to reassure Karla until his last statement.

"Let's discuss that later, shall we? We don't need to inconvenience these nice people any further. We really should get back home. Get your things together."

Karla tried to usher him from the room, but Leigh blocked their path. "I'm afraid it's not quite that simple. You need to answer my questions before I let him go, and there's a process through Children and Family Services and the courts."

"But he's my son."

"He's been gone ten days and you haven't even filed a missing-person report. That alone is cause for concern. You have to understand what that looks like from a law-enforcement perspective. We have to be sure it's safe and reasonable for him to return to your care."

Susan stepped between Karla and her. "Leigh, why don't you give them a few minutes. I'm sure they'd like to talk in private."

When had her mother become so concerned about others? But the scared look on Karla's face and the determined set of Jack's jaw made her think Susan could be right. "Okay, fine. I'll be here when you're ready to talk."

"Why don't you take your mother to your room, Jack?" Susan said.

As they ascended the stairs, Susan turned to Leigh. "I'm sorry if I overstepped."

"Nah, you're probably right." Alone with her mother again, Leigh was suddenly at a loss. She'd considered talking to her, but this didn't really seem like the right time. Would there ever be one? There was only one way to find out. Hopefully Hedy and Macy were right about Susan having a different perspective on the past. "Susan…"

"Yes?"

Her throat tightened and she wasn't sure she could speak. She remembered the times she'd pleaded with Susan and been ignored or had her concerns discounted. How could this woman reduce her emotionally to a prepubescent girl?

"How about a cup of coffee? It's a beautiful afternoon. We could sit on the deck and enjoy the spring air."

When they'd settled with their coffees, Leigh stared out across the yard, touched again by what a nice, homey place Susan had, unlike the dives they'd inhabited during her childhood. They sat in silence for several minutes until Susan spoke.

"I don't expect you to say anything, Leigh. I'd really just like you to listen, if you will."

Leigh clutched her coffee mug as if it would keep her from bolting and nodded.

"Thank you." Susan took a sip of coffee, and her hand shook so badly some of it sloshed over the rim of her cup. "Sorry. I'm really nervous."

She'd never seen her mother nervous to the point of clumsiness. She'd always been detached and totally controlled. The slip in composure would've been endearing in anyone else, but from Susan it seemed like a ploy.

"When your father...died..." Her voice cracked and she swallowed hard. "I was devastated and—"

"You didn't act devastated." The words leapt out quickly and her acidic tone sounded harsh. Her mother recoiled and guilt rushed through Leigh. "I'm sorry. I said I'd listen. Reflex, I guess. His death just didn't seem to affect you at all."

"You have a right to be angry, honey, but I assure you, it did. Your father was the love of my life, my soul mate. When he died, I wasn't sure I could go on. I considered...well, you don't need to hear that...but I had two children to think about."

"It didn't feel like you thought about us at all."

"I know it must've seemed that way to you, but I had to work to keep us together and to keep myself from going crazy with grief."

Her mother definitely hadn't been around much, but she'd always equated that with the men in her life. "What about those guys? If you loved my father so much, how could you...?"

"It was always about providing for you and Hedy. If I remarried I'd be able to stay home and take care of you, but after your father, I only attracted leeches and criminals."

"But *three* more husbands, Susan. Really?"

"I was desperate to get us out of public housing. That's no environment to raise children in, especially girls."

Susan sounded sincere and something inside Leigh wanted to believe her, but was it already too late? "What happened to the other three husbands?"

"I left the first two. Do you really want to hear this? It's not a pretty story. Suffice it to say they weren't good husbands or fathers."

"And the last one?"

Susan looked at her for the first time, and it was like seeing herself in a mirror twenty years later. Her emerald eyes had lost the spark of youth and hope for the future. Her copper hair was sprinkled with gray, as if each decision she'd made in life had left a trail. "Edwin Bryce was a good man and I stayed with him until he died. When he came along, Hedy was already in high school and you'd moved out. Most of the damage of my poor parenting had already been done." Before now, Susan had never conceded she'd made mistakes bringing up her children. She couldn't fake the sadness in her eyes.

The hard lump in Leigh's chest began to dissolve. "I know this is petty, but I have to ask. Remember the time I was sick and asked to stay home from school, but you made me go anyway? You said Hedy shouldn't walk alone."

Susan's eyes filled with tears. "Sending you off when you were sick was one of the hardest things I've ever done. I wanted to stay home and take care of you, but they were threatening to evict us if I missed one more payment, and I was already working two jobs. I couldn't leave you alone with husband number two. I didn't trust him."

"Why not?"

Looking down at her coffee mug, Susan seemed to be contemplating whether to answer. "Is that really important?"

"It is to me. In my mind that memory proved you really didn't care about me, even when I was sick."

"Oh, Leigh. You and Hedy were *all* I ever cared about after your father died. And you've grown into such amazing women, in spite of my failures. How have you both become so open and loving and successful when I was such a horrible example?"

She didn't remember getting compliments from her mother as a child, but it felt good to have her accomplishments recognized. "We've always been close, maybe that helped. Now, about husband number two?"

"I see why you're such a good detective." She fiddled with the hem of her blouse before finally answering. "He hit me, and I was afraid he'd do the same to you...or worse."

"Why did you stay with him?"

"I didn't. When it happened the first time, I told him I was leaving. It was perfect really, gave me the out I needed, but it took a few weeks to get the necessary paperwork through the system. In the meantime, I couldn't risk him hurting either of you."

The last stronghold of anger inside her collapsed. How many families had been torn apart or forever altered by domestic violence? She'd had no idea it existed in her home—a testament to her mother's strength and courage. "And then you met Edwin Bryce."

"Yes, too little too late for my children, but he provided a stable life for me."

"Good for you."

Susan placed her hand on top of Leigh's where it rested on the arm of her chair. "I'm so sorry I wasn't there for you. That's my greatest failure in life. I hope you can forgive me someday. I know it'll take time."

She was saved from answering when the doorbell sounded and Susan excused herself. Leigh followed her into the kitchen for more coffee, still reeling from their chat. She needed time to process what she'd heard and maybe talk with Hedy. She and Susan had kept in closer contact and Hedy might be able to provide more insight, now that she was willing to listen. When Susan returned, Pam and Macy were with her. "Macy...what are you doing here?"

"*Not* glad to see me then?"

"Of course I'm glad to see you. It's just a surprise...a good one. Macy, this is Susan Bryce...my mother." It was the first time she'd introduced Susan as her mother, and it felt strangely satisfying. "Susan, this is Pam Wilkinson from CFS." She turned to Macy and placed her hand protectively in the small of her back. "And this is Macy Sheridan, my...I'm not quite sure what we are at the moment, but—"

"Jack and I are ready to talk now." Karla and Jack entered the kitchen and stopped short.

Macy paled and looked as though she might pass out. Leigh pulled her closer. "Are you all right? What's wrong?"

Macy pointed. "J...Jesse..."

CHAPTER NINETEEN

Macy's knees trembled as she stood in Susan Bryce's kitchen staring at the woman she'd thought was dead for sixteen years. She felt faint. Maybe she was hallucinating. She'd finally decided to move on, to tell Leigh she loved her, and now this apparition appeared to remind her of what she'd left undone.

"Macy?" The apparition spoke.

"Jesse. It can't be. You're…"

"I'm right here."

Jesse moved toward her and she stepped back. "Not possible." But those crystal blue eyes, though ringed by dark circles and bloodshot from worry, were distinctive. She'd sketched those eyes so many times it was impossible to mistake them for anyone else's. "How?"

Jesse inched slowly closer until she stood within arm's length. "Can I hug you, please? I've missed you so much." Without waiting for a response, Jesse hugged her gently, as though afraid she might break. "I've thought about you every day since that night."

This wasn't happening. "Really? Then why haven't I heard from you in sixteen years? Why didn't you call? Send a note? Something? Do you have any idea what I've been through, thinking you were… dead?" Tears streamed down her face, and her heart pounded as fiercely as it had the night Jesse disappeared.

"I couldn't contact you, honey."

They rocked in each other's arms and she lost track of time, place, and everyone else in the room. She and Jesse were together, as they'd been so many times as teenagers. Life was as it should be again.

"It's okay, Macy. I'm here now," Jesse said.

When Jesse finally backed away, Macy thumbed the tears from her cheeks, memorizing the face she hadn't been able to portray on paper. Jesse's eyes were the same, but her features had matured into those of a beautiful woman. Her flashy blond hair had started to prematurely gray, but her small frame was still slender and fit, and she spoke with the same reassuring tone she'd used when trying to lure her into another hair-brained teenage adventure.

Macy blinked to clear her tears and to be certain her best friend was really standing in front of her. But why was she here? How could she be here? Where had she been? Once the questions started, they wouldn't stop. "Jesse, I—"

"I know you have a lot of questions, and I'll answer every one as soon as I can." Jesse turned toward the other people in the room, who'd moved to the far side of the kitchen. "But first, I need Detective Monroe to do something for me."

Hearing Jesse speak Leigh's name was surreal, like she was in a dream that didn't really make sense—her living and breathing best friend and the woman she loved standing in the same room about to have a conversation. God. She hadn't thought about Leigh since she'd seen Jesse.

Leigh moved closer to them. "I guess it's safe to assume your real name is Jesse Quinn? That answers one of my questions but raises a lot more."

Jesse looked around the room again and then directed her question to Leigh. "Can everyone here be trusted?"

Leigh hesitated, and Macy saw her glance at her mother before she answered. "With my life."

"I've just explained everything to my son, so maybe it's time to end this story once and for all. We should sit down. It'll take awhile."

Leigh herded everybody around the small kitchen table, and Susan set more coffee, water, sodas, and an assortment of cookies in the center. When they were settled, Macy noted that Leigh had purposely orchestrated the seating arrangement. She and Jack flanked Jesse, with Susan beside Jack, then Leigh, and Pam to Macy's right. She'd expected Leigh to sit next to her and was a little disappointed when she didn't.

Jesse looked down at the bottle of water caged in her hands. "You probably know part of the story, but believe me, you could never imagine what really happened. It's like something out of the twilight zone."

Macy held Jesse's hand to give her encouragement and to feel connected to her again. "Take your time."

"Macy and I went to the club that night. She didn't really want to go, but I insisted. I was supposed to meet a boy I liked. When we got there, I basically took off and left Macy on her own. Near closing time, I walked outside to get some air. I heard a commotion around the side of the building, so I went to take a look. A tall, muscular man was holding a shorter fellow at gunpoint. The tall guy said the smaller man owed someone money and he'd run out of patience. Then the tall guy shot the other man, three times."

The kitchen was as quiet as a funeral home until Susan spoke. "Oh, my God, honey. You could've been killed. What did you do?"

"Apparently, I screamed when the shots started. The tall guy chased me down before I could make it to the door of the club."

"Jesse, I'm so sorry I wasn't there." Macy stroked the back of Jesse's neck to calm her, kneading the bunched muscles along her shoulders.

"It's not your fault. I knew you'd blame yourself for my disappearance."

"I should've been with you."

"No. You weren't responsible for my teenage hormones and bad behavior. I shouldn't have taken you to that club in the first place. It was mostly a college hangout."

"What happened next?" Leigh's voice was very matter-of-fact, a tone Macy hadn't heard before. She couldn't determine if Leigh was just being professional or if she was annoyed.

"The guy took me hostage. I knew he was going to kill me and dump my body. He bound me with duct tape in a van, gagged and blindfolded me, and drove around for what seemed like hours. I had no idea where we were when he finally stopped. He made a call from a phone booth. I only caught snippets of his side of the conversation, but he asked to speak with a guy named Francisco."

"You're sure about that?" Leigh asked, not looking up from a small notepad she was writing on.

"Positive. He told this guy about me, waited, and then his voice got very loud. I heard him say, 'I didn't sign on to kill a kid. I won't do it.' Apparently Francisco didn't like that because they argued back and forth for several minutes. My guy gave Francisco directions about where to drop the money for the earlier hit and told Francisco he'd take care of me. I was so scared. If I could've just died, I probably would've."

"Why wouldn't this guy, this paid assassin, not just kill you right away and move on?" Leigh glanced up at Jesse but never looked her way.

"I don't know, Detective. Don't you believe me?" Jesse asked.

"She's not saying that," Macy said. "Are you?" Leigh still wouldn't meet her gaze.

"Well, if you don't believe me so far, you're certainly not going to believe the rest of what I have to say."

"Just get on with it." Leigh's tone had turned almost hostile.

"We waited all night."

"How do you know?" Leigh asked.

"Because I got chilly, and then the morning rush-hour traffic started and the van got warmer again. Wasn't hard to figure out. When you're tied up, you don't have anything else to do but pay attention to what's going on around you. Believe me, if you think you're going to die, every little thing becomes significant." Jesse's voice quivered.

"Shh, shh, it's okay, Jess." She scooted her chair closer and wrapped her arm around Jesse's shoulder. "You're safe."

"Get on with the rest of this unbelievable story."

"Leigh!" Susan gave Leigh a look that mothers had used for centuries to silently censure their offspring.

"My mother doesn't lie," Jack said.

"Evidence to the contrary," Leigh said. "She's apparently been doing it quite convincingly for sixteen years."

"It's okay, Jack." Jesse patted his arm. "When the guy got back in the van, I started talking to him, trying to connect in some way so he wouldn't want to kill me. I told him my name, and my best friend's name, where I went to school, and about my parents. He'd grunt occasionally but not really say anything. Later in the day, he went to the drop spot to pick up his money and I heard gunshots. Apparently, Francisco didn't trust him to take care of me. I heard the other shooters calling my guy Brewster as he dove back into the van. Bullets were pinging off the side of the vehicle. I thought I was a goner."

"Brewster," Leigh muttered, and scribbled on her pad.

"When he got back in the van, Brewster was a changed man. That's the only way I can describe it. He drove to a bank, and before you ask, Detective, I know because he told me. He put his cash in a safety-deposit box and said we needed to decide what to do next. *We needed to decide.* This was the first bright spot in the whole horrible event."

Macy stared at Jesse as she told her tale, unable to digest the convoluted story. One minute her heart was racing and the next she could barely breathe. She glanced at Leigh, willing her to look up so she could get a read on her reaction, but she was doodling—doodling. She didn't believe Jesse's story at all.

"And then?" Leigh said, her gaze locking on Macy. In that moment she saw a mixture of anger and pain in Leigh's eyes. She'd seen that expression in the mirror for sixteen years.

"Please go on, Jesse," she said.

"He drove awhile longer, but when he stopped this time, he opened the back of the van and took off the gag and blindfold. Before he untied me, he gave me his proposal, as he called it. He wanted to contact the federal authorities, release me, and testify against this Francisco guy in exchange for a lighter sentence. He asked if I'd be willing to stand up for him, swear he hadn't hurt me. I agreed. What else was I going to say under the circumstances? He explained I'd probably have to go into the witness-protection program. At that point, I would've agreed to anything. We made a pact of sorts and he starting making phone calls."

"An assassin with a conscience? Really?" Leigh's tone was one of total disbelief.

"It's the truth!" Jack said. "And Karla Chance was born, then she married my dad."

Leigh looked at Jesse, her face an unemotional mask. "And when did you decide it would be okay for your son to travel sixteen hundred miles alone to complete the family tree?"

"Leigh, that's not fair," Macy said.

Jesse shook her head at Macy. "You've been around my son long enough to know when he decides to do something, he's going to do it no matter what. I tried desperately to talk him out of it, but I couldn't tell him the whole story. I didn't know where he was going, had no idea he'd come *here*. How could I know he'd heard us talking about Greensboro? The first time he called we reached an understanding that he'd call me everyday and check in. He was supposed to tell me where he was, but that part didn't go so smoothly."

Pam spoke for the first time. "So, how did you end up here, Jack?"

"I told you the real story about that. But I got it wrong. When I heard my parents talking, it was about mom's past, not his. I thought this was the place to start looking. Guess I should've talked to my mom and got my story right."

"Was your husband from the Windsor area?" Leigh asked.

"Yes, but he was a foster child and had no real family. We'd never talked about that with Jack, for several reasons." She took Jack's hand. "If I'd had any idea he was coming here, I would've hogtied him to a bedpost or something. What if Francisco had a contract on me and found out I had a son? I couldn't bear it."

"And what about your parents?" Susan asked.

"The feds met me and Brewster at an old warehouse that night, heard our stories, and agreed to his terms. Then they took me home and explained the story to my parents. It was like we'd been dropped into some suspense-thriller. The feds explained I would have to disappear and, if my parents wanted to see me again, they'd have to do the same.

"The federal agents directed the local investigation, under the guise of cooperation, and made my disappearance look like a missing person. I stayed in a shabby hotel in Charlotte for two weeks, unable to call anyone or go out in public. Do you have any idea how difficult that is for a teenager? When the police department closed the case, my parents and I were relocated. The marshals said it would seem logical for a grieving family to move away after the loss of a child. But things didn't go as smoothly as they'd hoped. We ended up moving three times—first to Albuquerque, then Chicago, and finally Windsor, Colorado. But to answer your question, Susan, my parents died shortly after the last move, victims of a still-unsolved home invasion."

"Jess, I'm so sorry. How alone you must've felt," Macy said.

"Why so many moves?" Leigh raised her hand like a kid in class. "Wait. Let me guess. Someone was leaking your location to Francisco's people."

"Exactly. After my parents died, I was alone, scared, and ready to run when I met Steven Temple. He was a local builder working on our house. We became friends…and you know the rest."

Leigh was shaking her head. "Not exactly." Macy could see her mental wheels turning. "If my calculations are right…" She looked at Jack, then Jesse, and back down to her notepad. "Never mind."

"It's okay, Detective," Jesse said. "Jack now knows Steven wasn't his biological father. And you're right, I was pregnant when I left Greensboro, but it didn't bother Steven. He was quite a special man…and I loved him dearly." Jesse glanced at her, and Macy could almost see the guilt she'd carried all these years—the same burden she'd carried but for completely different reasons.

"It's all right, Jess," she said. "I'm just glad you had someone and that you're here now."

Leigh stood and folded her notepad. "This is quite a fantastic story, Mrs. Temple-slash-Chance-slash-Quinn, but I'm not sure I'm buying it. Why would the marshals still be interested in you after all these years? Did you eventually testify?"

"Yes. Brewster and I had to appear in closed session. Francisco's family threatened both of us. And the marshals have been getting information about threats against me for the past several years, but I refused to move again. Jack was a kid. We had friends in Windsor. Then about a week before Jack left, the marshals arrested a man outside our home. He had my name in his wallet, along with a picture.

Francisco's youngest son had apparently taken up the mantle to avenge his father."

Pam, who'd been particularly quiet, asked the question everyone must've had. "If the marshals thought you were in danger from a threat that originated in Greensboro, why wouldn't they have taken Jack home immediately? They had to have known where he was when Leigh and Nate started making inquiries about his father."

"That's what I want to know. If they used my son for bait, I'll—"

"They wouldn't do that," Macy said, looking to Leigh for confirmation.

"If this story of yours is true, there'll be documentation. I intend to find it," Leigh said.

"I hope you do. I want to put this nightmare behind me," Jesse said. "I'd really like to come back to Greensboro again, but only if I'm certain Jack and I will be safe. In the meantime, can you release my son? We'll need to find somewhere to stay until you clear this up."

"You'll stay with me," Macy said. She started toward Leigh, intending to set a time when they could talk about their situation, but Leigh turned to Pam.

"Can you handle the paperwork? I need to get to the station. We'll talk later." Before Macy or Pam had an opportunity to say anything, Leigh was gone.

❖

Leigh rushed from her mother's condo, desperate to breathe fresh air and see anything except Macy and Jesse making goo-goo eyes at each other. Her chest ached, and her eyes stung from holding back tears. Jesse was back and she was Macy's first love. Marriage to a man didn't necessarily erase Jesse's feelings for Macy. And the love Macy had carried for Jesse all these years was still painfully obvious. Her world had collapsed and Macy's nightmare had ended when Karla Temple turned into Jesse Quinn.

Feelings swirled inside her like a blender—her feelings for Macy, Susan's revelations, the whole Jesse Quinn story—how could she make sense of it? She was in love with Macy, but that was probably irrelevant now. She wanted to believe her mother but wasn't sure she ever could. Jesse's story was too strange not to be true, and so much of it made sense in the context of what she already knew about her case. Jesse's scenario would explain the apparent holes in the investigation and the feds' stonewalling. She needed to stay focused on the case, stifle her emotions, and let Macy and Jesse get on with their interrupted life.

She dialed Captain Howard's private mobile. "Captain, I need to see you ASAP."

"I'll be in the office in five minutes."

When she walked in, Howard closed her office door and did something she hadn't done since Leigh made detective. She hugged her, long and close. "Are you all right? You look completely shattered."

She couldn't speak. She was crying and there didn't seem to be enough air in the room. "Can't breathe." She clung to Anita. "She's alive. Oh, God, what am I going to do?"

Anita guided her to the sofa and eased her down. "It's okay. Just let it out." Anita handed her tissues, and she cried until she couldn't breathe through her nose and her mouth was dry.

So much for staying focused on the case. "I'm sorry, Captain." She'd never broken down in front of her boss, but she couldn't hold back her feelings any longer.

"Right now I'm your friend. We'll sit right here as long as you want."

"But…you have work—"

"Barbara knows not to interrupt us. What happened, Leigh? Is it Macy?"

"How do you know about Macy?"

"She came to see me yesterday, demanding I tell her where you were. Quite a feisty one, isn't she?"

"Yeah." She sniffled again and tried to smile.

"And…she told me she's in love with you."

"She said that?" Anita nodded, and Leigh's eyes filled with tears again. "That doesn't matter anymore. Jesse Quinn is alive, and Macy has been in love with her since they were kids."

"What? Jesse Quinn, alive? How?"

Between pauses to wipe her eyes and blow her nose, Leigh told Anita the entire complex story Jesse had relayed earlier. "So, whatever Macy and I had is over."

"Did she say that?"

Leigh shook her head.

"Did you even talk to Macy after all this came out?"

"No. She was too busy inviting Jesse and Jack to live with her. The inference was clear. I didn't need a signed declaration of no interest."

"Sometimes you can be as thick as Nathan Shaver about women, and that's not a good thing. Talk to her, Leigh, before it's too late."

"It already is. Can we get back to the case, please? I need to keep busy."

Anita hugged her again and then gave her some space. "Sure. What's your assessment of Jesse's story?"

"I'm not sure I believe it, but if we want the facts, we'll have to ruffle some feathers."

"We've waited too long to learn the truth about this case, Leigh. I'm not above causing a few waves. Some pompous asses think they can scare us off. They're wrong. Let's show them what we're made of, shall we?"

Anita called the Marshals Service. "I need to speak with the chief marshal for the district, please. Tell him it's about Jesse Quinn." Two sentences. A few seconds later, she'd been connected, and five minutes after that, she'd provided enough details to ensure a meeting that afternoon. When she hung up she turned back to Leigh. "You're welcome to be here. It's because of you that we finally know the truth."

Leigh considered the offer. "I don't think so, Captain. I've done my job and the rest is bureaucratic red tape, which is your department. No disrespect intended. I'd like to know the level of present danger to Jesse and Jack, and I think they should be informed. She wants to come back…home." The last word hung in her throat. "Will you let me know and see that she's notified as well?"

"Of course I will. Where are you going?"

"I'm at Pam's for a while, until I find something more permanent."

"You should still talk with Macy. Don't assume anything. You'll regret it."

"Thanks. I'll keep that in mind." As she made her way to her car and drove back to Pam's, she decided just the opposite. She didn't want to think about her situation with Macy. Jesse had always been the priority in Macy's life and would certainly be now that she'd returned.

Chapter Twenty

J esus, house hunting and pregnancy just don't mix. My feet
are the size of watermelons." Hedy dropped her purse on her
kitchen counter and plopped onto the banquette, propping her feet on
a side chair. "Fetch me some water, slave."

"Yes, master." Leigh poured them both a glass and sat across
from her sister. "I'm sorry. I shouldn't have let you do this. My
homelessness isn't your problem." She'd been at Pam's for a week
with no word from Macy and had finally decided to look for a house.

"Hey, pregnant women need exercise, and besides, who else
would I trust to help you find the perfect home?"

"Perfect is relative, isn't it?" To her perfect included the woman
she loved, which wasn't likely to happen anytime soon, if ever again.

"Have you heard from her?"

"No, and I don't expect to. She's got what she wants." She'd
said the same thing to herself every day, but hearing it aloud made
it more real and more painful. Macy's silent treatment made her feel
unimportant and practically invisible, much worse than not being a
priority. "Let's not talk about that, please."

Hedy held up her hands in resignation. "Doesn't make it go away,
any more than avoiding conversations about Susan did for all those
years." Her sister had managed to spend four hours with her without
mentioning their mother. The reprieve had to end. "Was dinner the
other night so awful?"

"No, not really." Surprisingly, Leigh meant it. Hedy had prepared
a nice meal and she, Bo, and Leigh had socialized with Susan for an

entire evening without relapsing into a family drama. Her hurt feelings had begun to ease, dulled by several talks with Susan and outings with Hedy and Bo. She had flashes of childhood memories, but for the most part, she regarded her mother as a stranger she was just getting to know. Interesting how a pending birth could change things.

"I guess Susan told you about the money. That would've come up at some point." The surprise on her face must've been clear. "Or not. Leave it to me to step in it."

"What money?" Leigh asked.

"Never mind. What about the houses today, anything?"

"That's not going to work, Hedy. Tell me."

"Susan will kill me. I promised not to say anything." She gave Hedy her you-can't-hide-anything-from-me look she'd used so successfully when they were children. "Oh, okay. The money we both got when we turned twenty-one came from Susan."

"How?"

"She paid for dad's burial on an installment plan and put the insurance money from his death into savings for us. Every year she'd add a bit more. She instructed an attorney to handle your part because she knew you wouldn't accept money from her, regardless of the circumstances. She gave me my share personally and explained everything."

"Your house?"

"Yep. That little windfall allowed me and Bo to buy this gorgeous love nest."

She'd bought her first house the same way. She replayed the memory of the day she'd gone to the attorney's office to collect her inheritance. She'd thought it odd she and Hedy would get sizeable amounts of money when their family had lived so close to the poverty line. She never imagined Susan had anything to do with her financial security. She'd seen her mother as a fiery, man-crazy redhead when she'd actually been just a mother desperate to protect and provide for her daughters—the same burning passion with completely different motives. Leigh's prejudices and hard feelings had formed easily but were proving difficult to let go of. She owed Susan more than one apology.

"So…" Hedy was waving her hands in front of her face.

"What, sorry."

"Did you see anything you liked today?"

"The little ranch in Sunset Hills was nice, though expensive."

Hedy nodded. "Yeah, but are you sure you want a house and yard to maintain with your work schedule? Wouldn't a condo or townhouse suit your lifestyle better? The one in Fisher Park was amazing, but no garage. I know you want one."

"I need a yard and a driveway so I can show my niece how to throw a ball and ride a bike. I'm not sure about a condo, maybe—" Her mobile rang and she dug into her back pocket. "Hello?"

"Leigh, it's Macy."

Leigh's face grew hot and her mouth dried. "Macy…"

"I was wondering if we could talk. I know it's been awhile, but we need to."

"I don't really think that's necessary. You've made it—ouch." Hedy kicked her under the table, nodded like one of those bobble-headed dog toys, and mouthed *talk to her.*

"Please." Macy's pleading whisper tumbled through her like a mini tornado kicking up feelings she'd tried to bury.

"When and where?" Jeez, she sounded like a lapdog, eager to please her owner.

"Could you come here? Whenever you're available. We'd have privacy. I know it's a long drive, but I'd really appreciate it."

"What about Jesse and Jack?"

"They're not here."

Did that mean not there *right now* or not there as in no longer living with her? The questions she'd tried to suppress resurfaced, and the deep pain returned. Did she need to hear Macy say she wasn't the one? She'd repeated those words until they were branded into her mind. Macy had chosen Jesse. End of story. But she heard herself say, "How about two?"

"Great. Thank you."

When she hung up, Hedy pumped the air with her fist. "Fantastic. She reached out, so don't throw it back in her face. Let her talk and listen with your heart. You're good at that."

"I'm not sure I can anymore."

Hedy leaned toward her. "Of course you can. You've always had a capacity for compassion and love, and right now it's more important than ever. You're clearing the air with Susan, and nothing's keeping you from having the life you want. Don't miss the chance because of pride, ego, or even a little pain. Promise me you'll be open."

Miracles were all around her—Hedy was having a baby, she and Susan were actually talking again, and she'd be going back to work—maybe she did have a chance with Macy. "I promise I'll try. That's the best I can do."

❖

Macy hung her latest painting, the one Leigh had inspired the day they drove around Belews Lake, over her fireplace. The twenty-by-twenty-four-inch canvas was covered with vibrant acrylic colors, and when she looked at it, she saw Leigh in its vitality and effervescence. New, smaller paintings hung on opposing walls, and the cottage was beginning to feel like an art gallery, her gallery. She'd called a gallerist friend of her parents, shown her portfolio, and was thrilled that the Ambleside Gallery had agreed to show her work. Only Leigh's absence diminished the excitement of her first public offering.

When she heard Leigh's vehicle pull into the driveway, she stripped off her painting coat and hung it on the hook by the studio. She brushed at imaginary lint on her black jeans as she walked toward the front door. She'd been this nervous when Leigh came to rent the apartment, but then she was afraid Leigh would stay. Now she was afraid she wouldn't. She had no idea what to say. For once in her life, she intended to go with her gut and speak from the heart. As she opened the door, she prayed that approach worked a miracle, because she'd need one.

She couldn't speak for several seconds when she saw Leigh standing on her stoop. She'd lost a few pounds, but her copper hair and emerald eyes were just as captivating as ever. This time a rusty nail was the furthest thing from her mind. Leigh looked like the woman she'd been waiting for all her life, her answer to a soul mate. "Thank you so much for coming."

Leigh nodded but passed silently into the room and dropped her jacket by the sofa. The familiar gesture that used to seem untidy now felt endearing, and she left it on the floor. "I know you're probably upset, hurt, and more than a little confused."

"Yes, I am."

The pain in Leigh's eyes stabbed at her, making it difficult to speak. "You...want to sit?"

"You've changed the place." She stood in the center of the room and turned in a circle, just like she'd done the first time she'd seen the cottage. "You rearranged the furniture and took down the dark curtains. Nice." Though her words were complimentary she delivered them in a tone devoid of emotion.

"Thank you." The sadness in Leigh's eyes gouged a raw spot in her soul, and she wanted desperately to revive the life she'd once seen there.

"And these are definitely new." She walked toward a wall of her most recent work. "Absolutely beautiful, lighter and more alive. When did you do all these?"

"This week." A blush started deep inside Macy and heated her body as it sprang forward. "Thanks to you. I'd never have had the courage to do this without your support."

"I'm glad you've gone back to what you love, Macy. It suits you. You look happier, but I suppose Jesse has something to do with that as well."

"She has, but probably not in the way you think. Thank you so much for bringing her back home. You have no idea how much that means to both of us." She motioned for her to sit on the small sofa that now faced the lake.

"I didn't do it, exactly. It was a team effort."

"Say what you want, but to us, you'll always be the one who reunited us." Leigh stared out at the lake, avoiding her gaze. The vitality and enthusiasm she'd always associated with Leigh was missing. She started to ask how she'd been, but Leigh spoke.

"I'd like to say something, if you don't mind, about Jesse's case."

"I know why you didn't tell me. I talked with Captain Howard. She'd ordered you not to discuss it. I jumped to conclusions, again. I'm sorry."

"You don't owe me an apology. But something else has puzzled me since I read your statement. You were listed as Macy Reynolds, and I wasn't sure for a while if that was you."

"After graduation from high school, I took my mother's maiden name, Sheridan. I didn't want any preferential treatment at college because of my family's money."

"That makes sense, but I didn't know at the time. You have to understand how important this case was to me, even before I met you. It's the reason I became a youth detective. I guess Jesse's case has haunted both of us, but I *was* going to tell you about my involvement in spite of Captain Howard's advice. I just hadn't found the right time."

"You were going to disobey your boss?"

"Some things are more important than rules. You were to me."

"Right." Leigh's use of the past tense disappointed her. She'd hoped Leigh cared enough to give them a chance, because she'd need more than her own courage to get through this conversation. "I guess you heard Brewster died from liver cancer in prison three years ago. And Francisco is on death watch."

"Yes. Captain Howard told me. Guess that's why his son was so anxious to settle the score. The gunman the marshals arrested in Windsor gave him up. And the marshals also located the leak that'd been selling Jesse's location all these years—a records clerk. Also in jail now."

All business, Leigh wasn't going to make this easy, but Macy couldn't blame her. She'd fought her every step of the way when Leigh tried so hard to engage, and she'd given her so little hope of a future. "The danger to Jesse and Jack is over. She's free for the first time in years."

"I'm happy for them. Everybody deserves an authentic life. Things would've been a lot easier if Jesse had been honest with Jack about her past, but I guess that's hard to do when you're on the run from organized crime."

"Yeah, he's a headstrong kid, but I think they'll be fine now," Macy said.

"Any idea what they plan to do?"

"They've gone back to Windsor to settle their affairs, and then she wants to move back to Greensboro, where she grew up and has the happiest memories. Your handsome partner, Nate, has been helping them arrange things with the marshals. He said they owed them a free plane ticket and moving expenses when they're ready. I think he might have a crush on my BFF."

For the first time since she arrived, Leigh stopped worrying the side of her finger with her thumbnail and looked at her. "Your BFF? You mean…you're not…"

She took Leigh's hands. "We were never lovers. She's always been straight. That fantasy was only in my mind. We've spent this week talking, crying, purging our guilt, and rebuilding our friendship. She's always been a huge part of my life and will continue to be. You need to accept that, if we're going to be together."

"Together?"

A fist of nerves bunched in Macy's stomach. *Leigh doesn't want me anymore.* She forced the negative thought from her mind and dug deep for courage and her true feelings. "I'm in love with you, Leigh Monroe, and I want to spend my life with you…or at least give it a try."

"Yeah?"

"Yes, my darling. And if you need confirmation, ask your captain, Pam, or Jesse. She saw it the first day we were together at Susan's."

"Really?"

"Are you in shock? I've never known you to resort to one-word answers about anything."

"Probably a little." Leigh's smile was tentative.

"What do you want, Leigh? You asked me that the last time we made love. Tell me."

She watched the emotional struggle on Leigh's face—the doubt, pain, fear, and hope. Her eyes drilled into Macy's until she apparently found the answer she was looking for. "I want someone who loves me as much as I love her. I want to be the number-one priority in my lover's life, as she'll be in mine. I want a true partnership, sharing the good and the bad. I want honesty, real communication, and intimacy. I want a stable home with my partner where we experience the ordinary and the extraordinary parts of life. I want a witness to my life, because the best bits aren't always the most exciting. They often happen when we least expect them, in a sunset, a quiet moment, or a deep conversation. I want someone who understands the quirkiness that makes me unique and loves me because of it, not in spite of it.

Aristotle said love is composed of a single soul inhabiting two bodies. That's what I want. Am I asking too much? Is that even possible?"

"I hope so, because I want those things too. Will you give us a chance?"

"Are you certain about Jesse? She's been the center of your life for years."

"I'm certain. I'd decided to move on before she came back, but now that we've cleared the air, I'm definitely ready…if you'll have me."

"Oh, I'm going to have you all right." The renewed sparkle in Leigh's eyes dissolved the tension between them and replaced it with playfulness. "You'll have to pass one little itsy-bitsy test."

"Really, and what would that be?"

"Let's go to bed."

She rose, took Leigh's hand, and led her into the small bedroom they'd never shared. The sun cast muted shadows through the trees into the room, which felt intimate and romantic. She ached for Leigh, had craved her all week, but with her so close, the need became urgent. She reached for the tail of Leigh's polo and started to peel it over her head.

Leigh stopped her and returned her hands to her sides. "Not so fast."

"But I need you, really bad."

"Good. Then you'll do as you're told for a change." Leigh's green eyes had turned the color of moss in a deep wood, dangerous and exciting. "Let's see if the décor is the only thing that's loosened up around here."

Before she had a chance to respond, Leigh shucked Macy's T-shirt off and she stood bare-breasted. She felt slightly uncomfortable, but the cool air dimpled her nipples and the sensation trickled down. "Oh." Leigh feathered her face with light kisses, avoiding her not-so-subtle attempts to capture her lips. "Kiss me, Leigh."

"Patience."

Leigh trailed kisses down her neck, across her collarbone, and to her left breast, sparking a burn that threatened to consume her. Leigh teased her flesh with her fingers and tongue and scraped the tip of her nipple with her teeth. She watched Leigh's mouth work at one breast and then the other. "That's so good." Leigh stared up at her as she knelt, slowly unbuttoned her jeans, and slid them to the floor, exposing her completely.

"Lie down on the bed and watch me undress."

She'd never allowed another woman to take charge of their lovemaking and was more frustrated and aroused than she'd imagined possible. Leigh pulled her polo off and slid her hands under her breasts, squeezing until she pinched her nipple between her thumb and forefinger.

Macy's clit twitched and she started to get up. "Let me do that for you."

"Stay put." Leigh kicked her jeans off and slid her finger through her slick folds. "I am so wet for you."

Macy reached between her own legs, unable to bear the prickly heat gathering there.

"Don't. That's my job."

"You better hurry. I'm about to lose it just watching you."

Leigh stepped closer to the bed, her eyes blazing a path over Macy's body, her hand still working between her legs. "You want this, don't you?"

"Oh, yes, I need you, Leigh. Come here."

The steely resolve in Leigh's eyes weakened and she lay down beside her. She gathered Leigh in her arms and pulled her on top, desperate for the contact that would ease her pain. Leigh resisted. She reached between them and tried to urge Leigh's leg between hers.

"Slow down, Macy."

"I can't. I want you."

Leigh straddled her thigh and worked her soaked center against her leg. Macy urged her higher so she could reciprocate, but Leigh remained just out of reach. "Would you do something for me, Macy?" She nodded. "Touch me, just here, and rub very slowly." Leigh guided Macy's hand to her clit.

The tone of her voice and the pleading look told Macy that Leigh needed her to do exactly as she said. She closed her hand over Leigh's center and firmly stroked, taking her lead from Leigh's responses.

"That's it. Good. Look at me." Their gazes locked and Leigh's breathing increased. She matched her pace. "Slow-ly. I want you to stretch it out as long as possible."

Teasing she could do, though she was desperate to be touched. She slowed her pace, stroked from the bottom of the shaft to the tip of Leigh's clit, paused, and started again. Leigh arched toward her, but she withheld her next touch until Leigh's moans filled the room. Then she started over, slowly but firmly coaxing Leigh's orgasm from deep inside.

"Oh, God, sooo good." Leigh raised Macy's other hand from her breast and sucked a finger into her mouth. Macy felt like she was deep inside the hot wetness between Leigh's legs, and she quickened her pace.

"Yes, Macy, faster now."

She wanted to keep teasing Leigh but sensed it was more important that she obey. She removed her finger slowly from Leigh's mouth and kissed her, matching the pace of her stroking with the in-and-out penetration of her tongue. Leigh humped her hand, her urgency driving Macy closer with each thrust. Leigh moaned deep in the throat, her entire body stiffened, and she collapsed against Macy.

"Ahhh…perfect."

She held Leigh as their bodies rocked and her lover stilled beside her. She'd given Leigh exactly what she wanted—slow, intimate, and intentional lovemaking. Macy had orchestrated their previous two sessions, desperate for the sex but unaware of the feelings underneath. Now her heart was so full of Leigh she couldn't imagine making love to her any other way than totally involved—mind, body, and soul.

She pressed her leg between Leigh's and attempted to top her, desperate to release her throbbing ache. "I need you, Leigh."

"Oh, no, you don't." Leigh pinned her against the bed and raised her arms above her head. "Hold on." She wrapped Macy's fingers around the metal headboard railings and pushed her legs apart.

"What are you doing? I can't do this."

"Do what, my darling?"

"Come…like this…" She nodded toward her body spread-eagled across the bed. How could she possibly climax when she felt so uncomfortable?

"But you'll try, for me, right?"

When Leigh smiled, Macy knew she'd do anything this woman asked as long as she kept that up. "Of course I will, but hurry."

Leigh trailed her fingers lightly down Macy's chest, around her nipples, toward the dark patch of hair between her legs, and back up. The touch was feather soft, but her nerves magnified the sensation. She tensed, then arched to meet Leigh's hands, to encourage a firmer touch, but the sweet torture continued.

Lowering herself along Macy's body, Leigh rubbed her breasts against Macy's rigid clit, gently back and forth and then up and down, but never with enough force to allow satisfaction.

"Please, Leigh." She released the headboard and reached for her clit.

"Stop."

"Touch me, really touch me, Leigh. I need to come."

"Put your hands back, please." When she did, Leigh lowered her head and captured Macy's clit between her lips.

"Awww…yes…more." She clenched the headboard rails so tight she thought they'd bend. Using the leverage they provided, she rocked against Leigh's mouth, quickening the pace, urging her climax toward the surface. "That's it, my darling. Make me come."

The pressure coalesced in her core as Leigh expertly sucked and flicked her clit. "Inside me." Leigh penetrated her slowly, withdrawing with equally agonizing speed. She pushed harder, digging her heels into the bed and locking her arms against the railing. "Faster. Oh, God, faster."

Leigh finally complied, her hand and mouth in exquisitely rapid sync. "Yes, baby, that's it. *That's it*." Macy looked down into Leigh's eyes, ablaze with passion, and as her orgasm rushed out, Leigh slid along her lower leg and, with one slow stroke, joined her. She had no doubt that Leigh Monroe was the perfect woman for her, now and always. "I love you."

"I love you too. The hard part is over, finding the love of your life. Everything else is just an exercise."

"Stop with the bumper stickers and come here." She pulled Leigh closer and they began again.

THE END

About the Author

A thirty-year veteran of a midsized police department, VK Powell was a police officer by necessity (it paid the bills) and a writer by desire (it didn't). Her career spanned numerous positions including beat officer, homicide detective, vice/narcotics lieutenant, and assistant chief of police. Now retired, she devotes her time to writing, traveling, home decorating, and volunteer work.

Books Available From Bold Strokes Books

Let the Lover Be by Sheree Greer. Kiana Lewis, a functional alcoholic on the verge of destruction, finally faces the demons of her past while finding love and earning redemption in New Orleans. (978-1-62639-077-5)

Blindsided by Karis Walsh. Blindsided by love, guide dog trainer Lenae McIntyre and media personality Cara Bradley learn to trust what they see with their hearts. (978-1-62639-078-2)

About Face by VK Powell. Forensic artist Macy Sheridan and Detective Leigh Monroe work on a case that has troubled them both for years, but they're hampered by the past and their unlikely yet undeniable attraction. (978-1-62639-079-9)

Blackstone by Shea Godfrey. For Darry and Jessa, their chance at a life of freedom is stolen by the arrival of war and an ancient prophecy that just might destroy their love. (978-1-62639-080-5)

Out of This World by Maggie Morton. Iris decided to cross an ocean to get over her ex. But instead, she ends up traveling much farther, all the way to another world. Once there, only a mysterious, sexy, and magical woman can help her return home. (978-1-62639-083-6)

Kiss The Girl by Melissa Brayden. Sleeping with the enemy has never been so complicated. Brooklyn Campbell and Jessica Lennox face off in love and advertising in fast-paced New York City. (978-1-62639-071-3)

Taking Fire: A First Responders Novel by Radclyffe. Hunted by extremists and under siege by nature's most virulent weapons, Navy medic Max de Milles and Red Cross worker Rachel Winslow join forces to survive and discover something far more lasting. (978-1-62639-072-0)

First Tango in Paris by Shelley Thrasher. When French law student Eva Laroche meets American call girl Brigitte Green in 1970s Paris, they have no idea how their pasts and futures will intersect. (978-1-62639-073-7)

The War Within by Yolanda Wallace. Army nurse Meredith Moser went to Vietnam in 1967 looking to help those in need; she didn't expect to meet the love of her life along the way. (978-1-62639-074-4)

Escapades by MJ Williamz. Two women, afraid to love again, must overcome their fears to find the happiness that awaits them. (978-1-62639-182-6)

Desire at Dawn by Fiona Zedde. For Kylie, love had always come armed with sharp teeth and claws. But with the human, Olivia, she bares her vampire heart for the very first time, sharing passion, lust, and a tenderness she'd never dared dream of before. (978-1-62639-064-5)

Visions by Larkin Rose. Sometimes the mysteries of love reveal themselves when you least expect it. Other times they hide behind a black satin mask. Can Paige unveil her masked stranger this time? (978-1-62639-065-2)

All In by Nell Stark. Internet poker champion Annie Navarro loses everything when the Feds shut down online gambling, and she turns to experienced casino host Vesper Blake for advice—but can Nova convince Vesper to take a gamble on romance? (978-1-62639-066-9)

Vermilion Justice by Sheri Lewis Wohl. What's a vampire to do when Dracula is no longer just a character in a novel? (978-1-62639-067-6)

Switchblade by Carsen Taite. Lines were meant to be crossed. Third in the Luca Bennett Bounty Hunter Series. (978-1-62639-058-4)

Nightingale by Andrea Bramhall. Culture, faith, and duty conspire to tear two young lovers apart, yet fate seems to have different plans for them both. (978-1-62639-059-1)

No Boundaries by Donna K. Ford. A chance meeting and a nightmare from the past threaten more than Andi Massey's solitude as she and Gwen Palmer struggle to understand the complexity of love without boundaries. (978-1-62639-060-7)

Timeless by Rachel Spangler. When Stevie Geller returns to her hometown, will she do things differently the second time around or will she be in such a hurry to leave her past that she misses out on a better future? (978-1-62639-050-8)

Second to None by L.T. Marie. Can a physical therapist and a custom motorcycle designer conquer their pasts and build a future with one another? (978-1-62639-051-5)

Seneca Falls by Jesse Thoma. Together, two women discover love truly can conquer all evil. (978-1-62639-052-2)

A Kingdom Lost by Barbara Ann Wright. Without knowing each other's fates, Princess Katya and her consort Starbride seek to reclaim their kingdom from the magic-wielding madman who seized the throne and is murdering their people. (978-1-62639-053-9)

Season of the Wolf by Robin Summers. Two women running from their pasts are thrust together by an unimaginable evil. Can they overcome the horrors that haunt them in time to save each other? (978-1-62639-043-0)

The Heat of Angels by Lisa Girolami. Fires burn in more than one place in Los Angeles. (978-1-62639-042-3)

Desperate Measures by P. J. Trebelhorn. Homicide detective Kay Griffith and contractor Brenda Jansen meet amidst turmoil neither of them is aware of until murder suspect Tommy Rayne makes his move to exact revenge on Kay. (978-1-62639-044-7)

The Magic Hunt by L.L. Raand. With her Pack being hunted by human extremists and beset by enemies masquerading as friends, can Sylvan protect them and her mate, or will she succumb to the feral rage that threatens to turn her rogue, destroying them all? A Midnight Hunters novel. (978-1-62639-045-4)

Wingspan by Karis Walsh. Wildlife biologist Bailey Chase is content to live at the wild bird sanctuary she has created on Washington's Olympic Peninsula until she is lured beyond the safety of isolation by architect Kendall Pearson. (978-1-60282-983-1)

Windigo Thrall by Cate Culpepper. Six women trapped in a mountain cabin by a blizzard, stalked by an ancient cannibal demon bent on stealing their sanity—and their lives. (978-1-60282-950-3)

The Blush Factor by Gun Brooke. Ice-cold business tycoon Eleanor Ashcroft only cares about the three Ps—Power, Profit, and Prosperity—until young Addison Garr makes her doubt both that and the state of her frostbitten heart. (978-1-60282-985-5)

Slash and Burn by Valerie Bronwen. The murder of a roundly despised author at an LGBT writers' conference in New Orleans turns Winter Lovelace's relaxing weekend hobnobbing with her peers into a nightmare of suspense—especially when her ex turns up. (978-1-60282-986-2)

The Quickening: A Sisters of Spirits novel by Yvonne Heidt. Ghosts, visions, and demons are all in a day's work for Tiffany. But when Kat asks for help on a serial killer case, life takes on another dimension altogether. (978-1-60282-975-6)

Smoke and Fire by Julie Cannon. Oil and water, passion and desire, a combustible combination. Can two women fight the fire that draws them together and threatens to keep them apart? (978-1-60282-977-0)

Love and Devotion by Jove Belle. KC Hall trips her way through life, stumbling into an affair with a married bombshell twice her age. Thankfully, her best friend, Emma Reynolds, is there to show her the true meaning of Love and Devotion. (978-1-60282-965-7)

The Shoal of Time by J.M. Redmann. It sounded too easy. Micky Knight is reluctant to take the case because the easy ones often turn into the hard ones, and the hard ones turn into the dangerous ones. In this one, easy turns hard without warning. (978-1-60282-967-1)

In Between by Jane Hoppen. At the age of fourteen, Sophie Schmidt discovers that she was born an intersexual baby and sets off on a journey to find her place in a world that denies her true existence. (978-1-60282-968-8)

Under Her Spell by Maggie Morton. The magic of love brought Terra and Athene together, but now a magical quest stands between them—a quest for Athene's hand in marriage. Will their passion keep them together, or will stronger magic tear them apart? (978-1-60282-973-2)